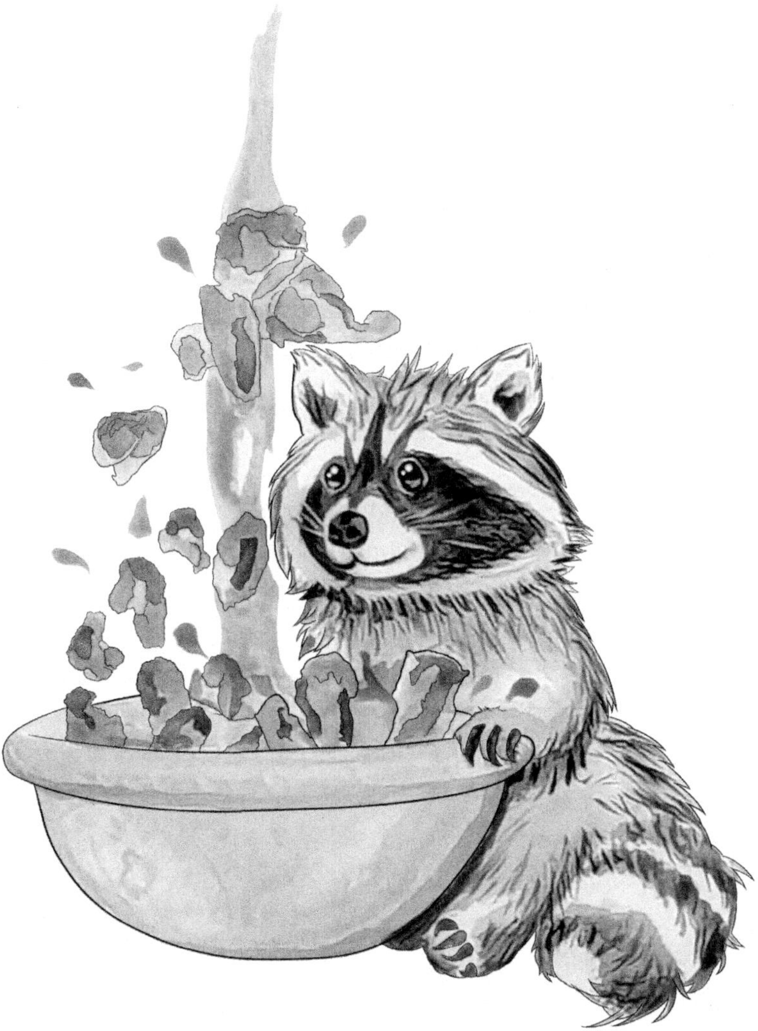

By C. B. Alice

Breeder Babes Happy Husbandry: Roulette
House Rules
All In
Double Down

Wilmington Juggernauts
Christmas Cheer
Good Guy Gabe

Stand-Alone Romance
Holly Jolly Cake Fight

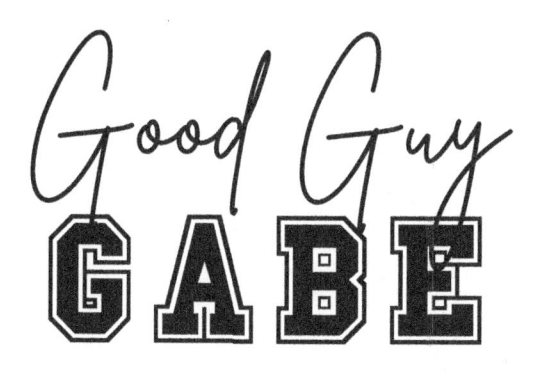

Good Guy GABE

C. B. ALICE

"Good Guy Gabe"

Copyright © 2024 by C. B. Alice

All rights reserved.

No part of this publication may be reproduced, distributed, or transmitted in any form or by any means, including photocopying, recording, or other electronic or mechanical methods, without the prior written permission of the publisher, except as permitted by U.S. copyright law.

The story, all names, characters, and incidents portrayed in this production are fictitious. No identification with actual persons (living or deceased), places, buildings, and products is intended or should be inferred.

First print edition 2024

Content Warning

Good Guy Gabe is a fairly fluffy opening to a series that will get progressively darker. That being said, this does include a wide range of potentially triggering content surrounding pregnancy, including mani-pulation with the intent to impregnate and references to stillbirth. There are also references to abuse and accidental death of patients of a pediatric surgeon, references to suicide, and mild on-page social ostracization/bullying, stalking, and suicidal ideation. Please be advised.

For an updated list of warnings for the Wilmington Juggernauts series, Did you find this content warning to be lacking? Please let me know! Contact info also available on my website.

Listen, "Good Guy" is a relative term. Gabe is a relatively good guy in comparison to his friends. Trust me, if Gabe's friends have any sway on his moral compass, he's the goodest guy possible.

Just wait until you see the shit Merrick pulls.

Chapter One
GABE

"Seventeen," I call out. "Sixteen. Fifteen," clicking the button each time Blaise Sinclair reaches forward, grabs the ball in front of him, and slides his torso over it. The rules state his abdomen must be on the ball for it to count, and I'm a stickler for rules, so I make sure he's already there before calling out the next number.

My entire life is rules and timing, every action occurring in a blink that has the world riding on it. I may look like a gigantic oaf, but my reflexes are every bit as sharp as Sinclair's.

I'm mostly stationary, having started at the middle of the line so I wouldn't need to work so hard to keep up. On the other side, Merrick Briggs is running to stay flush, watching not where he's going but Blaise's progress, but Merrick's used to running in one direction while looking in another. On his head is a GoPro filming this. I studied the rules before we set this up. As long as it's filmed and the angle makes it clear that Blaise isn't touching the ground, it's valid. To that end, I'm also strapped with a camera. We don't want the committee claiming that Blaise's left hand touched the ground.

Seriously, though, Blaise's left hand is insured at one hundred million dollars. It's not touching the ground.

"Eight!" I yell. "Seven! Six!" Excitement, the familiar, addictive buzz of adrenaline, has my heart pounding. I wasn't initially into this, just doing what Blaise asked me to do because my life is all about protecting Blaise, and with a guy like Blaise, there's no clocking out. But there's that point where it becomes real, where this is an *actual* thing, he's going to go down in *actual* record books, *I'm* going to be a part of this, and yeah. I'm excited.

"Four! Three—!"

A sudden explosion behind us. Gigantic rubber exercise balls go scattering all across the gymnasium, several of them flying through the air, one of them slamming so hard into a wall it gets skewered on a peg and deflates sadly.

Merrick trips over his own feet and falls on his ass. Blaise nearly dodges a similar fate — or worse, smashing that nine-figure hand under his exercise ball as he rolls off it — only because I dive down to catch him, hitting the floor hard, but it's that recycled tire stuff. I get smashed by walls of flesh all day. This is fine.

Except I hear a rip as something on Blaise catches on my cooldown hoodie. It's definitely a fabric rip, not a muscular one, but I frown. I love this hoodie. It's really hard to find anything in this color in my size.

"What in the name of god and all that is holy are you dipshits doing?"

Some good news here: that's not the voice of Head Coach Keenan or any of the other coaches or higher-ups on the corporate side of the Wilmington Juggernauts, the NFL's most recent expansion team. It is, however, Lin Huang, the kicker, and he can be a bit of a dick. He duked it out with Blaise and Merrick a lot last year during our inaugural season, where we didn't quite make it to playoffs but at least finished with a respectable 8-5. You can't expect much more from a first-year expansion. But he's also a dancer, showed his dick to an entire audience and they saw it as artistic. Last time Blaise tried that, I had to go down to the courthouse and bail his ass out. Only difference for Blaise was it was in a bar instead of a theater.

I'm mostly cool with Huang. His girl's tight with the wife of Evan Allore, a good buddy of mine, so we hang out sometimes. But Blaise and Merrick hate him.

"I was setting a world record," Blaise huffs as he jams the heel of his hand right into my sternum to lift himself off me, "until you ruined it."

"You suck so much, Huang," Merrick grumbles from a few feet away. I roll to my side to see if he's okay — as the wide receiver, his ankles are worth nearly as much as Blaise's hand — but he's already popping back up.

I'm slower to rise. I'm the oldest of the three of us, only by a few years, but those years seem a lot longer with the extra hundred-plus pounds I've got on them. It doesn't help that I'm also the one constantly running into men just as big as me to keep them off those two. And being the center, having no choice but to take that hit to my head and shoulders every single time because once that ball leaves my hand, the guy across from me is going to try to tear through me to get to Blaise?

Yeah, I'm already feeling the creaks at 29. It was a fucking miracle that the Colts picked me up at 27 and then transferred me alongside Blaise to the Juggernauts the following year. When this contract is up at the end of this season, I'm gonna be 30. There will be a batch of recruits a decade younger than me chomping at the bit to take my place, and experience only does so much to compensate for worn joints and growing concussion counts.

This might be my last year.

"What are you doing?" Huang repeats as Blaise and Merrick each take one of my hands to drag my three-hundred-pound ass off the floor.

"Clearly I was attempting to break the Guinness World Record for the greatest number of exercise balls ridden across without touching the ground," Blaise snaps back, and yeah, when he says it like that, it does sound pretty dumb. Still, I stand tall, crossing my arms over my chest, defending my QB against injury, ridicule, and his own stupidity. That's my job, and I'm one of the few guys who's done well at it. There was a reason Blaise and I were a combo pack. Blaise could be a Super Bowl worthy-quarterback, but he's a loose cannon.

And kind of an idiot.

Huang drops his head back to stare up at the cosmic beyond. "You are the starting quarterback for the sixteenth-ranked team. As much as I die on the inside admitting this, you are an incredible quarterback who could be legendary if you got your shit together. You could be breaking actual, important, memorable records that would land your ass in Canton if you grew the fuck up, and instead you stole all the exercise balls from the studio to ride them like some drunk frat boy?"

Listen. Huang and I have had some good moments. I know he has his own inner demons, that he's plagued by his father, who still doesn't fully accept his choices even though, to turn his words back around, he's the kicker for the sixteenth-ranked NFL team. That's dead center but also dead center of a pool of only thirty-two men of the thousands who dreamed of this since their peewee football days.

But I've met his father. I know that when Huang yells at us like this, he picks up his father's accent, like this is how he learned to chew people out. And that's sad but just a little funny.

I snort.

Just a little.

But I'm a big guy. I'm not loud, but my sounds carry.

He glares at me, and I hang my head.

"*You* know better," he says, and he's definitely talking to me.

I firm up my lips and nod sharply. I do know better, but it's easier rolling with Blaise's shenanigans than trying to reason with him. And it's not like Merrick is going to stop Blaise. They come together like sulfur and oxygen. I wish I could be a fire extinguisher, but I'm just the farmer mowing over his field to keep the brushfire from spreading.

"We're done," I assure Huang. "Just a stupid thing to try. We'll clean it up before we head out."

I expect him to be mollified by that, but instead he says, "Not you. Emily Hess wants to see you."

"Ooh," Blaise and Merrick sing out in unison as though I've just been called down to the principal's office.

I glare at them, but I have to look over my shoulders to do that. Of course they're using me as a meat wall. Blaise is shaking out the twists he just had done, his preferred hairstyle during football season so he can bring the afro back out from February to July. Merrick winks one blue eye and blows me a kiss.

"Who's Emily Hess?" I ask them, nervous. This is the final season of my current contract. I can't be messing up now.

"She's in PR," Blaise says.

"You're in trouble, dude," Merrick adds.

Huang has to shout, "She's the director of events!" over another chorus of oohs, saving me additional stress. It wouldn't be the first time I've gotten chewed out by PR about some social media nonsense that wasn't my fault.

It's almost always Blaise's fault. When it's not, it's Merrick's.

"What does the director of events need me for?" I mutter as I head out of the gym. Huang barks orders out behind me, and I'd fully expect a fistfight to break out if it wasn't mid-August, with only one more pre-season game before the second season of the Wilmington Juggernauts officially starts.

Emily Hess, Director of Events, has an office that is simultaneously spacious and cluttered. The offensive line could fit in here comfortably, but right now, there's barely enough room for just me because of the stacks of crates, all labeled KICK-OFF GALA, plus an entire team's worth of life-sized pop-up replicas of us. I come face-to-face with myself, and even cardboard me took twice the materials of Merrick standing nearby. Merrick's looking all sleek and suave and dangerous in that way that gets his fangirls dropping panties. Cardboard me is red-faced and jolly and tubby, Santa Claus working his part-time gig.

Yeah, I got fangirls, and yeah, I mostly get cookies from them. Don't get me wrong, I appreciate the cookies. But I wouldn't say no to some panties.

I frown when I notice this photo must have been from this past summer, before I noticed the patch of silver sprouting at the edge of the ginger and started using a shampoo that makes it less a beacon pointing to my advanced years. I meander over to the desk and open the top drawer to see if there's a Sharpie or red pen or dark nail polish, anything to color in that spot. Only then do I hear a hissing sound and realize I'm not alone.

Lurking between Dom Morales, second-string QB, and Micah Oliver, running back, is a very petite, very angry middle-aged woman. She has one very angry finger pointed at me, another pointed at the headset in her ear, I guess to indicate she's on a call. She's got one of those haircuts that tells me she's complained to the manager so many times she's *become* management.

I ease the drawer closed and sheepishly lower myself into her seat, but the creak it makes has me shooting back up. I fold my arms in and keep my head hung in acknowledgment of her eye daggers as I wait for her to finish her call.

When she talks, it's pleasant, upbeat, go-getter platitudes, assuring whomever is on the other end of the call that everything is right on schedule and the Kick-Off Gala is going to go off without a hitch. They've even added extra security in case any disruptive elements need to be removed.

That's the team. We're the disruptive elements. We've already been told that we will be served exactly two alcoholic drinks aside from the champagne toast, to not even try to bribe the bartenders because there will be cameras, and that we're all going to be sent through metal detectors and manually searched upon entry.

C. B. Alice

When her call is over, her voice jumps an octave as she gestures for me to leave, like I wasn't told to come here by the least likely Jug to prank me. "You, the Quilted Flower, now."

I pat myself down, wondering if I've somehow picked up some fabric brooch of hers or something. Nope, just my usual athletic shorts and my baby pink Party Animal hoodie with the screen print of a DJ cat in Deal-With-It sunglasses.

And a giant rip on the side.

"Go to. The Quilted Flower. Right now. The quilt we're auctioning for the Kick-Off fundraiser is coming from there, and I haven't been able to get in touch with the quilter in four days."

"The quilter?" I repeat. The only quilter I've ever known was my great-gram, who passed a couple years back at the ripe old age of 92. Even died with a quilt in her lap, halfway through a stitch. Grams tried to pass it off to my sisters, but they all agreed the thing was cursed. I don't know what ever happened to it.

"Yes, the quilter. The person who makes quilts. They're called quilters."

"Well, right, but what if she's . . ." I lean in and whisper, ". . . dead? I don't want to find a dead body."

"She's not dead!" Emily screeches, punching cardboard Kai Bodley right in the face, triggering a domino effect that knocks over half the team. "Her name's Jocelyn Page. She's very much alive, she's just not returning my calls. Now go!"

I shouldn't push my luck, but I have to ask, "Why me? I'm supposed to be packing for Cleveland."

I've seen defensive tackles driven to the brink of madness by Blaise's taunts, to the point of five-yard penalties for offsides, who look less like raging bulls than this woman. She breathes several times. I'm not sure if she's calming herself or stoking an internal fire. Finally, she says, "The store is in Camden. You live in Camden. It's on your way home."

"I mean, Sinclair and Briggs live there too. Plus Bodley and Jennings and Vedder." I grumble as I head back out of the office, but even I know that's a bad line. They'd terrorize the poor granny.

I pull out my phone and search for The Quilted Flower. The picture taken from the street is an old farmhouse with weathered clapboard siding and a wraparound porch that has several quilts draped over the railing. Some look like the ones Great-Gran Bernie made, washed-out pastels and antique tones in fussy patterns, but others are bright and sophisticated murals more like what I'd expect at a modern art gallery. One of the quilts looks like a clean fade from baby pink to a nightmarish neon melon, but when I zoom in, what looked like bad camera pixels is actually intricate designs stitched together from tangerine- and dragonfruit-colored fabric.

I haven't had a ton of girlfriends, no wives to speak of, but I do have four sisters. If I didn't know my colors, I'd never have survived the emergency nail polish runs to CVS in high school.

The shop is a block away from the Camden Square pizza place I like. I'm genuinely surprised I've never noticed it before. There's no way that quilt wouldn't have caught my eye.

I flip over to my text messages, needing to let Merrick know he has to get a ride home with Blaise. I don't get a single word typed before Emily yells from down the hall, "And Shaunessy?"

"Ma'am?" I call back.

"You got a date for the gala, right?"

Crud. That was something else they've told us at least three times now. Dates are required so no one's trying to pick up any senators again this year.

"Yes, ma'am," I say as sweetly as possible.

"You're lying to me, Shaunessy. Find yourself a date."

Like it's that easy.

Chapter Two
JOSS

"You can't live forever without a phone," Tilly says from hundreds of miles away, disproving the very point she's trying to make.

I line up my project in my sewing machine, nudge the thick fold of fabric into the narrow space, and drop the foot. "I'll get it when I get my car."

"I just saw Jimmy Dawson yesterday, and he says you haven't called him to approve repairs yet," Cora says, ratting me out.

"Well, how can I do that if I don't have a phone?" Okay, there's a landline right in the shop. But that even better proves this isn't urgent.

"You can't hide forever," Tilly says more gently.

I gesture to the room around me. They're not physically with me, but they're the ones who help me set everything up every time I update equipment. They know what I'm pointing at. "I'm not exactly hiding."

"Honey, you've been hiding for almost a decade," Cora says. Tilly nods in agreement, and I decide not to argue the point that it's only been six years. I can't really say I haven't been hiding in my own home, either.

This place has a long and colorful history. Despite the farmhouse exterior and the massive barn behind it, the property has never been a farm. The first resident was a blacksmith who gained some notoriety for allegedly supplying bullets and cannons to the wrong side during the Civil War. That ultimately led to his shop getting razed, but the main house survived, only to literally explode half a century later by a drugstore owner who fancied himself a thoroughly educated chemist. He was nothing of the sort and learned the hard way that vinegar and baking soda can make a surprisingly powerful bomb when enough are combined and sealed up tight.

He did not live to share this discovery with the world, but the world at large already knew that.

The house that was built to replace it — the farm-house with the clapboard siding and the wraparound porch — was initially a bed and breakfast. The owners didn't make enough money to keep it running, so it bounced from hand to hand, ultimately getting ren-ovated into a veterinary clinic with an apartment upstairs.

When the vet retired, the old animal clinic sat for nearly a decade, the smell too pungent for most. Ultimately, a pediatric oral surgeon spent an obscene amount of money to gut and remodel the downstairs, setting up a quaint practice where he and his pageant queen wife could settle down and build a future together. He planned to only live in the apartment upstairs for a few years, promised his wife that it was temporary, even vowed to rush it once the baby was on the way, although he did set up a nursery for the baby, just in case things didn't work the way he hoped.

They didn't.

Because he was a disgusting pervert.

And the biggest mistake I've ever made.

"Stop it right now, missy."

I blink and look back up at the monitor mounted above my Husqvarna domestic. One half of the screen is Tilly Reinhardt, currently in Atlanta, hiding in the dark recesses of the wardrobe of the set she's been working on for the last month, going absolutely ham on a jar of pickles after having already eaten half a tub of Greek yogurt. Cora Prasad, meanwhile, is all of twelve minutes away from me if she takes the highway, but she's driving herself crazy putting together twenty-four outfits for a runway for December. I'm going live in an hour to demonstrate this modern cathedral window quilt technique that I've been partially assembling units for.

This works. We live in the time of virtual meetings. We got this.

Up in the corner are two smaller video feeds. One shows my fingers guiding my fabric under the presser foot, the needle rhythmically punching through at sixteenth-inch increments along the edge of the folded-over fabric. The other miniature video is of my face, the scowl on it the one Cora and Tilly refer to as The Ex.

Ex human, unfortunately. The jackass didn't give me a chance to divorce him before he exed himself from life. The only good thing he did for me was gifting me the house when he initially bought it. I thought it was a grand gesture, a wedding gift. Ended up being the only thing I had left after the lawsuits from his victims were wrapped up.

But I digress.

I give myself a full upper-body shake that fluffs up my blonde ponytail and pinks up my pale cheeks. With a dazzling smile, I'm myself again.

Tilly says, "Ulk, that's just as bad," through pickle-stuffed cheeks. "Just be you."

My smile droops only a notch as I say, "But this is me." I've been besties with Tilly for five years, but I had already recreated myself at that point, first as Cora's pattern drafter and then in the quilting field when I realized this was where my passion truly lay. Tilly thinks I'm always giving pageant energy to hide some 'true' self deep inside.

I'm not. It's been a decade since I last competed, but I spent almost twenty years on that stage. My first time, I had to hold my mother's hand because I hadn't mastered walking yet. And I get how cheesy it was. I get why the industry gets such a bad rap. There really weren't too many toxic moms and even fewer toxic girls, but the bad apples did spoil the bunch. Still, I loved it.

Every time I proudly said *world peace*, I meant it.

"Don't you do it!" Tilly suddenly screeches. "If you leak a single tear, I'll be bawling like a baby. Again. Pregnancy hormones suck."

"I wasn't going to cry," I say quickly, even though yeah, it takes hardly anything to get the waterworks going.

"You think because your eyes are blue, we can't see the water pooling?" Tilly snaps.

"Play nice," Cora says.

I can see the fight in Tilly's eyes, but she chomps down on her pickle instead. "Sorry, I just need to get laid. We all need to get laid."

"You got laid five weeks ago, and look what happened," Cora jokes.

"Well, you two need to get laid."

I don't. I really, truly don't. I've had three boyfriends since my nightmare of a husband took his trash self out, and they were three too many. I'm done. I roll myself away from my workbench and pick up the two Cathedral Window lap quilts I squared up yesterday. "Kona Mermaid Shores or Island Batiks Hocus Pocus for my display style?"

Cora says, "Mermaid," and Tilly says, "Hocus Pocus."

The debate explodes immediately. Tilly loves anything Halloween, and I've fussy-cut the Hocus Pocus fabrics so the Cathedral Window diamonds each have a featured Halloween element while the leaves are soft patterns in the traditional purple, green, and orange palette. Cora's more of a solids girl, especially when an ombre effect can be pulled off. I've already tested both samples and found they film well, and they both clearly show the elements of the pattern. In my mind, they're equal.

Well, not exactly. While Cora and Tilly bicker, I thread a needle with black and settle back in my seat to whip-stitch the backside of the binding down on the Hocus Pocus. Sorry, Cora, but this is a livestream for my subscribers, and we're in Halloween craft season.

"Natalie, you back here? We got an emergency!" a masculine voice can be heard yelling faintly in Tilly's feed.

She rolls her eyes and stuffs one last pickle in her mouth before screwing the jar shut. She calls out that she'll be there in a minute as she does a quick reset of her orange hair.

Neon orange, not redhead orange. With black roots. 'Tis the season, and all that.

"He was such a bang until he started calling me *Natalie*, and now he's a total kill," she mutters as she reaches for her phone to end the feed. "See you bitches later!"

The screen drops before I can say anything to her. "I'm sorry, is she about to go kill that guy?" I ask Cora.

Cora snorts. Now that the screen isn't being shared and I can see the full width of her camera frame, her current project is visible. Once upon a time, it would have been an avant-garde asymmetric gown with some trick to it to wow the photogs at the Met Gala. Today's ensemble is a three-piece women's business suit that's formal enough for a lawyer to wear to court but fashionable and trendy enough to stop for drinks at a high-end bar after the trial. This must be the line she's doing for Neiman Marcus. It's nearly done, with completed pants and shirt. The jacket is assembled but unlined, and Cora is fussing with the fit. "You know, the Bang, Marry, Kill game."

Reaching the end of my sample, I ease the fabric out of the machine. "The what?"

"Oh come on, we've definitely played this before. Where you're given a list of three people and you decide who you'd bang, who you'd marry, and who you'd kill?"

I gasp. "Why would you kill one of them?"

"I don't know, that's just the game. Gotta kill one."

"Wait, which am I?"

"What?"

"Am I the bang, the marry, or the kill?"

"No, it doesn't work like that."

"Well, there's three of us: you, me, and Tilly. So—"

"Erm, Joss?" Cora says, her eyes trained just below the camera, meaning she's looking at me.

But I'm not done. She's talking like this is a well-known thing that she and Tilly do often, but I've *never* heard of it before, which means they have a fun thing they do that I've been excluded from. Or, I guess fun, but how awful does this sound? Bang, Marry, or Kill? What kind of options are those? Can you not be friends with someone? Or just not have a relationship at all? What if they're already married, or if they don't want to marry you? "So one of us has to be banged, and one married—"

"Right, but behind you. There's a giant—"

"—and one killed, so what am I?" I finish before what she's saying hits my brain.

"Marry, definitely," a deep, gravelly voice says from behind me.

I spin around and let out a yelp at the sight of the red-haired, hazel-eyed giant.

Chapter Three
GABE

While the Quilted Flower looks roughly the same as the street view photo — a couple of quilts have changed, but that melon-looking one still hangs outside — the interior is nothing like the hobby shops and discount department store craft aisles my sisters used to drag me through in their quests for teenage individuality.

The floor is occupied by two large tables with gridded mats that ladies are cutting panels of fabric on. Both tables are flanked by shelves stacked with coordinated bundles of fabric tied together with ribbons, packs of thin strips rolled together, and mismatched fabrics tightly folded into triangles and kept in vintage cigar boxes. Toward the back of the room, there's a doorframe but no door and a window frame with no window, giving the distinct impression of the reception desk at a doctor's office. There's a vintage cash

C. B. Alice

register alongside a tablet payment system, and although the shop is open and doing business, no one's actually running the register.

Between the doorway and the window is a tall display of threads, the same colors seeming to repeat over and over again in more brands than anyone would think thread needs. The rest of the walls are covered by floor-to-ceiling shelves the exact height of the cardboard holders the fabric is wrapped around, not an inch of space wasted. It ranges from solid fabrics to wild patterns: swirly skulls, stars and moons, those leafy things that are all over the douchey shirts Blaise wears when we're boating, random household items.

I'm looking more closely at a teacup next to a pocket watch, checking the others in the set to see if my suspicions are correct and they've all got Alice in Wonderland images, when a voice as soft and high-pitched as the drunk mouse in the teapot says, "Um, excuse me? Can I help you?"

I turn to see a woman old enough to be my grams with short white hair and a pair of sharp-looking filigreed scissors hanging from her necklace. "Hey, I'm Gabe Shaunessy!" I say with a big smile. I bet it looks really weird that I took one step into the shop and froze. I look past the woman and notice there are two others with shopping bags in their hands looking ready to leave.

I'm blocking the exit. I didn't mean to, but it's what I do. This lady is probably Joss since she's the one willing to say something to me.

"I was sent here by Emily Hess," I continue as I let the ladies through. "She sent me up here to check on a donation you're making to the Jugs — err, Juggernauts — fundraiser?" When the lady continues to stare blankly, I say, "You're Jocelyn, right?"

"Jocelyn? I don't know—oh, ha! Joss. No. That's sweet of you. She's out in the barn. Just cut through to the back and follow the path."

I'm not sure what's so sweet about thinking she's Joss, but I follow the lady's directions, discovering that behind that first wall is at least twice as much fabric in little rooms off the main hall. There's a room of hand-dyed fabrics that look kind of like tie-dye, but the fanciest and least hippie tie-dye ever. What Merrick wears when we're boating. There are sewing machines with price tags I have to look twice at. One of them is giant with this crazy rig attached to it that's $10,000 *used*. Hanging from the walls is thousands of supplies that I can't identify.

I follow a path lined with wilting snapdragons and pansies to the barn. Inside is a large, open room filled with six pods of worktables, mostly cleared off. There are also four of those crazy expensive machines in here. The weird frames? Two of the machines have quilts wound onto them. One of the machines is even running on its own, sewing through the center of the quilt, and I can see the frame slowly moving to make a pattern.

Wild.

At one work station, two octogenarians are working at together to . . . I don't know what they're doing, to be honest, but they have a bedsheet-sized layer of stuffing, and they're attempting to wrangle a big, unfinished piece of fabric over it.

A quilt? Is that fluff the inside of the quilt? Either way, they're struggling, so I hustle over to them, startling them both when they notice me, but the squat, pink-haired grandma lets go of her side, giving me the opportunity to take hold of it.

The willowy, lavender-haired grandma says, "Oh are you helping us? What a sweet young man!"

C. B. Alice

"And a big 'un!" says Pinky. Hopefully the other one is Joss. I've found that ladies who think I'm sweet give me cookies while the ones who go right for my size are more likely to give me more larger treats, like pies and cakes.

And that makes me feel fat.

I get it enough from my teammates, since I'm one of the biggest guys and do have a gut, but I need that gut.

I need my cookies.

I spend at least twenty minutes helping them with the quilt. Purple slides me a pile of pins while Pinky tells me this is for a granddaughter who's marrying another gal next month, and isn't that just the coolest thing. I don't understand why they call what we're doing basting when it's not a turkey and there's no turkey juice, but that's okay. When they trim away some of the fluff, Pinky takes a handful of it and tosses it outside with the explanation that it's for 'Jerry,' which sounds an awful lot like spilled alcohol on the ground for one's homies. Finally, Purple says, "Where are my manners? I'm Rose."

"And I'm Iris," says Pinky.

Huh.

"Gabe," I offer, stretching my hand out.

Rose takes it and giggles like a schoolgirl when I grip hers just right to show I'm a strong man but I won't hurt her. "I know who you are, young man. My Carl has season tickets to the Jugs. He thinks you boys are making it to the playoffs this year."

"I certainly hope so, ma'am." And I can't wait to tell the guys that old people are calling us the Jugs now, too. PR has been hating it, but it's not our fault they gave the team a stupid name. "But I'm actually here to see Joss. Can you point me in her direction?"

Good Guy Gabe

"Ooh," Iris murmurs, and they share a pointed look at my left ring finger.

Oh dear. This is not the first time a little old lady has attempted to match me with her recently widowed daughter who's still plenty old enough to be my mother, but I put a big smile on my face and head through the door they pointed at.

It opens into a short, narrow hallway with a room a few feet ahead that seems to be oriented sideways. Fabric cubbies topped with framed pictures of orchids line the walls. When I step closer to see if I'm right about there not being glass in the frames, I realize they're not pictures at all. They're tiny quilts made from hundreds of slivers of fabric. I get now why there were so many shades of solid fabrics in the shop.

They're for painting with fabric.

I glance the other way and find half a dozen lights pointed roughly in my direction. They share a wall with a spider web of cables, multiple mounted cameras, and a big screen TV currently occupied with a petite, dark-haired woman stitching a jacket on a mannequin. There's a picture-in-picture at the top corner of the screen, and although the image is smaller, it's perfectly lit to show every detail of the big blue eyes, button nose, and pink cheeks of the blonde woman on camera.

Oh, and she's seated right in front of me but distracted by both the conversation and the small quilt in her lap. Visible on the screen is a simple V-neck tee with the logo of the Quilted Flower, but behind her workbench, I can see she's paired it with a patchwork skirt with enough length and volume that she's tucked it between her legs.

"So one of us has to be banged, one of us married, and one of us killed," she's saying, her voice soft and sweet and just a little bit Southern. Exotic for a guy originally from Minnesota. "So which one am I?"

"Marry, definitely," I blurt out.

She lets out a squeaky yelp and spins around too quickly in her swivel chair, going an extra ninety degrees before I catch her and spin her back to face me.

Our eyes meet, and my breath is stolen. She is, quite literally, breathtaking. She's startled by me, understandably so, but something in those gentle blue eyes makes me want to take her in my arms and keep her there forever.

To hold and to protect, is that the line? No, it's to have and to hold, but I would hold and protect her whether I have her or not.

"Are you Joss?" I ask.

She nods silently.

"I've been looking for you all day."

Chapter Four
JOSS

I don't know that I've ever seen such a big man in my life. It doesn't help that I'm sitting and he's leaning over me, but it's like he's eclipsed my world in one move.

I should be frightened of him. His bushy copper beard and undercut, the gleam in his hazel eyes, even the bulk of his shoulders exude a menacing aura. But his casual smile looks genuine, and he's in a baby pink hoodie with a juvenile screen print on it and athletic shorts. That undercut is messy and overgrown enough that it invites my fingers to run through it. I don't think I need to be frightened of him.

Besides, Rose and Iris are like ancient pit bulls. Iris has mace in her bag. I'm pretty sure Rose could do some damage with her arthritis-friendly rotary blade.

So, no, I don't have to fear him. But my heart is pounding harder than it has in a long time.

"I'm Gabe," he says, his smile widening when his eyes drop to my hands in my lap.

"Your sweatshirt is ripped," I squeak out, pointing down near the hem. "Just there."

He looks down and frowns, but even that is incredibly inviting. His mustache covers his upper lip, but his bottom lip is as welcoming to my fingertips as his hair is. "Blaise did that when he rolled off the exercise ball," he explains.

I have no idea what to say. I have no idea who Blaise is. "Oh."

"He didn't break the record."

"I can fix it for you," I whisper, unsure if I'm breathless or just dumbfounded. He's all mass and harsh lines, but my god, those eyes.

"The record?"

"The sweatshirt. I can sew it up for you?"

He lights up like a kid on Christmas who's just unwrapped tickets to Disney. "Really?"

I nod and say, as stupidly as possible, "I have a sewing machine."

"I'd like that."

"Who's Blaise?" I ask.

"My quarterback."

I blink a couple times as I process this, as the wheels start to turn and click into place. "Oh!" I cry out, releasing a laugh on the breath that had stilled in my lungs. "You're with the Juggernauts? That's why you're so big."

"I'm the center."

I don't know what a center is. I've never had any interest in sports. I lived on a treadmill in high school, and once I retired from competition, I did everything I could to avoid any physical pursuits. Cora drags me on walks just to make sure I don't get too sedentary.

But he's here for the quilt, not to . . . sweep me off my feet? Rescue me from my hermitude? Ride off into the sunset with me and the feral raccoon I feed my table scraps to?

"The quilt for the fundraiser, right? It's not ready yet. I was told they didn't need it until day of. Did something change?" I start to stand up. "I have to throw it on the longarm, the computerized ones are both running, but I can run it on a manual." The calculations begin. Today's show is for subscribers. They're generally happy with any content, so if I demo some new free motion quilting on the longarm, I can do something simple but fun with the fundraiser quilt. "Tomorrow, I can have it ready—"

Panic must have leaked into my voice because Gabe rests a gigantic hand on my shoulder, its weight alone enough to keep me seated, its warmth calming, its grip reassuring. "No, no, you don't need to rush it. Emily Hess was worried when you didn't return her calls and asked me to check in on you."

"Oh dear. My car broke down last week, and I left my phone in it."

"See, I told you!" Cora says.

We both snap to her, Gabe with a little wave. "Hey, I'm Gabe."

"Yeah, I caught that. Gabe the center. Joss, I'm telling Jimmy to fix your car."

I sigh. "Fine, fine. Sorry for making you drive out here, Gabe. If you've got an extra minute, I can fix that sweatshirt now. Won't take a minute."

The sweatshirt is suddenly shoved at me, and I catch a light scent off it. Soap, definitely; Gabe must have just showered. There's also a soft, inviting musk with notes of rosemary and freshly cut wood. Masculine but gentle. I glance back to say something, hopefully not anything insane, but my jaw drops.

Gabe is shirtless.

And he is *big*.

Like, okay, we've already established this, but there's a difference between broad-shouldered in a baggy hoodie and seeing it wasn't actually all that baggy. He's got wide, well-defined pecs and a round belly that lacks a six-pack but has the vertical divots proving that the undefined layer is the mass needed to support the strongman build. He looks like he could flip tractor tires and drag firetrucks around on ropes. All that covered with skin lightly bronzed, the sort of tan one gets from working outside all summer instead of deliberately tanning, and lightly dusted in coppery curls that match his messy hair and bushy beard.

My former husband, may demons eat his soul for all of eternity, looked like an evening mug of warm milk in comparison.

Gabe frowns. "I shouldn't have taken that off."

"You absolutely should have," Cora pipes up. "That's just her cocksucker Brian face. She was comparing you to her ex-husband."

"I wish she'd kept that thought to herself," I mutter to Gabe. "But yeah, you look great. I mean, not in a creepy way, I'm not like, thirsting, or—oh but I'm not saying you're not attractive." I spin right back to my sewing table, distracting myself with matching thread with its coordinating bobbin. I also grab one of my business card magnets. "That's my shop number. Please give Emily my apologies and this card."

As he takes the magnet from me, our fingertips brush, and I swear we generate a current. "Yes, ma'am," he rumbles.

At 30, I don't very much appreciate being called *ma'am*, especially when so many of the people I work with are over twice my age, but that current shoots right up my spine the way Gabe says it, so I don't correct him. I'm looping the thread into my machine when Cora makes a soft tutting sound. I raise an eyebrow at her, and she says, "I mean, you should really darn that."

"You can do it however you want," Gabe assures me. "It's just a sweatshirt."

I nearly agree with that. It is just a sweatshirt, and it's in rough shape beyond the tear. The cuffs are splitting; one of the metal grommets has fallen off. It should be retired.

But it's pink and has that silly cat print on it. It's definitely for a girl. The tag has faded to pure white so I can't check to see what size it is, but I'm guessing it's a ridiculous one. This wasn't something just plucked off the rack at Walmart. Maybe it was a gift from someone. Could be a rare find of his. Even a custom order. Whatever it was, it has sentimental value.

Sentimental value deserves darning.

I smile up at him. "Nah, I like darning." Totally a lie.

"Totally a lie," Cora says, and before I can glare at her, she throws in, "I gotta go, you got a show to do, love ya, bye!" and disconnects.

"You have a show? Do you need me to leave?" Gabe asks.

"Nope, I got your hoodie." I begin whipping through the stitches. "I'd say I could make the show about garment repair — definitely not a topic I discuss, but my viewers would probably enjoy it — but I can't have you shirtless on camera. Nobody would learn anything."

Not only do his cheeks flush, but so does his chest, a weirdly intimate thing for me to know about a complete stranger who probably has a line of girlfriends around the block. Everyone went nuts about the Juggernauts when they did well their first year. I overheard plenty of chatter and have already sold through four bolts of fabric with their logo.

"What's your show about?" he asks, his voice going uncomfortable to match his color.

I laugh. "Quilting, of course! But today's for my subscribers, so I can be a little more flexible. I was going to preview the Cathedral Window tutorial I have coming out next month." At his confused look, I nod to the Hocus Pocus quilt. "That's Cathedral Window."

"Ohh," he says, reaching for it but bringing his hand back to ask, "May I?" before grabbing it at my nod. His eyes shift between it and the one I just pulled off my machine. He looks at one of the earlier ones where it's just white squares folded into triangles and stitched to colorful, unfolded squares the same size. "This is pretty. How do you turn that into this?"

"If you subscribe to me, you can find out at seven p.m. Eastern," I say with a wink.

"Yes, ma'am. What's your screen name?"

I smack his phone out of his hand probably harder than I should, immediately returning to the darning because my god, why am I this awkward? "That was a joke. You don't have to subscribe to me. You can Google it. But, like, you don't sew, so that would be weird. Just trust the process." I finish the last stitch, tightening the threads to make sure the hole has closed up but isn't puckering. "Here, you're all set. Does Emily need me to call her? Does she need the quilt early?"

"No ma'am, I think she was just worried something was wrong." He holds the sweatshirt close to his face, studying the tear. "That's so good. I can hardly tell." He slides it back on, wiggling his head through the collar and popping back out, the hood catching so he briefly looks cozy with his head covered in baby pink. He pushes it back and takes hold of the bottom of the sweatshirt, tugging it out so he can look at the patch again.

He glances up at me and then back down. One more glance at me, this time blurting out, *"Doyouwantmetopickyouupforthefundraiser?"* before he looks back down at the sweatshirt.

"What?"

"Do you want me to—"

"Oh!" I squawk out over him, realizing that I just told him my car's in the shop. He was offering to pick the quilt up before the fundraiser. "Yeah, absolutely. That would be fantastic."

"Awesome, it's a date!" he says with way more energy than I think the moment needs. "Well then, I'll look forward to seeing you next Saturday. Good luck with your video tonight."

"Good luck with your, umm, game? Do you have a game this weekend?"

"Yeah, pre-season. We're flying out to Cleveland tomorrow morning. I should probably go pack. It was really nice meeting you, Joss."

"You too, Gabe."

I'm still thinking about him when I launch my stream and, mixed in with the greetings from my regular subscribers, I see a new subscriber flag on the message *I really do want you to show me how to make a cathedral window.*

The new subscriber's screen name is GabeShaunessy, followed by the smiling face with hearts emoji, and then YourFavoriteJug.

"Okay, walk to the wall and back. I need a snappy spin this time. And a stomp. Angry catwalk. I want you pissed that I made you do this and ready to go home. Make the cameras fight to get the good shot. Make them know they are not worthy of you. You're not a model. You're a *super*model. A queen. Why the fuck are you on this runway? You have a goddamn reality show to film and an agent to fire. That's it, bitch, that's it. That's—nope, I fucking hate this length."

I sigh as I hoist myself back up on the platform.

Tilly starts pulling pins from the hem. She's home for three days, and she got roped into working anyway.

Cora scowls at both of us. "This is important. I realize that you just need it to work on film for ten minutes of screen time," she says to Tilly before looking at me and adding, "and you will happily die in a patchwork swing dress, but I need perfection on this runway. I need every single outfit to look great in full motion, full body, all angles, and I need this two-piece dress to look every bit as perfect on a size 8 as it does on a size 2, or I will get roasted for not understanding the everyday woman and still being stuck in my bespoke phase."

"I don't think you're stuck in your bespoke phase," Tilly says as empathetically as she can. As a professional costumer, her only phase is bespoke.

"My feet are just hurting," I add to explain my own sigh.

Cora glares up at me. "Why do you insist on lying when you suck so bad at it?"

"I don't know." It's a fair question. My feet don't hurt. I haven't worn heels regularly in six years and prefer to not put the extra thirty pounds I've gained in that time in stilettos, but no. I've only been in these heels for an hour. I'm fine. "I'm just concerned you're about to drop the hem a quarter inch that no one will see."

"Says the point queen," Cora huffs, but points are super important on quilts. People see when lines don't match. They don't see a quarter inch dusting around the ankles. "Tilly, can you do me a solid and fix that funny seam on the boning casing? See how it's bunching a little?"

Tilly loosens the laces in the back and drops the side zipper, catching the bustier before it falls on the ground. There's no catching my boobs, though.

And listen, there was a point in pageant life where we all dressed in front of each other. I even did some modeling for Cora back in the day, which meant lightning-fast wardrobe changes. It's not like I have any issues being topless in front of my friends. They both make garments. I am apparently a perfectly proportioned size 8, according to Cora, right down to the reasonable height of 5'7". I am their Barbie doll when they need one.

But I'm 30. I have the boobs of a 30-year-old. They are boobs that need either a bra or a far freer spirit than I possess. Of all the things I regret about marrying that asshole monster I married, the one that bothers me the most now is the fact that I wasted my good boob years on a criminally perverted man who was so weak he refused to even live to face the consequences of his actions.

I cross my arms over my chest, not even to cover them so much as to fluff them up as casually as I can, but Cora sees everything.

"I bet Gabe Shaunessy would love to see those gals just how they are."

"Gabe *Shaunessy?*" Tilly repeats, her eyes brightening right up at the prospect of hot gossip.

I groan. I was hoping that what Cora witnessed would end there and not make it to Tilly. Tilly is a dog looking for a bone, but there's no bone here. Gabe was cute and sweet and just enough of an oaf that I got the feeling that he doesn't do anything criminal. He looks safe. He paid for my highest level of subscription and even watched some of my streams this week, which was really sweet of him.

But I can't do this. I have tried to date a few times, and it's always been a disaster. I tell myself I've moved on, but there's a point where things become too real, our lives start to merge, and it hits me that if he's another monster, I'll be destroyed again.

I'm safe here.

"He stopped by on Friday right after you had to go, and he thinks Joss is a marry."

Tilly's jaw drops. "Gabe is totally a marry."

Cora nods as she goes back to adjust the hem down a hair. "Agreed."

Oh god, not this again. "I'm still so confused. Who are the other two?"

"Blaise Sinclair and—" Cora starts.

"Kill," Tilly says immediately.

Cora gasps, stopping what she's doing so she can look Tilly in the eye as she says, "Merrick Briggs is the kill."

"No way! I would ride that man like a show pony. Blaise is crazy."

Cora shrugs. "Yeah, crazy hot."

"Merrick's hot and not crazy."

"Are you sure? Are you really sure? Because I think he's a secret psychopath."

"Whatever," Tilly huffs. "I need Doritos." With that graceless adieu, she stomps her way down the set of stairs and through the door that leads outside. There should be a door at the top of the landing, too, but it got requisitioned for an art project back during the quarantine days, same as this spot that used to be my dining room and is now set up with a platform and circle of mirrors for Cora's tailoring. Since it's a full flight of stairs and the exit is on the opposite side of the building from the path to the barn, it's not like anyone is going to see me standing here topless.

"Leave some Doritos out there for Jerry!" I yell as the door slams.

"You really need to stop feeding the raccoons," Cora chides.

"I'm not feeding raccoons, I'm feeding raccoon. Jerry. And before you say anything, I got some rabies vaccine treats from the SPCA. He's fine."

I can tell Cora doesn't believe me but recognizes a losing fight when she sees one. "So what *is* up with you and Gabe?"

"Nothing." Have I spent way too much time thinking about him this week? Yes. Have I gotten excited seeing him in the chats? Yes. But it's not real.

"Lift your arms," she says, and I swear it's punishment for being grouchy.

"Your model isn't going to be walking down the catwalk with her arms like this."

"First of all, I still want you to be the model, and don't give me that *too old* shit. Second of all, Gabe liked you so much he subscribed to your channel. I saw him in the comments. He was flirting with you."

"He wasn't flirting with me! He was asking for demonstrations."

"And considering you don't even have a phone right now, that was the closest thing to flirting he could do without being a creeper. You should ask him out when he comes to get that quilt."

"Too late. It's today. I left it with Barb in the shop."

"You sneaky bitch, you," Cora gasps. "That's why you wanted to do this today. So you could hide from him."

"I am absolutely not hiding! I am—" I'm interrupted by a knock on the door downstairs.

"Oh for fuck's sake, did Tilly lock herself out and forget the passcode?"

"Pregnancy brain?" I reason, not sure if that's a thing at only six weeks. She's having a rough time in general, has for a few years now. The pregnancy was a one-night stand gone wrong. She's excited but scared, and she's a contractor, so there's no maternity leave. Thankfully, the baby will have two aunties right here. One of them even has a nursery.

That's been dormant for six years.

My apartment is mostly normal. Nice kitchen, little breakfast nook that's more than enough for me, two whole bedrooms and a comfy living room I'm hardly ever in. But that nursery is the one thing from my past I will not let go.

"9317!" I yell down as Cora smacks my underarm to get it up in the air again. "Why could you possibly need me to do this?" I grumble over heavy stomps up the stairs. "It's the dumbest—"

"Oh no," someone who is definitely not Tilly says, and through the reflections in the mirrors set up around me, my eyes meet Gabe's a dozen times.

I shriek, attempting to cover myself. One of my stupid heels slips. I start to tumble, only to be caught in Gabe's arms.

His massive, strong, secure arms.

I see his eyes first, of course, noticing this time that they're the sort of hazel that starts blue in the center before feathering out to an earthy green.

His beard has been trimmed up, the ginger frizz tapered down to a long but tidy strip on his chin.

He's in a tux.

He smells really nice.

I swallow hard and cover my chest with my arm. "Um, hi."

"You gave me the code."

"I thought you were Tilly."

"I'm not."

He gently sets me back on my feet, his hands skimming my sides to make sure I'm solid before he lets go of me.

"That was fucking hot," Cora whispers.

I give her the most pained look while Gabe scrubs the back of his head sheepishly. "Sorry, I thought you'd be ready by now."

As Cora mutters something about how he's even bigger in real life, I bring my hands up to my mouth to cover my gasp. "Oh my god, no, this is my fault. The quilt's ready. I told Barb where it was. She must have forgotten."

"Oh, she gave it to me. I meant you. I thought *you'd* be ready now."

I shake my head. "I'm not going."

He furrows his brows, and then his face goes red, his eyes giant, and he juts his hands out.

To cover my chest.

Because my arms were covering them until my brain thought it was more important to cover my face.

"You have to go," he says with a scowl. "You made the quilt."

I let out a nervous laugh, unsure if I should cover my boobs myself, but he didn't leave space for my hands there. If I put mine over his, I'm basically making him grope me.

Perish the thought.

"Vendors don't go to these sorts of things."

"You said you'd go with me. I asked if you wanted me to pick you up, and you said yes."

He's so giant that even with the platform and the heels, I'm only a few inches above him. But he starts to look incredibly small, like he's deflating before my very eyes.

There's nothing more terrifying to me than a society function in Wilmington. This is the sort of event that attracts money and influence. A decade ago, my husband surely would have wanted us to go, and I would have loved an excuse to don a pageant gown.

The thought now has my lungs tightening, my breaths going shallow as I shrink back, replacing his hands with my arm once more. Still, I feel bad for Gabe as I say, "I meant the quilt. I thought you meant the quilt."

"Right, well." He doesn't say anything else, just bends down in his nice tux and his polished shoes to pick up a small box he must have dropped to catch me. It contains a corsage matching the boutonniere I'm only now noticing on his jacket. It's simple but elegant and modern, a sprig of orchids with a bit of green.

The flower projects I have framed in my studio, the two central ones, they're both orchids.

I gnaw at my bottom lip as I exchange a look with Cora.

"Wait!" she pipes up. "She'd love to go!"

I don't have a dress! I mouth at her, but Gabe is already returning, this time looking cautiously hopeful.

"Honey, you're in a dress."

"I am in a skirt. I really don't think Gabe wants to hold my chest all evening!"

Gabe wisely stays quiet as, from the bottom of the stairs, Tilly yells, "I'm all over that boning!"

"This is for your show," I remind Cora. "I can't—" I look back to Gabe. "I'm sorry, I sound like I don't want to go with you. That's not true. But this is for Cora's runway next month."

"I'll make it different colors," Cora says.

Gabe holds up the corsage. "You match the flower."

I look down at myself as though I'm not surrounded by mirrors and haven't been in this for the past hour. Both the bustier and ruffly, asymmetrical skirt are colorblocked in white and fuchsia. I really do match it.

"But you can say no, I won't be offended," Gabe adds.

But he will be. Or, he should be. It all clicks now; he's been hanging out in my stream to get to know me as best as he can. Cora was right. He did it as appropriately as he could. He's a good guy.

I shoot a desperate look to Cora. "It's in Wilmington."

Cora's lips thin down. She approaches Gabe, and it's impossible not to notice how gigantic he is when Cora, barely five feet and thin as a breeze, faces him.

"You need to protect her."

Gabe recoils. "I would *never* hurt her."

"It's not you. It's the world."

Puzzlement crosses his features, but he shakes it away like it doesn't matter why I need protection. It's enough for him to know I do. He fluffs up his chest, taking up the entire room with his presence. "I will protect her with my life."

Cora gives me a look I can't fight.

But I don't think I want to after that proclamation. "I'd love to go with you, Gabe."

"Awesome," he says on a big exhale. "I'll be back in an hour. Does that work?"

I cringe. Tilly's pulling a seam apart; Cora needs to stitch the hem. That's the better part of an hour right there, and I still need hair and makeup.

"I just saw Sherry Hunt in the shop," Tilly says. "I'll drag her up to do your hair."

Chapter Five
GABE

The good news: Joss agreed to go to the Kick-Off Gala with me and does seem to agree that it's a date.

The bad news: her friends bullied her into it.

A win is a win. And it's certainly not the biggest dating disaster I've ever had. I kept the same girlfriend throughout most of high school and college even though my sisters all hated her and, admittedly, she was kind of mean to me, until one of my high school football buddies sent me pictures of her sucking him off.

He apologized because he didn't know until after the fact that we'd never broken up. It was good intentions on his part, I get that, but she almost never gave me blow jobs, and that stung as much as the cheating itself.

Oh, another thing that I'm not sure how to rate because I could argue that it's both good and bad? I touched Joss's boobs. I didn't mean to. I'd already seen them by that point and wish I hadn't — because that made my dick get really excited about life — and I wanted to be a gentleman. The best solution seemed to be holding my hands in front of them. I just forgot how long my arms were for a second, and squash.

Super squash. Warm and soft. A nice round shape to them. And no matter how hard I tried to ignore it, this little voice in the back of my head — possibly the voice of my dick — had to keep pointing out the fact that the longer we stood there, the more her nipples prodded at my palms. So yeah, I really wish I hadn't grabbed her tits in a gentlemanly way, but her nips and my dick were on the same page there, and that's gotta mean something.

Okay, what it means in the immediate moment is that the hour I gave her to get ready? I run home and rub one out.

I'm not proud, but you do what you gotta do.

Even following that up with a cold shower, the moment I think about Joss's nipples again, my dick starts seriously considering things. I need a long-term solution: a minor but critical wardrobe change.

I feel even better about this decision when I return to her place and discover that the top of her dress is one of those form-fitting, waist-tucking bustiers that puts her breasts in cups that only cover so much. Now that she's in five-inch heels but no platform, it's clear that I'm going to be staring down at soft, jiggly, porcelain flesh all evening, and it's going to be inviting me to touch it at every opportunity.

Most of her soft blonde hair's been pulled back in a ponytail and left to hang in wide curls that bounce between her shoulder blades as we walk to the car. What's been used for a hair tie is the wrist corsage I got her after asking Huang if this is the sort of event that requires corsages. He's got a girl; he should know this stuff.

"I didn't make us a reservation anywhere," I have to admit sheepishly when I realize we're in the sort of fancy dress that calls for fancy restaurants. "I'm sorry, I should have done that. I don't even know what you like. If I'd asked you that, you would have known I was inviting both the quilt and you to this."

Her laugh is light and sweet. Her elegant fingers, with their simple, white-tipped nails, wrap around my bicep. It helps calm me, although my thoughts immediately stray to the other places her hand could go. "I'm happy anywhere. I even brought my lipstick to freshen up."

She holds up her purse, and I say, "It's crazy how quickly your friends threw that together. It looks like it came from the store." Seriously, they must have grabbed one of the framed orchids from her workroom and slapped it onto a purse.

"What, this? Nah, I made it years ago. For one of Cora's shows, actually."

"Wait, you make purses?"

"Don't get any ideas. I loathe making purses."

"And you make your own patterns, too?"

"Not the purse pattern. Just the orchid."

"You're amazing. I am absolutely amazed by you."

She's flustered by that. I get the idea that she's not one to handle compliments well, but that's crazy. She's got this whole business going on here. Yeah, she's got the actual shop, but she also has an online store that has hundreds of items and thousands of ratings. She's got that subscription content, and the streams I've watched live have gotten at least fifty viewers each time. Some of the replay videos have thousands

C. B. ALICE

of views, and again, they're all paid subscribers. She's making big money just teaching people how to quilt.

She's amazing.

"You're a professional athlete!" she counters. "A starter. I know nothing about sports, so I didn't really know who you are, but Cora and Tilly do. *That's* amazing!"

I shrug. "I throw a ball between my legs and hit people really hard. It's not that amazing."

"It's way more complicated than that."

I take a glance at her and see the sincerity in her expression. I was just regurgitating what I've heard hundreds of times in my life. Mostly from people who don't care about football, but I've gotten it from my own quarterbacks before, too. One of the things that drew me to Blaise was the fact that he might be chaotic and hard to rein in at the best of times, but he's only ever been respectful to me.

"I like to think it is," I say gently before resting my hand over hers and driving to my favorite pizza place.

Chapter Six
JOSS

I shamelessly don the garbage bag that the pizza place provides me with and even cuts a neck hole out at my request. I'm rewarded with Gabe's praise of, "That's the smartest thing I've ever seen," when I'm halfway through my chicken wing flight and drop one. There's a Louisiana dry rub and a crispy adobo, but it's the juicy, greasy, sticky raspberry habanero wing that goes splat in my lap. Thanks to the industrial-sized trash bag poncho, the only tragedy is I feel like I shouldn't eat the wing off the trash bag, even if it is clean. It's a principle thing.

If I were home alone, I'd do it. But I don't want Gabe to think I'm a total trash panda. We'll leave that for Jerry.

"If you think dropping a wing is smart, wait 'til you see me try to peel shrimp."

Gabe's hazel eyes glitter at that. "You want some shrimp?"

I look down at the table. It's just the two of us, but the hostess took one look at Gabe and sat us at a six-top. The plastic red-and-white tablecloth is now barely visible beneath my wings, Gabe's pizza, my margarita, his hard seltzer, the nachos and mozzarella sticks we got as an appetizer, and the basket of bread. Gabe's had the lion's share of it, but I've had plenty myself. I'm about to steal a slice of his Hawaiian pizza.

But shrimp? "Ummm, yes?"

"They're bacon-wrapped coconut shrimp."

I gasp. "Oh my god, yes!"

At that, Gabe laughs boldly and loudly, attracting the attention of our fellow diners. People have taken note of us the entire time we've been here. Before we even sat, three separate tables stopped us to ask Gabe about the upcoming season and request signatures. The woman at the table next to us slides her eyes up and down Gabe as he laughs, the third time she's done it.

And why shouldn't she? He's hot. Every man I've been in a relationship with in the past has been the intellectual sort. Attractive men, but smaller and more polished. Gabe is an absolute beast, an aesthetic I'd never think I'd be attracted to until he walked into my life. Now, I can't stop staring at him.

It's been six years since I last went to Wilmington. Only a twenty-minute drive, but I was so traumatized last time I was here that none of my friends or employees question why I refuse to drive those couple miles. It's rare for me to even leave my property. I get almost everything delivered.

Gabe doesn't know why I need to be protected, but Cora certainly did, and he's taking his promise seriously. He's been incredibly polite with his fans, so I don't think anyone has even noticed the way he's placed himself between me and them except me. I feel safe with him in a way I haven't in a very long time. Certainly not with any other man.

So I take no offense when he says, "I don't think I seen another woman get so excited about trash food. Except Leah, my baby sister. This is awesome. If you like ethnic stuff too, I have so many places I wanna take you. And I wasn't talking about the wing. I meant the bag. That's genius. I need to tell my mom about that. She'll throw us all in bags at the Christmas party this year."

I giggle. Honest to goodness giggle. "I can't take credit for it. I did pageants growing up, and it's an old pageant mom trick."

Gabe folds a slice of pizza in half and takes a single bite that's half the slice, washing it down with water. He's barely touched his seltzer. "Oh yeah? Phoebe — that's my older sister — she was obsessed with Toddlers and Tiaras, made me watch it with her. Was it any of those pageants?"

I duck my head down to hide my blush. "Yeah, I'm way older than them, but I met most of the kids on the show when I was Miss Alabama."

Gabe freezes in the middle of lifting a stack of at least six nachos, somehow masterfully balancing them so not a single jalapeno falls off. "Holy crap, you were a Miss Alabama? Like, *the* Miss Alabama?"

"Like, was I Miss Alabama in the Miss America pageant? Yeah," I admit, wishing I'd insisted on an opaque foundation for today. There's no way he's not seeing my face go beet red. "But I lost terribly. I was basically a back-up dancer."

"That's still incredible," Gabe says with a giant, enamored grin that I can't help but warm up to. "Do you still do it? Is there an adult version of pageants?"

"God no. I mean, yes, there are adult pageants. But I'm certainly not competing. Look at me!"

"I am."

He says it so gravely that my breath catches in my throat. He's staring hard at me, his lids going heavy like he's thinking thoughts far darker than this ridiculous moment of a grease buffet between us and a black trash bag for a dress. My thoughts go straight to my dining room when I forgot that I was topless and bared myself for him, and he did the gentlemanly thing and covered me from his eyes.

But his gruff, gigantic, sinfully warm palms grazed my breasts, and for a second, every forgotten, abandoned nerve ending there lit up, pebbling my flesh to push back into him, begging for more touch, forgetting that we were nearly strangers and Cora stood there watching.

I had to run to the restroom the moment he left to clean myself up, and thank goodness the morning required no more wardrobe changes, because Cora certainly would have noticed I changed my underwear during my potty break.

"I, umm, I was on a diet my whole childhood," I whisper, needing to pull myself away from thoughts I shouldn't be having in a family restaurant. "Nothing crazy when I was little, just portion control, but then it got strict when I was a teenager, and I practically lived on a treadmill. So when I quit and then . . . ended up being by myself, I just stopped worrying about it." I grin down at the feast between us. "I guess I do get really excited about food, but it's so good. I want it all."

Gabe nods in understanding. "I'm gonna get it all for you, then." He waves his hand for our server, on the opposite side of the room and clearly busy entering another table's order into the computer. The server gestures that she saw him, but instead of waiting for her to come over, Gabe yells, "An order of bacon-wrapped coconut shrimp for the lady!"

Not a single person seems put out by him interrupting their conversations, but I'm quickly realizing that the entire city of Wilmington knows Gabe's a good guy. And maybe, just maybe, that'll protect me. Maybe Wilmington has forgotten who I am.

Chapter Seven
GABE

The moment we enter the ballroom, Joss tenses, and I don't like it.

I mean, I love the way she holds my arm. I want to feel her arms around me as we snuggle under a blanket in front of the TV as much as I want those perfectly manicured nails digging into my bare arms as she screams my name, but I don't want her to feel scared of a social event.

I want her to feel safe.

I find Merrick in the crowd. I'll put my arm around Joss and give her the opportunity to join the conversation with Merrick and me but not force it. I'll make her comfortable. Merrick is one of my closest friends on the team, along with Blaise, Evan Allore, and Dom Morales. I'd rather spend the night introducing her to my friends than forcing her to deal with strangers who are being weird with her.

C. B. Alice

Some people are shooting us seriously evil eyes, and I just don't get it. I don't care to, either. Joss is great.

Merrick is with his on-again, off-again girlfriend Selene. Last I heard, he hated her. Based on their body language, that's still true. Selene's a bitch, so it's understandable, just like Merrick is sadistic with a sprinkling of masochism, so it makes sense for him to fly someone he hates into town just to do this thing.

Oh, and I'll have to listen to them hate-fuck tonight before he sends her packing tomorrow. Not even because the walls are thin between our bedrooms. They're probably going to do it in the kitchen or the living room or the bar, and they're going to be stupidly loud about it. I don't know why he's like this, but it's exhausting.

I'm concerned I shouldn't be introducing Joss to Merrick while Selene's here, but then Joss responds to Selene's cultivated disdain with her bright, unassuming smile. She even loosens her grip on my arm, giving me the opportunity to drop my hand to the small of her back. She blows right past the roll of Selene's eyes when she says, "Oh my gosh, I know you! You're the, oh gosh, the lady with the thing, the big ball thing!"

Selene's groan would make me think she was furious with Joss if I didn't know how much she loves being recognized and has even staged this kind of encounter in the past. "It's a Scandinavian mercury detoxifier," she says in her most bored voice.

It's not Scandinavian or mercury, and the sound it makes when you touch it isn't the toxins getting drawn out of your bloodstream; it's a texture on the surface. She's sold thousands of the stupid things in her luxury holistic spa shop, and she knows it's all a scam.

"Right, yeah, a Scandinavian mercury detoxifier." Joss gives her the biggest doe eyes, so big I'm thinking she might be baiting Selene and says, "I've always wondered how you made the mercury solid like that. And how do you prevent mercury poisoning? Like, it's just so smart."

Selene huffs and says, "It's an alloy," as she turns to Merrick, giving Joss the literal cold shoulder. "Babe, can you—"

"What's an alloy?" Joss asks as Merrick says, "I vomit-burped when you called me *babe.*"

This is possibly the greatest thing I have ever seen. Selene, with her ill-fitting, inappropriately sheer dress that barely covers her panties, her hair pulled back so tightly it's doubling as a facelift and her contouring makeup that makes her nose look like the back of a skunk from the side, is getting trounced by Joss. I don't know how Joss is so good at destroying mean girls, but it's hilarious.

Selene's stuck, and when she's stuck, she lashes out at the person who looks the weakest. She's also sort of dumb about it, usually going after Blaise when, admittedly, I'm the one who lacks the snappy comebacks. She fails again now, going for Joss. "Who even are you, and why are you talking to me right now?"

"Oh, I'm Joss Page. I'm a quiltfluencer."

She says it all with a happy bob of the head, like it's the most normal thing in the world and she's genuinely excited to talk to Selene. But as she says it, a couple of older, sour-faced ladies pass behind me, and one of them says, "She's still Jocelyn Edgars," to her companion just loudly enough that I can hear it, too.

Joss's hand clenches, and if she was going to say anything else, it's cut off, giving Selene the chance to dig in with, "That's not even a thing."

"Not really. You're right. I've only got four hundred thousand followers, and I think I'm at three thousand paid subscriptions. It's nothing, really."

If Selene was wearing less make-up, I'm sure I'd see her pale at that. She's got more followers for sure, but followers are easy. It's a click of a button, no financial burden. Three thousand paid subscriptions means a minimum $15,000 monthly, less the processing fees, for Joss. I paid $300 for a full year of her highest tier, and she has plenty of others at that price point. She's making well into the six figures from that alone.

I know for a fact that Selene isn't doing that well. She sells nudes and private cam time to make ends meet. Yeah, she looks like money, but most of it is gifts and product endorsements.

Whatever she's about to say, Merrick cuts her off by pounding the rest of his beer, turning to her, and belching obnoxiously in her face. "I need another drink, let's do this." He even goes as far as to slap her ass to get her moving before he nods to Joss. "We'll talk later."

Joss stands there frozen for several seconds before saying, "I don't think I like Merrick."

"He grows on you."

"So does fungus."

I scan the crowd for other people to introduce her to, landing on the Allores. They're a younger couple, Evan having been drafted by the Jugs straight out of college last year, but Keira's got a good head on her shoulders. Strangely, though, when Keira spots us approaching, she grabs him by the arm and drags him straight out of the ballroom.

Huh.

I shrug it aside and find Blaise and Candy, who's definitely a stripper but is also nice and happy to meet Joss.

Joss, in turn, is really excited when Candy says her mom is a subscriber.

"Oh? What's her name?" Joss asks.

"Oh, I can't imagine you know her. I don't think she talks or anything. Lisbet Rosser?"

Joss gasps. "What are you talking about, I love Lisbet! Oh my gosh, that means you're, oh god, lemme think. You're Tara? The radiologist?"

Candy — or Tara — is shocked and delighted. "I am! I am a radiologist!"

"Really?" Blaise asks, as surprised as I am. I guess we both thought she was a stripper.

She gives him a little shove. "I do exist outside of Red Ripple. I told you I was there to pay off student loans. The Firebugs aren't just a bunch of sluts."

"What's a Firebug?" Joss asks way too gleefully for my comfort. I don't need her getting sucked into that circle. By all accounts, Blaise is a better catch than I am. I would never tell Joss she can't be friends with his fangirls, but I really don't want her head getting filled with all the reasons she should ditch me for him.

"It's this asshole's fan club," Tara says with a jab of her thumb at Blaise. "You know, 'cause his name is Blaise? Like, *blaze?* I don't know why we do it. He's such a prick to us. He's lucky he's so good in bed. Are you one of Gabriel's Angels?"

Joss drops her jaw in exaggerated shock as she tugs on my sleeve. "Do you have a fan club, too?"

I shift uncomfortably. I don't want her to get the wrong idea about me. "I don't have sex with any of them."

"He's just in it for the cookies," Blaise jokes, using his left hand to smack my gut.

C. B. Alice

Perfect. Didn't want her to get the *right* idea about me either. Thanks, Blaise.

Tara shoots eyeball daggers at Blaise. At least she's got my back. "Did you really make that quilt, Joss? Are you selling the pattern?"

I can see from here that the quilt is a long, skinny design with the Jugs wheel and roses logo. Now that I've found someone for Joss to talk to — and ignore the weird glances she's been getting — I take the opportunity to get a closer look at it, offering to get a plate of snacks for everyone if Blaise is good to watch Joss. He shoos me off with a request for a tray of fig pockets.

An actual tray. Like straight off the table.

I'm not doing that. That will absolutely get me in trouble.

The quilted Jugs logo is, as expected, incredible. From a distance, it looked like the team colors of ruby and saffron, lit with a spotlight to give it depth, but there aren't extra lights on it. Joss has mastered creating shadows and texture out of solid fabrics. An even closer inspection reveals that it's been quilted on one of those giant machines — longarms, I know they're called now — with a pattern of vines and roses that Joss would have had to trace by hand instead of leaving to the computer to guide it through the machine.

On the bidding app, it's described as a family stadium throw, with the thought that up to four fans can warm up under it during the colder games. It's a nice thought, but I'm thinking it would be even better on the sidelines for some of us to huddle under in Buffalo in December, so I drop a bid of $5,000. The current price jumps from $2,400 to $5,100, which means at least one other person is recognizing how goddamn incredible this thing is.

It takes a bid of $7,100 for me to take the top position. I set a timer to check on it in an hour and head toward the hors d'oeuvres, but I'm intercepted by Emily Hess.

Obviously, I'm not a fan of interceptions.

"What is Jocelyn Page doing here?"

I swear the tone comes right from that speak-to-the-manager haircut, but I straighten myself up so I can look as down on Emily as much as I can. "You told me to get a date, so I got a date. In fact, you told me to get a date and then sent me straight to Joss. So if anything, you told me to ask Joss to be my date."

"I told you to make sure she was alive, not to date her."

"You said it wasn't a proof-of-life check! I'm not dating her. Yet. But I'm working on it."

Emily covers her face, no doubt smudging her makeup, but honestly? It had that aging-schoolteacher-who's-trying-too-hard look to it, so it's no tragedy. "No, you can't date her. Seriously, Gabe. You can't. And she can't be here."

"Why, because she's the hired help?" I fire back, recalling how Joss said vendors aren't invited to events. "Well, news flash, the entire team is hired help. The only difference is we were forced to be here. Did you see how much that quilt is going for now? My photo ops were fifty a pop. She's going to make more than half the team combined."

Emily's shoulders sag. If she wasn't trying to kick Joss out for the stupidest reason ever, I'd say she actually felt bad. "Joss is a really nice woman. I want the best for her. But she's not going to have that here."

"Why not? You're being ridiculous."

"You don't know the story, Gabe. Wilmington is a big place, but it's still got small-town issues. They're never going to forget her husband."

"The ex? From the sounds of it, she hates the guy, too. That's why she's divorced."

"Not divorced. Widowed. He was . . . a very bad man. And I promise you, I don't think she did anything wrong. Most people don't. But there are enough people who do—"

She suddenly cuts herself off, and if I thought she might have been feeling bad before, I can definitely tell she's feeling bad now when she gasps and covers her mouth as her gaze goes past me.

A hand lands on the back of my arm. I already know it's Joss before she says, "I'm not feeling well, but you should stay. I'll call for a ride."

I don't need to look at her to hear how upset she is. It took me all of ten seconds in her shop to imagine us on a giant sofa in oversized sweaters with three kids and two dogs cuddling around us while we watch game reels and sip cocoa. I'm not going to drop that because she was once married to a criminal. We all make bad choices. So I don't get upset, I get pissed.

Emily stiffens up. Her lips purse into a scowl. The gleam in her eye tells me that any compassion she might have felt died with the grip I put on Joss's waist. "You understand it's nothing personal."

Incredibly, Joss nods. Even smiles apologetically. "Of course. I hope the quilt does well."

Absolutely not. This isn't happening. Joss is mine. Where I go, she's going. No one's going to get me without her, and Joss needs to know right now that she is my utmost concern.

I nearly open the app to retract my bid so it doesn't do well, because Emily doesn't deserve that victory, but I can't ruin charity.

I *can* ruin a charity event.

I move my hand from Joss's bicep to her waist, shoot one more pointed glare at Emily, and turn away. I head toward Merrick, who's dicking around on his phone to piss Selene off. Even better, there's a door not far behind him marked EMPLOYEES ONLY.

When Merrick sees me approaching, I mouth, "Barbecue Express," at him.

Several other teammates catch it and casually grab their dates, easing their way toward the wall as though they're concerned a grenade might be pitched into the crowd.

Merrick grabs Selene's shoulder to pull her from her conversation with the team owner's daughter to scream, "When were you going to tell me about the video you're selling of getting fucked in the ass by Darren Whiting and Corey Devine at the same time and then showing off your stretched asshole to the world?"

Well, shit. I have no idea if that's a real video or not, but I asked him to ruin the event, and he delivered. Gasps ripple across the crowd. Everyone's repeating it to everyone else, spreading it like wildfire, giving me the opportunity to lead Joss toward that Employees Only door without anyone noticing.

Chapter Eight
JOSS

Emily's right. I think that's the hardest part about this. She was looking out for me by not inviting me. I should have told Gabe immediately, cut things off cleanly.

Now it's going to hurt. Because no matter how I feel about him, no matter how charming and funny he is, no matter how safe he feels, no matter how hard my heart pounds every time his giant hands sweep down my sides, he is in the public light where I'm not welcome.

"Is this a back way out?" I ask, distracted by the shift to linoleum and primer paint.

He hurries me down the hall. "Not sure," he says, his head turning to look at the doors we pass, reading the signs on them until he comes to a dead halt.

I attempt to stop myself, but my heels don't have a lot of traction. They skid, and I bump into him. He catches me and pivots me into a door, using my ass to push it open. I don't need to turn around to recognize the distinct, peculiar scent of cleaning supplies, water, metal, and paper. A public restroom.

He sits me down on the counter next to the sink. His hands settle on either side of my thighs, containing me, but I'm not one to get claustrophobic. The containment is comforting in a way.

"Do you want to talk about it?" he asks, his deep, resonant voice echoing on the tile walls.

"About the exit? I'm sure if we keep going, we'll—"

"About what Emily said. And what your friend said. What people were gossiping about."

I frown. Right. *That.* "No, but—"

"Then you don't have to," Gabe says like it's the easiest thing in the world. Like he's just asked me if I want to tell him what my first car was or what color my underwear is.

"Really?" I croak out, my throat dried from the emotions I refused to let myself succumb to in the ballroom in front of everyone else. He looks so sympathetic and supportive that I could forget about it all.

Except I can't. Gabe does need to know. The sooner the better. Rip that Band-Aid right off before it's completely buried beneath the skin.

"I do need to tell you. Emily isn't wrong. I'm . . . I'm hated in Wilmington." Everything I've done in the last six years was with that in mind. It's why I started out in social media before opening my shop in the remnants of my ex-nightmare's practice. It hits different saying it out loud, though.

My sinuses tingle. I tell myself not to make a big, soppy mess of myself, but the only thing that stops it from happening is Gabe's lips.

Crashing into mine.

I'm not a prude. I've had my share of first kisses. The ones I'm most familiar with are the end of the date, in the front seat of the car or at my doorstep. There have been a couple terribly romantic, impulsive ones in public places. But this kiss?

This is a different beast entirely.

This isn't romantic, this is *passionate*. The way Gabe's thick, soft lips slide over my gloss, I wouldn't say it's a desperate motion, but it's an intense one. One of his hands goes to the back of my neck, digging into the base there, the other at my waist, supporting me and keeping me close.

I take hold of his shirt, keeping him close as I demand more from him and he obliges, flicking his tongue over my teeth, seeking passage I happily give. Our tongues meet and tangle like this is what they were meant for, like this is shared space, like everything that's his and mine is ours. Like we haven't only just met but have always known each other; it's only taken this long to finally share the space that was always designated for us both.

It's so damn easy for me to lose myself in our kiss and forget that there's a whole world out there that hates me, that I can't just curl myself up inside him and vanish for more than these couple stolen moments.

But when he pulls away so we can rest our foreheads against each other as we catch our breaths, it all comes right back. I reach up into his beard, enjoying the softness of it even as I perversely hope the scratch of it shows around my mouth. I don't want everyone to know we snuck off to make out in the bathroom like teenagers, but I want them to see his mark on me. "Why did you bring me in here? We have to go."

His hand has somehow made its way through the slit in my skirt to my upper thigh, so natural I didn't notice it except to be thankful it's finally where it belongs, on my bare skin. His hand has been mostly on my waist tonight, and despite the divide in my dress, he's been careful to keep his fingers atop the fabric when it would have been oh so easy to slide a digit beneath my bodice. "We all have bad shit in our past," he says, tilting my head up for a softer kiss as he kneads into my thigh with slow, hypnotic circles. "Maybe yours is worse. I don't know, and I don't care. It sounds like it was a long time ago and nothing you had control over. And even if you did, it's the past. The only thing I care about is your future. Our future."

It's such a big word. *Our*. I've been a *my* for a very long time. When my nightmare came to life, I had no choice except to dig my roots into salted earth. Cora and Tilly are immune only because their world isn't here, just their homes. And Tilly's about to be glued to this spot for long enough that I'm concerned about what my reputation is going to do to her as well. She doesn't have a choice now, either, not when her family may as well be in the bottom of the ocean for as useful as they are, but she might end up wrecked by her association with me.

Gabe will end up wrecked, too.

But I want him. The very second I first saw him, even while I was so startled I couldn't catch my breath, I felt something I don't know that I've ever felt before. It's taking everything I have not to launch myself at him.

"We can't have a future," I protest, although the words are short and cut off by heavy breaths as Gabe's thumb shifts a critical inch to rest against my panties. It's all overwhelming, and the rumbling sound he makes, no doubt at the discovery that my panties are damp, is enough to make me whimper. "You don't understand. I'll ruin you."

His thumb stays separated from me by the thin stretch of cotton between my legs, but it finds the path of my labia and traces it up and down, making me clench at the delicate pressure. "Ma'am, I was undrafted."

"I don't know what that means."

"My football career might never have happened. I wasn't good enough in college. No one wanted me. It took five years to get signed. Most men give up. Some pros are already retiring, or their contracts ended and they weren't picked up again."

He pinches the crotch of my panties, forcing it between my labia so the fabric which seemed so slick a moment ago is rough against my clit.

I should stop him. This is terribly inappropriate. We're in a bathroom anyone could walk into with a phone and turn this into the biggest scandal the Jugs have had since Blaise slapping a senator's ass and inviting her up to his room at last year's formal event.

I should push him away and insist he let me go for both our sakes, but I wrap my arms around his neck. It's as much to bring him closer as to dispel the chokehold he put on my heart by saying no one wanted him. I know he's talking about football, but it feels deeper than that.

He rubs his free hand briskly across my shoulder blades, skin on skin, as he slides a finger in the crevice alongside the cotton, sending shivers through me. I can't stop this, no matter how inappropriate this is.

"It's a miracle I got signed, and it was another miracle when the Jugs picked me up. This is my last season I'm contracted for, and if that miracle doesn't happen again, it'll be because of what I did on the field, not because of anything that happened in your life before I ever met you. I promise you that."

With a pinch of my clit between his fingers, I cry out, and he takes the chance to claim my mouth roughly. Our teeth clash as he drags his thumb along my clit and folds his middle finger to dig the whole knuckle into the rim of my pussy.

I want his words to be true. He's so big and bold and demanding, but just as laid-back and unruffled that it's impressive that my tiny life could impact his. It all seems so ridiculously plausible right now.

I can have this life.

I can be his girl.

I can stand right behind him, where his spotlight won't touch me.

I can come right here on the counter of the employee restroom.

"Are you close, sweet girl?" he whispers against my cheek as the pulses start to get me and I struggle to breathe. I'm overwhelmed by the need for everything, but I need more. I reach for his pants, only peripherally noting that the hardness my fingers brush against feels not quite organic, but he easily pins my wrists together with one hand. "No, no. This is for you."

"Gabe!" I whine, but there's nothing left in me except fireworks racing up and down my body, curling my toes and tingling the roots of my heart. The world goes white behind my eyelids. I lean back against the mirror as both of Gabe's hands go to my thighs, rubbing them to ease me through it.

"Are you my girl, Joss?" he asks once I've settled and he's lowered my skirt back down. "You're mine now, yeah?"

I nod, about the best I can do in the moment.

He pulls some paper towels out of the dispenser, I'm thinking to clean me up, and I'm sort of right. A second later, they're damp and being scrubbed around my mouth, removing my trashed lipstick.

"That makes me really happy," he says.

I'm happy, too.

Chapter Nine
GABE

The way Joss holds my hand between hers and leans against me as we walk back down the corridor, not a thought — or at least not a word — of protest to returning to the crowd, is everything. And the decision I made back at the house when I decided that rubbing one out wasn't going to get the job done? Absolutely the right call, even if I've spent the night chafed and missed out on an opportunity for a hand job.

It was for the best. I would have made a mess of her pretty dress and not been able to return to the gala. Probably pissed Cora off, too. I know she's already planning to make a different dress for her show, but I imagine she'll want this back in one not-cummed-on piece.

Two pieces.

Everything seems to have settled back down to the typical din of polite conversation when we return to the ballroom, but key people are missing, including Merrick and Selene. Emily Hess is attempting to fire up her laser eyes at me, and I'm wondering if we should be making our own exit before the gossips get to speculate too much about why we were absent for so long. I pull out my phone, place another bid on Joss's quilt to take it over $12,000, and look back up to see Blaise barreling toward me, his date in tow and gesturing like we should go *now*.

I don't get why, though, so I stand my ground, not comprehending why Blaise has his right hand low at his hip, fisted and cocked back slightly, until it's too late.

He punches me right in the dick hard enough that I hear a cracking sound I'm not sure is knuckle or plastic.

Blaise yelps and backs up, hopping up and down and shaking his fist out.

I buckle over, the protection I went with to keep from tenting my tuxedo pants pinching one of my balls enough to knock the wind out of me.

We already have half the room staring at us. It's not even the hushed whispers and attempts to ignore scandal from Merrick's distraction. This is full record scratch, everyone freezing and staring at us, with no idea of what happened. Hell, I don't know what happened.

"Are you wearing a cup?" Blaise shrieks, his pitch too high, as though he was the one who just clipped his manhood.

"Why did you punch me in the dick?" I fire back, anchoring my hands on my thighs and crouching slightly, which has the dual effect of helping me catch my breath while also comforting me and preparing my body to take another hit because seriously, who knows what Blaise is about to do. But bent knees? Crouched down? This is a position my body knows well. This is safe.

"*Whyyyyyy* are you wearing a cup?" Blaise screams again. Now the entire room is turned to us. They heard that. I'm gonna have to explain that.

"You . . . punched me . . . in the dick," I grind out.

Joss rubs my back. Hopefully her attention is more on the punch than the cup.

"You left me out of chaos," Blaise whines. He actually whines. Like a toddler. "And you're wearing a cup! You're in a tux, and you're wearing a cup. Who does that?"

I finally get the momentum to straighten myself back up, and fair credit to Blaise, he looks more upset than angry. I might have hurt his feelings. That doesn't excuse this. I don't know if anything does. And the idiot is still shaking his right hand out, which has to be scaring any onlooker who doesn't realize he's a lefty.

I grab hold of the front of his shirt, yanking him up to me, forcing him on his tiptoes with the extra four inches I have over him. "You need to cool the fuck off," I snarl at him before shoving him back, making him stumble. I'm not stupid enough to do anything that would hurt him — it's literally my job to protect his stupid ass — but he needs to remember that I *can* hurt him far more easily than he can hurt me. Linemen don't lose entire seasons because of hits from quarterbacks, but that's something he has to fear with every single play.

The motion is enough to galvanize the nearby teammates. Reuben Janns, defensive line, is the closest to me, and he's a fair fight. He's not a fighter, though, not off the field. Neither of us is. So when he puts one hand on my chest, flat against me, not even pushing, and nods once at me, I lift my hands and nod back. On my other side, Kai Bodley takes hold of Joss's arm and starts to pull her away from me.

It's a smart move. He's doing the right thing. If things blow up, it's better if Joss is out of the danger zone.

But I don't like it. She doesn't need protection from me. I protect her. Not Kai. "Gabriel," Reuben says with an air of warning and a firmer hand when my attention snaps to Kai. I have to swallow the knot in my throat.

Meanwhile, Blaise is still running his mouth. "It was a joke! What's a nut shot between friends? You're the asshole for wearing a cup!"

He's as yet unrestrained. Protect the quarterback. Take down anyone trying to hurt him. He takes one foolish, arrogant step toward me, putting himself in range for me to dart my hand out before anyone can stop me and grab his shirt to pull him in. "Get fucked, Sinclair," I yell in his face, and he's lucky I don't headbutt his stupid face for good measure.

Reuben manages to grab me by the elbows and pin them behind me, restraining me, and Blaise sees it as an opportunity to clock me. He brings his already-bloody right hand back and swings.

Just as Lin Huang attempts to pull him back.

And gets punched right in the face.

"Oh, you little shit!" Lin hisses and then, despite being the smallest and usually most timid guy on the team, launches himself at Blaise, knocking him to the ground.

Reuben and Kai forget about me as everyone dives in, attempting to separate the two, but both are slippery as eels, on and off the field. I take the opportunity to grab Joss and hustle her out of the venue. We're halfway to the exit when I hear Blaise bellow, "Barbecue Express, bitches!"

This is a disaster.

Outside, I keep a close hold on Joss while we wait for the valet to bring the car around. A lot of people are standing out here with us. They're all glaring at me, like they know I was the one who set off the chain of events that ruined the fundraiser.

"Fuck, the fundraiser," I mutter and dig out my phone.

"It's okay, everyone can still bid whether they're here or not," Joss says. "I'm sure everyone already decided what they want and are tracking."

"Right, I'm tracking." I'm already pissed that Blaise had to go so extreme and make it a point to embarrass me in the process. If I lose the quilt, I'll be livid.

"Oh? What are you tracking?"

I start to tell her what her quilt is going for when I notice the Allores nearby. Good people. Their little one started walking a few weeks ago so they never hang out at the Jug House where several of us single guys live, but I'm Uncle Gabe to baby Shelby. Hell, I'm babysitter #3 after his parents and the Moraleses.

I've nearly forgotten the way they seemed to give me the cold shoulder inside. I'm sure I misread it. Keira talks constantly about hooking me up with one of the cheerleaders she manages. I always laugh it off because I don't want them to be disappointed that it's not one of the younger, more attractive guys. I'm sure she's happy I brought a legitimate date.

But her scowl says otherwise. The look on Evan's face after she whispers something to him and then pushes him toward me confirms it.

He looks between us as he approaches, scratches the back of his burgundy mohawk, laughs awkwardly. Evan's not a nervous guy by nature. If I'm being honest, he's usually too dumb to know when he should be worried. But there's a wobble in his voice when he says, "Hey, big guy. Mind a quick bro-to-bro chat?"

C. B. Alice

My side cools as Joss shrinks away from it.

I don't care that what we know about each other is casual anecdotes shared over pizza and wings or that to everyone else, it looks like I'm desperate and clinging to the first pretty girl who would give me the time of day. She's made me happy today, and it's been a very, very long time since I've been this excited to find out where things might go.

I reach out to pull Joss right back to my side. "You wanna say something, say it."

Evan's a big guy for his position, but he's not as big as me. It's not mass so much as momentum that he relies on. This close, there's no contest.

But he looks back at Keira, and she gives him this bitchy little mean girl pout that just about sets me off, and it's enough for him to brave it. "Listen, Shaunessy, I get that you're new to Wilmington, and I'm sure you're a real nice lady, Miss Edgars, but—"

"It's Page now, Joss Page," she says so softly that I doubt Allore can even hear her.

And I don't like that. She's so intimidated that she's not even comfortable correcting her name? Fuck that.

Evan scowls, his thick eyebrows dropping low, but I know that face enough to know he's not mad, he's trapped. "With all due respect, ma'am—"

I cut him off right there because I know exactly where a phrase like that goes. I step in and take hold of his shirt so he can't back away. My left eye is momentarily blinded by a cellphone flash. "You will treat her with all due respect. What happened in the past is in the past. I don't fucking care—"

"I don't want you to be hurt!"

There are several cameras turned our way now. We're gonna be lucky if this doesn't make it to SportsCenter. Evan is the second-highest-paid safety in the league. This is definitely going to be in the gossip rags' sports sections within the hour.

"Then you either apologize to Joss for whatever you were thinking about saying or you go the fuck away."

He swallows and looks to Joss, has the audacity to lead with, "I'm sorry, Miss . . . Miss Page, but my wife's best friend was one of your husband's victims."

Victims.

Goddammit.

I do not want to know.

"I'll go," she blurts out, and I hear the warble in her voice. I hear the unshed tears.

I shove Evan back so hard he stumbles into someone holding up their phone, knocking him on his ass, but we're saved by valet.

"We're leaving," I tell Joss as I help her into my truck. "Together."

Chapter Ten
JOSS

I feel sick. Actually nauseous. Gabe's knuckles are white on the steering wheel, as are the ones on my thigh. I think he wants the touch to be calming, but he's too pissed to be comforting.

"I'm so sorry," I whisper once we're out of the parking lot and heading toward the suburbs and I finally find my voice again.

"Don't—" he snarls, only to cut himself off short. He takes a deep breath, rubs his palm on my thigh to loosen his fingers, and starts over. "That voice wasn't for you. It was for Evan. And Emily and everyone else. Don't apologize for them and don't apologize for what your husband did."

"He was a monster. You have no idea."

He laces our fingers together on the console between us. "I'm not very smart. I do and say a lot of dumb things. But one thing I do know is people who are horrible, it's the ones closest to them who get hurt the most, whether it's because they're the biggest victims or because they're the ones who get destroyed by the fallout. Sure, sometimes their loved ones are in on it, but that's not you. No way."

"How do you know that?" He's not wrong; I was quite literally the one who had to pay for Brian's crimes. But Gabe barely knows me. And I knew my husband for years but had no idea what he was doing to his own patients right under my nose.

"Because you hate Tammy Buckner."

"I do not!" I protest before it hits me how irrelevant that is. Tammy's one of my subscribers. I don't know how he even knows her name.

He shoots me a playful grin, one of his many larger-than-life expressions because everything he does is larger than life. "Ma'am, I have watched four of your livestreams, and every single one of them, Tammy said something I can only guess was asinine. I don't know anything about quilting, so I couldn't say for sure, but I got that vibe. And you thanked her and told her you'd take her advice into consideration, and every single time, you looked like you were about to burst a capillary for all the restraint you were putting on yourself."

"You can't even tell binding is machine stitched on the first side!"

He takes the stop sign as an opportunity to lean across the console and steal a swift, unexpected kiss, but the car behind us lays on the horn when we sit a half second longer than appropriate.

"You wear your heart on your sleeve. Plenty enough locals love you so much that I can tell everyone else is wrong about you. And I'm really excited to prove them wrong, too."

He's finally relaxed, melting back into his seat and loosening his grip on the wheel, absently rubbing his giant, rough thumb up and down the back of my comparatively dwarfed hand. His lips are curled into a natural smile, like that's his default, and he's just happy to be here.

Happy to be with me.

I'm happy to be with him. I want to pinch myself to see if this is real. He makes me feel good.

And thinking about that has my mind going to how *good* he made me feel in the bathroom. "Why are you wearing a cup, anyway?"

I don't know what I'm expecting, if it's going to turn out that the quarterback has a history of punching his teammates in the crotch or if he's going to be embarrassed about a medical condition or if this is going to be the thing he won't tell me so I can feel like we're even on secrets. Instead, he replies immediately with, "Because I got to start my day by holding your boobs, and I figured that every time I thought about that, I'd get a boner. I didn't want to be dealing with that all day."

I'm the one blushing with his confession. Of course he's attracted to me. He's made that clear enough already. He's already kissed me and defended me and made me orgasm. Did I feel a twinge of self-consciousness when he wouldn't let me touch him back? Yes, absolutely, but now I get why. The poor man's probably been uncomfortable all night.

We're far enough from downtown that the road is mostly empty. Wilmington has highways that reach out to the suburbs, but they've been built along slower-moving surface roads. We're on one of those, and we have several miles lined with undeveloped woods ahead of us.

Brian, the asshole, valued nothing more than propriety from me. I never did anything considered lewd, and he never asked or expected me to. So when I scoot toward Gabe in my seat and pivot myself to face him, my conscience is telling me to stop. What I'm thinking isn't okay. Gabe is going to reject me.

Gabe glances at me, his eyes dipping to my cleavage. I see the twinkling there.

I grab for his belt.

He rests his giant hand over mine yet again, not necessarily stopping me but slowing me down, at least. "Whatcha doing there?"

"Seeing if I can figure out how cups come off."

He chuckles, the sound low and husky. He looks around, gaze traveling from one side of the road to the other, before he flips his blinker on. "Not too much of a challenge, that, but you should take your skirt off instead."

My heart races at the challenge he proposes so easily, without a thought to whether we should do this or not.

I can't be nearly so casual though, and I'm terrified my words are going to get stuck in my throat. I am not a bold person. This is not who I am.

But it's who Gabe makes me want to be.

"It's your turn," I insist.

He guides his truck onto a service road that leads us into the woods. There's no sign saying we can't be here, but it feels a bit like a horror movie. He parks and kills the headlights but leaves the engine running, the dashboard providing just enough illumination. "I'm not going to have Cora kill me because I tore or stained your skirt. Take it off."

He's so laid-back and friendly that the bite to his tone now catches my attention. It's not rude or demanding. It's patient but leaves no room to counter.

I unbuckle my seatbelt and shimmy out of my skirt.

He holds his hand out to me, so I hand it to him and watch, intrigued, as he handles it delicately, finding the seams where he can fold it without leaving ugly creases and laying it on his back seat.

"Now your panties."

Is he going to dictate everything we do? I'm a pacifist down to my bones and have never found myself attracted to aggressive guys, but the way he defended me against both Blaise and Evan has me thinking I might be willing to do whatever he tells me to.

Not only does he fold my panties neatly, he tucks them under my skirt. He doesn't leer at them or do anything else that might turn me off. Only once they're hidden away does he say, "Are you wet for me, Joss?"

The reflection of the dashboard speckles in green and blue starbursts in his eyes.

I nod.

"Does that leather seat feel nice on your pussy?"

My eyes widen at the awareness. I never would have noticed if he hadn't said it, but now, the cool, smooth leather is all I can think about. My core clenches, and the suction from my slickness tugs at me. Tiny bubbles of air tickle up and down the length of my slit, making me even wetter.

Gabe's smile is a knowing one. He unbuckles his seatbelt and pushes the seat back as far as it'll go, reclining it a couple notches. With a flip up of the center console, opening up more space next to him, he pats his thighs. "Now come see how your pussy feels here."

My nerves frizzle slightly on that. I'd been thinking a hand job or even a blow job. He takes up so much space that I'm not sure how well I'll fit there. We're only twenty minutes from home; wouldn't it make more sense to invite him in?

I've never invited a man in. I once brought a guy to the barn just to avoid bringing him up to my apartment. But I doubt the workbench could take Gabe's weight.

He must see my hesitation, but he's nothing less than casual with, "Or we could do something else if you don't want this."

He tucks his hands behind his head, relaxing back, waiting patiently, and it's exactly what I need. My eyes travel up his form, so at odds with himself with his hulking form and his sleek suit, his friendly face and his heavy eyes, laid-back but fully aware that I'm going to take his offer.

He helps me position myself, strong hands deftly maneuvering my legs so that my thighs hug his. A faint draft wicks between my legs, parted enough by his broad lap that I'm spread open.

He flicks my clit, just once, but it's enough to have my back curling around the steering wheel.

That husky laugh. A teasing, "Were you really planning to just jerk me off?"

I wasn't planning on anything. I'm flying blind here. But I can't resist pointing out, "How is that different from what you did in the bathroom?"

"Oh, so you're gonna catch an attitude now?"

I steadfastly fight and fail to hold back my pout, which results in Gabe hooking my top by the gore and pulling me down onto him. It gives him enough space to smack my ass just enough to make my flesh sing as our lips meet.

Momentum and gravity drop me onto him, and he's so big that there's nothing for me to brace myself on but his shoulders. I rest my forearms on him, but it only leaves a sliver of space between us. I slide on his lap, and the coarseness of his pants rubs along my sensitive, swollen slit.

He's still zipped up, and now the hard shell within is obvious. I grind against it, a part of me wishing it was his cock that I felt there, but the purely sensation-driven nerve endings in my clit forcing me to moan into his mouth.

"You are so fucking hot," Gabe groans. "You're about to come all over my pants, aren't you?"

I'll be embarrassed about this later. I'll get all stuck in my head trying to figure out why I'm so easily set off by him. For now, I bear down on him, mindlessly working myself to orgasm.

Gabe doesn't seem to be bothered. In fact, he digs his hands into my ass, pulling my cheeks apart to expose me further to the chilled air pumping through the a/c and giving him plenty of space to sink two thick fingers into my pussy.

I cry out, pushing into him in shock and then shifting back against his hand to force him to go deeper.

"Take it," he encourages me, bending and spreading his fingers, lighting me up. "Take everything you want before I take what I want."

I'm going to come. I'm right there. And I want more. I want it all. Pushing my weight off of him sinks his fingers further, making it worth it to relieve the pressure from my clit. I fight with his belt as I bounce on his lap, obsessed with the way his splayed fingers stretch my rim and dig into my inner walls.

He does nothing to help me get into his pants, but the intensity of his gaze tells me this is exactly what he wants me to do. He wants me to loosen myself up so I'm ready to take him once I get his cock free.

"Do it, Joss."

I'm not sure if he's talking about coming or getting into his pants, but they both happen at the same time. I lift right off him, squeaking out his name as my hand hits snug synthetic shorts with a pocket the cup's tucked into. I manage to pull it out, finally feeling the shape of his hard, thick cock attempting to unfurl itself.

My orgasm has me shaking and bucking and desperate for more. It's right there, I can feel it, and I know *I know* I'm going to feel so much better once that thing is stuffed inside me, but I can't seem to get to it. "Why are these so fucking tight?" I screech.

"That's so cute when you swear."

And then I'm whimpering because Gabe's taken his fingers away, but he needs them to get into those stupidly tight shorts.

I salivate at the sight of his cock once it springs free, thick and veiny, and I swear it looks angrily red even though there's barely light between us. I grab for it, and pre-cum sputters out.

Gabe grunts. "I'm not gonna make it."

He's going to make it. I need to feel him inside me, I need to split myself open on him. I need him buried to the hilt for a second. That's it.

I don't hesitate, holding his cock steady and lurching myself up, hitting my head on the roof of the truck as I notch him at my entrance and sinking my full weight on him.

Loud sounds come from us both, and I'm thinking I'm not the only one this was too much for. He's big, but I didn't give myself time to think about that, as desperate as I was. Pain shoots through me, immediately leveling out to an ache that makes every muscle tighten, strangling his cock.

But it's exactly what I want.

We both struggle to catch our breaths, but I finally settle myself enough to keep going only to realize the mistake we made. I lift myself up off him with a curse. "Dammit, is there a condom here?"

Gabe lurches up out of his seat, his eyes wild and dazed, his cock already nudging at my core again. After a second, he blinks. "I had a vasectomy."

"What?" I don't even understand what the word means at first. I just need something between us so we don't regret this later, and that's a condom. But then it clicks.

Birth control.

He so emphatically doesn't want kids that he's had surgery to prevent them.

And I don't want to get pregnant tonight, of course, that's part of why a condom is so critical. I barely know Gabe. This has been such a crazy whirlwind that I threw out my usual inhibitions, but we're nowhere close to being ready for kids. I can't even say we're officially dating. We haven't had a full date yet.

But I do want kids. Desperately. I always have. And I got so close, only to have the opportunity stolen from me in the most devastating way possible. So it's sobering to know Gabe has gone to such extremes to prevent it.

This is a problem. A big one. A problem that potentially ends the relationship we're not even in.

But it's a problem for another day.

"Oh, and I just had a physical with the works," he adds. "We all get them. Negative for STDs. And everything else. Except my blood pressure's high. But I'm good here."

I nod. "Right. Good. So am I."

He snags me by the chin, tilts me to meet his eyes and then draws me to his lips again. "We can stop if you want."

I shake my head and kiss him back. "No, I want this."

He guides his cock back into me and grabs my ass, setting a pace between us that has any thoughts of the future vanishing for the moment. One day, we'll need to discuss this, but for now?

For now, I take what I want. I crush his shirt in my fingers and demand his kisses and long not for babies but for naked flesh against flesh. His sounds echo my motions, enthusiastically responding to what I do, making me feel truly appreciated, like the bridges he may have burned this evening were truly worth it for him.

Like whatever this is between us is worth it.

He comes suddenly, no warning except a tightening of his fingers, bruising my ass, no doubt. He tips his head back over the head rest and groans up at the roof, the sound of relief enough to quell any lingering doubts about whether we should have done this. And when he tips me back against the steering wheel to rub my clit until I come while his cock is still pulsing inside me?

I barely even notice the horn blaring outside until he finally relaxes and draws me back onto his chest to doze and the beeping finally stops.

It was the truck. I was sitting right on that horn.

Chapter Eleven
GABE

I have no idea why I said that. I don't even know if they'd give a single, childless man my age a vasectomy. My little sister Abby never stops complaining about how she's had three kids and they still refuse to tie her tubes.

I wouldn't want a vasectomy. I love kids. I've always thought I'd have two or three of them myself by now, with at least one more on the horizon before I called it a day.

I don't know where there's a condom in my car. There should be a couple in the glovebox and one in my gym bag behind the seat, but Blaise has a habit of nicking them. Another in my wallet, but I can't attest to the date on it. Still, that doesn't excuse lying to Joss about something so important, and now I need to admit that I lied and deal with the fallout from that.

Instead, I'm taking the slowest route possible home while Joss lounges next to me. Her seat is halfway reclined, her arm is thrown over her head, and her left leg is sprawled onto my side, her pussy bared and spread for me to continue to tease.

I push my cum back into her, guiding it as deep as I can.

Her sigh is one of dozy content, like she's absolutely loving being filled with my fingers and my semen, and I can't ruin the moment.

I'm an honest person to a fault. I suck at keeping secrets, and I just plain don't like it. Every lie I've ever attempted to pull off, I've gotten caught for, and that sucks enough that I don't do it. But every vision of my possible future with Joss is filled with a great big belly on her or a bassinet set up next to her sewing machine or a herd of blonde kiddos running circles around me in the yard. She didn't like it when I told her I'd had a vasectomy, so I'm thinking she's wants a family, too.

I need to figure out the right way to spin this so I can confess the truth — or something close enough — so that she won't get mad. I can do this.

The little rumble from Joss as I begin to circle her clit with the pad of my thumb, absolutely loving the puddle on the seat beneath my knuckles, has me smiling. I can't remember the last time a woman was so wanton with me. "I can't believe it's only eleven."

The time triggers something in me. When I see the 10:56 on the clock, I realize the auction's about to end. I take advantage of a red light at a deserted intersection to fish my phone out of the cupholder with my left hand to pull up the app.

"Everything okay?" she asks.

"Sure is, just putting the winning bid in on your quilt."

Joss snaps straight up at that. "You don't need to bid on that! I don't care if it doesn't go for much."

The fact that she looks more terrified about that than the brawl we left behind at the hotel is enough to warm my heart back up. "I'm not doing it to stroke your ego. I want it. And you don't have to worry about how much it's going for."

Whether I deliberately intended to goad her into grabbing my phone from me or not, the result is the same. She grabs it out of my hand and gasps when she sees the bid I'm about to place. "Oh my god, how do I cancel this? Where's the cancel button?"

I laugh, enjoying seeing her so flustered and wondering if, in her panic, she ended up submitting the $50,000 bid. The current winning bid is just shy of 25, but I want to make sure I end this. "I'm good for it. I'm fine." I was poor but comfortable for so long that when I finally got selected and lucked out with my seven-figure contract, I didn't see any reason to change my life too much. And Merrick refuses to take rent money from us; he paid cash upfront for the house and insists he didn't buy the monster to be a landlord. He figured it'd be useful since there were so many players moving to Wilmington at the same time, many of us without families or connections. The rest of us split utilities and any other expenses that pop up. Blaise and I went in together on the pool.

Joss has the cutest scowl, like an angry puppy. "I don't care if you're good for it, it's too much money. I'll make you one."

I scoff, trying to push down any fluffy feelings about how casually she offered — not even offered, unquestionably stated — to make this for me. "You've already made one. How great would it be on the sidelines, a bunch of the guys huddled under it? The photo ops alone would get you media coverage. Way better than it hiding in the stands."

She turns back, and though she still clutches my phone, she's brought it up to her chest, looking positively angelic as she looks up at me and says, "No, I want to make one just for you."

Okay, yeah. That's fluffy feelings right there. "Don't these take a long time?"

"I can have it done in a month."

"But you have other stuff to do. I couldn't ask you to make me a quilt."

Her eyes shimmer up at me, evoking all kinds of crazy emotions inside me. I've already told her she's my girlfriend. It's clear I want to see how far we can go. But that vision I have of her and me and kids? It's coming right back, with the addition of that quilt for our family to cozy up under.

"You didn't ask me," she says. "I offered. And I won't let you say no."

If she won't let me say no, I won't let her, either. I steal a quick kiss and hand her a wad of paper napkins for a quick clean-up while I grab her panties and skirt. I pass them to her and then continue on down the road.

Once she's gotten herself dressed, I reclaim her hand. "I hope you know this isn't some fling for me, Joss. I've got a mandatory practice at six a.m. tomorrow, so—"

She gasps, horrified. "But you're all going to be out late tonight! And it's Sunday!"

"Yeah, that was management's attempt to keep us from getting into trouble. And I am going to be in a bit of trouble, so I'm going to roll in at 5 to kiss some serious ass. But I need you to know that what's between us, it's not what we just did. I want more than that. I'm absolutely not going to spend the night with you, because I'm not going to sneak off in the middle of the night like a criminal or wake you up before sunrise."

She gives my hand a squeeze, and in my rearview, I see she has the biggest grin, like she's absolutely smitten.

I hope she is. I am.

"I'm going to hop in your stream tomorrow if I can. And I'm sure my life's going to be a living hell this week because of the Kick-Off Gala, so I'm going to buy your one-on-one tutorial package so I can say good night—"

"Do not do that!" She tries to be firm, but she can't quite smother her laughter.

"I am doing that. Because you probably still haven't gotten your phone and I want to tell you good night every night face-to-face. And I know that this is probably a big ask, but if it's at all possible for you to come to the game next Sunday, I'm going to give you two tickets for the WAG section."

"What's the WAG section?"

"Where the wives and girlfriends like to sit."

"Gabe, are you asking me to be your girlfriend?"

"Ma'am, you already are my girlfriend. I'm asking you to come see what I do and then come out to dinner with me and my buddies so I can show you off and get to know one of your friends better and then ditch your friend to spend the night at my place."

She strains across the seat, a far bigger distance for her than me, to peck my cheek. "It's super hot when you call me *ma'am*."

Chapter Twelve
JOSS

Cora and I arrive at the stadium several hours early, at 10 a.m., like Gabe advised. There's already a massive line of cars to get in, so I see he was right. "They're here to tailgate," Cora explains. "They'll all get drunk in the parking lot, have a good party, save themselves money at concessions."

"It's a little early to drink, isn't it?"

Although truth be told, I could go for something to take the edge off right now. I only got a quick goodnight from Gabe last night. He was apologetic about not being able to stop by the shop as he'd done a couple other days this week, and not that I expected him to, but now I'm wishing I'd gotten a chance to see him once more. Or even a quick chat with him today. He calms me.

C. B. Alice

Cora and I are stuck in traffic for half an hour, the roads surrounding the stadium on all four sides in gridlock, but eventually we see a sign for Lot P. Cora passes my ID to the man at the gate and, just like Gabe promised, is handed two tickets.

The road leads to a valet and on to a VIP tailgate area. Instead of sitting in camping chairs, drinking beers out of coolers while people scream and carry on and blow their horns, we're offered complimentary mixed drinks and an assortment of charcuterie and tapas catered by local fine dining. There are several giant TVs showing pre-game stuff as well as a gaming area where a bunch of people are playing video game football. There's something for fantasy football, a fancy playground for kids, even a DJ. As for the people tailgating here, I get the impression that it's a mix of people like us — people with some connection to the team, be it personal or professional — and fans who paid a lot of money for the privilege.

I'm enjoying myself as we stroll around, taking it all in, but I start to get this feeling that I'm being watched. There are too many people around for me to pinpoint who it is, and Cora is a well-known fashion designer, so it could be someone watching her. Even so, the moment she gets drawn into a sales pitch from one of the vendors, I run to the bar, just to see if I'm still getting that feeling.

It sticks with me. I've sucked down half my second mimosa by the time I scurry back to Cora, who thrusts a bag at me.

"What's this?" I hand her my drink, which she finishes as I open the bag and pull out the ruby red polyester shirt folded up inside. The slippery material unfolds on its own, revealing the saffron accents at the sleeves and around the white writing. A giant 72 with SHAUNESSY on the yoke.

It's Gabe's jersey.

While Blaise's last name and number are far and away the most popular, I've seen a half dozen people with Gabe's already. Still, this feels like a big deal.

"Go on, put it on," Cora coaxes.

"I feel like I should have done team color make-up now. And not this skirt." I gesture to my frumpy, floor-dusting patchwork skirt, which seemed easy and casual this morning but looks crazy against the sea of jeans and leggings. "Whose did you get?" I ask, nodding to the bag she's still holding.

"Okay, so I didn't want to get Sinclair because everyone's wearing Sinclair, and I thought it'd be weird if I also got Shaunessy. Like, people are going to think we're having three-ways or something."

I blanch, wishing the jersey was Gabe's size so I could bury myself inside it. People heard that. Two nearby fans in unnamed jerseys and beer hats look right at us, and one nods his stupid hat at me as the other waggles his eyebrow.

"I ended up getting a Briggs jersey."

"He was your kill," I remind her. She said she'd bang Blaise and kill Merrick. "And rightfully so. I told you how disgusting his girlfriend is, right?"

"Yeah, but he was Tilly's bang. I can give it to her. I'm in Tokyo in December. You'll need someone to go to games with you. And Tilly could use some action."

I do my best not to recoil, but good grief. Last time Tilly got some action, she ended up pregnant. She's not even going to fit into that jersey much longer. There's a baby bump incoming.

Not that baby bumps aren't welcome here, of course. Lin Huang's wife, Wren, looked about ready to give birth at the gala, and I've already seen her a couple times since we got here. She's been in a group of women who all look vaguely familiar, so I'm guessing that's the wives and girlfriends gang. She's hard to miss with her dancer's build, miles of silky black hair, warm olive skin, and long, visually striking face, but all the women are stunning.

And I am broken. I've stitched myself back together, but it's like a ripped shirt. Patch it up all you want, but the tear is still there, and it's only ever going to be weak, no matter how well it's patched.

I give up and put the jersey on, and that's when I hear, from behind me, "Oh my goodness, it *is* her!"

That kind of excitement I hear out of the feminine voice, the sort of soft, awed reverence, can't be for me. Cora's got a fan base who goes nuts for her. She's iconic in her corner of the world.

But then I hear, "Fuck yeah, it's her. Stop pussy-footing and give it to her already."

I look over my shoulder and see a dozen women, all roughly my age, the youngest college aged while the oldest might be in her 40s. They're all wearing Gabe's jersey, and they all have halos on their heads and angel wings in the team's colors drawn on their cheeks. Two hold bags of cookies; one has an extra halo in her hand. It's secured to a headband. Next to her is Tara, Blaise's date from the gala.

She's not wearing a halo. She's wearing deely-bobbers, one of those headbands that have little trinkets attached to them by springs so they dance around like antennae, and on her cheek, under her winged eyeliner, is a small, expertly-drawn flame. Because she's one of Blaise's Firebugs. The other women must be Gabriel's Angels.

She gives the Angel with the extra halo a gentle shove forward along with a small wave, a wiggle of the fingers like no one can know she's waving at me. I don't wave back, for fear of breaking some unspoken rule, but I grin at her and take a mental note to have her mom pass my number on to her. I'm thinking I made need some help from her to navigate this new world.

The Angel, a petite brunette in her thirties with a nervous smile and giant eyes, thrusts the halo at me. "I'm Rachel," she blurts out. "You're one of us now. Whether you like it or not."

The squeak she makes after announcing that tells me she probably didn't mean to say it in such a threatening way, so I take the halo from her and ask, "Because of the jersey?" It seems like a low bar for a fan club, although maybe not in VIP and with Gabe's jersey. Again, there aren't a lot of us sporting 72.

She shakes her head and, with another glance back at the other girls, who mostly seem to be having a good laugh at this one's torment but still give her supportive thumbs-ups, leans close. "What was it like kissing Gabe? Is he soft and squishy? It looked like the sweetest kiss ever! What did you say to him that made him kiss you like that? Are you two for-real dating now?"

The questions fly out of her mouth before I get a chance to process them all, then it's my turn to look thoroughly terrorized. There was media coverage from the Kick-Off Gala. The ladies in my Tuesday night paper-piecing class told me about it. I made an announcement that yes, I was seeing one of the Juggernauts, but that wouldn't affect my classes, and that stopped the conversation. I have no idea what the picture was that this girl saw, but it was no doubt some trauma — since the Gala was a total disaster — so I lie with, "Oh, I told him I'd make him a quilt so he'd stop bidding on the one that was being auctioned."

"That's so much better than cookies," one Angel grumbles, while another looks at her bag of cookies and pouts.

"Did you make those for him?" I ask her.

The girl, one of the youngest ones, still in braces and with a blemished face although she's got a hard seltzer in her hand, nods sullenly.

"I can make sure he gets them after the game if you want. What's your name?"

She lights up like I told her I'm going to bring her whole body to him. "Really? Tell him those are from Desi. Tell him they're his special recipe! I added extra pecans because I know how much he likes them in his chocolate chip cookies."

"He does?" I look around at the other haloed women, and they're all nodding. Most of them are happy I'm talking with them, but I can tell a few are miffed at me and would rather I not exist. Gabe made it sound like the Angels were a bunch of sweet old ladies who randomly chose him as the guy to root for, but I'm thinking that's not the case after all, and they'd be every bit as excited to go on a date — and more — with him as Tara and the Firebugs are for Blaise.

"He's new to me," I confide in Desi. "I really like him, but I don't know much about him. Maybe you and the other Angels can help me with that?" Can't bake to save my life so I'm not sure how far I'll get on cookie advice, but I'll take what I can get.

"His favorite color is pink, and he always tells the other players they did a good job when he helps them up, even if they're on the other team," Desi rattles off as she takes the halo out of my hands to plop it on my head.

Tara slips around me to link arms with Cora and pass her a set of deely-boppers. "I know you're rocking the Menace jersey, but let me tell you about the Firebugs. Trust when I say you're gonna wanna gag over the fluffy bunny nonsense coming from the Angels."

"Let's go, let's go, let's go! Fucking run, bitch!" Cora screams at the top of her lungs.

I glance back at Mel Cohen with an apologetic grimace. When Cora agreed to come to the game with me, I wasn't expecting her to get so worked up. I didn't even know until we got here that she's a football fan. I guess it's her family's secret shame, that although they say they're all about cricket and field hockey — "proper Indian sports," her brother even told me once — they all watch football when no one is around.

I'm trying to enjoy it, and honestly? I probably would in a different scenario. There's so much energy and tension. I thought it would feel slow since I knew it was done in plays that needed a reset after each one. Instead, the crowd is so animated and the score volleys so dramatically that I barely notice the downtime. What I do notice, and what ruins the excitement for me, is the way Gabe gets hit in every single play.

So, while Cora is screaming and calling the running back a bitch, I'm watching Gabe to make sure he gets back up.

"That's it, bitch!" Cora screams, her voice raw, as Drew Cohen is knocked off the field by one of the defensive linemen from the Patriots.

I shoot Drew's wife another apology, but she waves it off. "He's a bitch. He'll be whining up a storm tonight because the grocery store was out of the dairy-free butter pecan ice cream. And he did good. He got that first down. He looks great today." She says it so proudly, like a three-hundred-pound wrecking ball didn't just slam into him.

"And look, he's fine," Cora says. At first, I'm thinking she's talking about Drew, but then she squeezes my hand back — oh Lord, I was squeezing too hard again — and points to Gabe.

"He was just taking a break," Wren agrees from my other side. She's got one hand on her heavy, protruding belly, and the way she breathes makes me concerned she's already in labor, but it could be simple excitement.

I've done my best not to stare at her belly, but there's a difference between knowing Tilly is pregnant and *seeing* Wren's pregnancy. In my line of work, I see pregnant women frequently, usually when their quilt-minded friends bring them along to pick out fabrics for baby blankets. I try not to let it bother me, but there's that constant tickle of how that could be me. That was me; I should have a five-year-old now, turning six some-time in the winter.

I don't know how to talk to Gabe about this. I don't want to look like a psycho by making it a problem that I want kids and he doesn't when we didn't even know each other three weeks ago, but he's been emphatic that he's dead serious about us.

"They do that sometimes if they know the clock's stopped," Wren adds as she continues rubbing that belly. "Lin says they're being lazy, and I usually agree with him just to appease him, but come on. Lin's on the field for like forty-five seconds of—*where the fuck was the offsides?*" she suddenly erupts, as does everyone around us.

Penalties are a common thing, I've learned. Mostly what's gotten everyone upset is holding and false start, but when Cora explained the false start thing to me, she went ahead and explained offsides, too. I now know that when Gabe is on the field, he's the one who starts the clock. No one is allowed to move before him. I'm confused about his job in general — like, I don't get why he's the one starting with the ball when the only thing he does is toss it between his legs to Blaise — but it's kind of cool that he has that power.

And if anyone moves before him, that team loses five yards. Wren's been clear about that being an extremely big deal.

The rest of it? I don't get it. I get soccer and basketball and hockey. Get the thing in the net. Baseball? Hit the ball and run to the safe spot before the ball gets there. Got it. But this? These downs and the scoring system and all the resets? I think I'm going to need a tutorial.

Hopefully Gabe isn't offended when I ask him for that.

"You know, I thought I hated football until last year," Wren says with a laugh once that offsides *is* called. "I was a dancer growing up, so I had to perform at football games, but I never watched the game. Couldn't stand cheerleaders — sorry, Keira."

My throat catches when Evan Allore's wife turns toward us. I've seen her a lot today, prowling the sidelines in a smart suit in the Juggernaut ruby color. She works with the cheerleaders who are stationed at the four corners of the field, one pod directly in front of where we sit next to the tunnel. Cora and I are in the fourth row, but since she was down on the field and it felt like a whole other world between the seats and the field, I thought I'd fly under the radar.

Five minutes ago, she appeared in the second row to pass off a diaper bag to the blue-haired girl who's had her hands full wrangling four kids, two of which are babies in giant noise-cancelling headphones. I've watched Keira nearly leave three times now before getting sucked back in to snuggling with the ruby-and-saffron-tutued baby.

Now she's glaring right at me despite responding to Wren. "Nah, you're good. I hated cheerleaders, too, even after I became one. But then I realized they're mostly good, unlike *some* people."

She and the blue-haired girl have a quick exchange before the entire group packs up and leaves their seats. Keira casts one last venomous glare at me as they pass by, and the rest of the ladies surrounding us watch, stunned.

"What the heck was that about?" Mel bursts out once they've vanished, and then everyone's talking at once, but no one seems to know it's because of me. Why would it be? I'm new. And since this is the Jugs' second year, these women probably all moved here last year.

"Maybe we should go," I whisper to Cora.

Wren grabs my shoulder to hold me in place. "Absolutely not! Tomorrow I've got a lunch date with Keira and Cadence — that's the other lady, the one with the blue hair, Morales's girl — and I'll talk some sense into her. You shouldn't be blamed for what someone else did."

"You know who I am?"

"Yeah, I live up in Salem. It was a pretty big deal there, too. Some of the, ahh—"

"Victims?" I supply for her. In the beginning, when I had lawyers, they insisted I use *patients,* but I never understood how that was a better word. It just reminded me that my husband's victims trusted him to care for them properly.

"Yeah. Some were from Salem. But that's not why I didn't talk to you at the gala! I wasn't even sure it was you. You look a lot different from your old pictures."

I nod. "I gained a bunch of weight."

Wren looks horrified and backpedals with, "I just meant the make-up and the hair."

Cora gives me a hard shove. "You talk like thirty pounds is a natural disaster. Can we just watch the game? This is the good part."

"Is it? I don't know if I can handle the stress of this." My heart's been pounding the entire time, if not because of Gabe's constant hits then because of the score that's bounced back and forth the entire game. The Juggernauts are losing right now, but they were winning a couple minutes ago, and there was already so little time on the clock that it seemed impossible the score would flip. One good pass, though, one slip of the Patriots' wide receiver past our defense, and they got their touchdown with only forty-five seconds on the clock.

That's since dwindled to nineteen seconds. One more play, maybe two. I feel sick watching this. Is everyone going to be in a terrible mood tonight? Will Gabe still want me to come over?

Do I want to come over? What if everyone else there is friends with Allore or Morales? I don't want to mess things up with the team or worse, get Gabe in trouble.

"It's the adrenaline," Mel says, "and the wins feel amazing for it. And if they lose, I'll give Drew a blow job in the parking lot, and that'll make him feel better. So you gotta look at it that way."

Despite the mess I made of Gabe's seat last weekend, I don't think I'm at the blowies-in-the-parking-lot phase of our relationship, but I've got this bag of cookies.

The boys get themselves back in position as the play clock ticks down. Gabe waits until almost the very last second — literally two seconds left — before passing the ball off to Blaise, setting the play in motion.

He spreads his arms wide, taking on two of the Patriots' defensive linemen, freeing up another offensive lineman to shoot off to the side. Blaise takes several steps back as he scans the field, looking for his target.

Mel screams as Drew takes down a defensive player, but that knocks him out of position to take the ball.

I'm watching the middle of the field, stressing about Gabe, especially when one of his targets breaks free and charges for Blaise, still holding the ball. I barely notice the streak of deep red dashing toward the end zone with two white shirts chasing as best as they can.

Blaise fires the ball off just as the guy that slipped past Gabe slams into him. My heart flutters. I'm worried he's not getting back up.

Cora starts shrieking, "Oh my god, oh my god, oh my god!" and it's enough for me to look to the other end of the field.

Merrick has the ball, and he is running for his life, hugging the sideline so if the men chasing him get to him, he'll be knocked out of bounds and stop the clock.

That clock is ticking, though. I don't know if they'll have enough time for another play.

One of the Pats leaps through the air, attempting to knock him down. They manage to get an ankle, and Cora lets out a weak gasp, only to scream, "Yeah!" as Merrick slips past and keeps running. The other Pat has to jump over his teammate, but it's too late for them.

The crowd goes wild as Merrick sprints into the end zone and spikes the ball.

They won.

Holy crap.

They won.

Our whole section is filled with family members cheering and hugging and crying. I'm not there, but not because I don't feel what they're feeling. Or, I don't know if I am, but I'm so overwhelmed that I'm stuck in my spot. From our position at the end zone, by the tunnel, I can see almost the entire stadium, tens of thousands of people, sharing this same experience with us, all feeling this same sensation of triumph, like together we've gone through some harrowing battle and we've all won together. Like we're a part of this thing they're doing on the field.

There are so many of us in the stands, but it's really the eleven men on the field. They did this, and now they're being swapped out for the men who will make sure that Huang can get that extra point. Tens of thousands of people are cheering for them. Who knows how many people are watching at home? It's incredible.

I look over to Cora, and I swear she has hearts in her eyes. I'm not sure who they're for, but I'm thinking next time she's here, she's going to be rocking some deely-bobbers or a halo. I'm doubting it'll be the devil horns that Merrick's Menace girls wear, but the thought of that has me laughing.

"What's so funny?" she asks.

"Nothing. Everything? I don't know if I like football, but my goodness, that was . . . that was something. I feel like I'm gonna need yoga to get through the next game."

"But you're gonna be at the next game?" Wren asks as she waves down to the field, where Huang has just kicked that extra point and has paused to tap his face guard and wave back.

I think he just blew her a kiss. That's pretty much the sweetest thing ever.

"Yeah, if he invites me."

"Oh, he's gonna invite you."

"Why do you say that?" Yes, I absolutely think he'll invite me, but I didn't think the feelings between us were so obvious.

"He did ruin the Kick-Off Gala because Emily Hess said he couldn't date you."

I shake my head, confused. "No, that was Blaise. He attacked Gabe out of nowhere. It was nuts. Yelled something crazy about a barbecue and threw a punch."

Wren laughs at that even as she takes my hand for the very final play. Donnie Thompson, the punter, kicks the ball into Pats territory. "Barbecue Express. It was a play they did last year that was a total mess but worked because the Raiders were too confused to figure out where the ball was going, but it's one of those things that can't be done often because everyone covered it so heavily and prepared for it after that."

One of the Pats catches the ball and starts running.

"That's what their little gang — Blaise, Merrick, and Gabe — say to each other if they need a distraction. But Blaise always goes too far with it."

The Pats runner is tackled at their 45. Game over.

"Gabe did that for you. Lin saw him mouth it to Merrick before Merrick called Selene a . . . whatever he called her. Gabe's going to fight for you."

"He'll burn the world for you," Mel says with way too much glee for how horrific that statement is.

So why does it feel so warm and happy in my belly?

Chapter Thirteen
GABE

I have one of the equipment guys help me out of my jersey and shoulder pads before hopping in the shower, taking extra time to scrub my hair and beard and the bottoms of my feet and the undercarriage, making sure I'm smelling as good as possible for my night with Joss.

Not that I walk around stinky usually or anything, but I end up in the pool or the hot tub after a lot of games, so there's no point in putting a ton of extra work in when I know I'm going to be washing up again later.

I don't see the text until I've returned to my locker, which I'm glad for. I probably would have rushed if I'd seen Cora's message asking me if I'd mind taking Joss home tonight; Cora's had something come up, and she won't be able to go out with us tonight.

I dress as fast as possible, shake my hair out, pack my bags, and run out with a quick "Gotta go!" to the guys. There wasn't an announcement about a team meeting yet, so it's on them if I didn't know about it.

I find Joss waiting at the gate by the employee parking lot, as close as she can get to me without security stopping her. She's all prettied up with her fancy skirt, an angel's halo, and her jersey, my number proudly blazoned on her chest. She lights up when she sees me, but I can tell she's stressing about something. Cora's waiting with her, but she's on her phone, her other ear plugged, having what appears to be a heated conversation.

And Joss is tangled up in her thoughts.

"What happened?" I yell as I approach, already plotting the death of whoever upset her.

"It's not . . . it's nothing," Joss protests, only for Cora to yell from behind her, "That cheerleader bitch is a bitch."

"Fuck." I pull up Evan's number on my phone, ready to rip him a new one. If I go directly to Keira, that'll open up a whole other fight.

Joss yelps and nips the phone out of my hands. "It's fine."

It's not fine. And the more I fight for her — I've had to fight all week because everyone knows there's beef between Allore and me now — the more I absolutely do not care where this is coming from.

It doesn't fucking matter what happened in the past.

I nearly march right back into the stadium, where I know Evan and Keira both are, and demand an apology, but Joss puts her foot down. "Everyone else was really nice to me, I swear. But can we do something together tonight, just you and me?"

Behind her, Cora shoots two thumbs up and then skitters off as though I might say no and she's making sure I don't have the option.

But I could never say no to Joss.

―――※―――

I want a nice, wholesome, relaxing date night that will take some of the pressure off the fact that Joss is sleeping at my place tonight. I thought deciding this in advance would cut down on the stress of guessing at what each other wants, and instead, the anticipation has become a rock in my gut, and I feel like a damn virgin even though we literally had sex already.

Unprotected sex.

That Joss doesn't realize was unprotected. She might already be pregnant, and I should hate myself for lying about this, but I don't. The more time I spend with her, the less I want her to make friends with my roommates, all single, all wealthy except Vedder — whose child support payments are astronomical — and all far more attractive than I am.

And the more appealing the idea of getting her pregnant sooner rather than later becomes. Which is despicable, but I've lost women to my teammates before, and I don't want to lose Joss.

So by the time we've filled ourselves up on Korean barbecue and groped each other heavily at the movie theater, I'm fighting to focus on anything except filling Joss's pussy with my cum. But that's all wrecked when we get back to my place, where Rydell is vomiting in the bushes. Vedder's launching empty beer cans at him from the balcony off his bedroom.

Joss stares wide-eyed. "Gosh, it's like a frat house."

I cringe at that, wondering if it's too late to ask if we'd be better off at her place, but then Blaise opens the front door and screams at Joss specifically to come do a shot with him because Rydell is a 'little bitch man.'

Blaise talks her into exactly two shots before I cut them both off, frustrated that now that's she's been drinking, I'm going to have to be the good guy and put the brakes on our plans for at least a few more hours.

"I'm fine," Joss protests, pouting as I toss her shot glass into the sink.

"Ma'am, I will throw you over my shoulder and spank your ass if you don't walk it down to my bedroom immediately."

Joss's cheeks flush at the threat, but her pupils dilate and her lips part, as well. She's already told me she likes when I call her *ma'am,* but now I'm intrigued about what else she likes. She pretends to drag her feet like she thinks I'm being ridiculous and has no intention of fucking tonight, but as soon as she starts walking, it's a race.

I don't think a lot about my bedroom. It's a room to sleep in. There's a TV, but I hardly ever use it when there's a wall-sized screen and theater seating down the hall. My walls are mostly undecorated aside from a goal tracking calendar that's three months behind. I never got proper curtains, just the blinds that were already installed. My California King doesn't have a headboard. The simple blanket covering it is threadbare and in desperate need of retirement. There's a laundry chute in my bathroom so there aren't any dirty clothes, but a stack of folded tee-shirts sits on my chair. Too many pairs of sneakers prevent my closet doors from fully closing. I don't even know why I keep buying them.

Good Guy Gabe

There's a treadmill I got because even in the weight room here, Blaise is a dick about my pace, but the jacket I wore last weekend still hangs from it.

It's not much different from my bedroom in college; Joss was married and probably dates men who have corporate jobs and thought-out condos. This is embarrassing.

I'm about to apologize when Joss silences me with a single flourish of movement that has her jersey vanishing. I was worried about her being timid without the adrenaline from high emotions running through us like they did last week, but she stands proudly before me in a bra with a cute blueberry print on it that's cut low enough that it shows ample flesh. Her frilly, colorful skirt goes next, and beneath it is matching panties in that cut that sits low on the hips but covers enough that she could almost get away with wearing them in the gym if she was feeling particularly brazen.

The set isn't sexy, not in the classic Victoria Secrets barely-there lace style, but she's cute as fuck in it. Immediately, my cock stirs. Any concerns about the room or those two shots of vodka vanish as quickly as the vodka did.

"Did you know my favorite fruit is blueberries?"

I step up to her. Considering the fact that Joss is the one who undressed, I'm more than a little surprised that she places her palm on my chest to hold me back. It's not a caress; it's a push. An adorably weak, dainty push, but she's keeping me away. She's also touching me and leaving space between us for me to admire the jiggle of her boobs, the gentle curves of her hips, the soft pooch of her tummy, so I'm not complaining. Her hand is nice and warm, and I can't wait to be all over her.

She more effectively stops me with her words than her hand. "Nope, your turn."

C. B. Alice

I furrow my brow. *My turn.* For my turn, I choose to wrap one hand around her leg to lift her thigh and widen her stance.

She sidesteps me, but seriously, it's only my manners that keep me from grabbing her anyway. She is tiny. My reach is vast. "No, no, no. This." She gestures to my clothes. "You've seen me naked. Now it's your turn."

Because she's being sassy, I have no qualms sassing right back. "Technically, I've never seen you completely naked."

"You have seen every single part of me."

"And I'm sure I've seen every single second of *Frozen,* but I've never seen it from front to back, and honestly, I couldn't tell you what the plot is."

Her jaw drops, fully affronted. Before I can stop her, she launches herself over my bed, belly-flopping across it to grab my TV remote. "Well then, we have to watch it! Right now!"

I know she's joking. She better be joking. But she rolls onto her side and actually turns the TV on, and seeing her there? Propped up on one elbow, her legs crooked just right into a casually seductive pose, all long lines and cheeky lingerie?

No fucking way we're watching Disney princess shit right now. I *lived* that my entire childhood.

I'm not gentle, but I'm careful not to be too rough with her when I grab her by the ankles and slide her on her belly toward the edge of the bed. I smack her ass firmly enough the sound echoes through my room.

She shrieks and flips over, again propping herself up on her elbows. The soft of her stomach gathers a little, in a way I'm sure she'd think terribly unflattering, but it's sweet and makes me think of how much better she'd look with even more.

Like, if there wasn't any folding there because there's a baby taking up all the space.

I spent the week obsessing about this.

And it turns out that sometimes vasectomies fail. It's not like I would know if it did until it was too late.

Joss bites her lip playfully and lifts her foot to rub it up and down my thigh, hugging along the bulge of my throbbing cock.

I groan and rip my tee-shirt off without any more hesitation. But I have to pause there, give her time to accept who I am. I know she won't reject me; I would never be plotting what I'm plotting if I was concerned she would run off because I don't have the physique most of my friends do.

But I don't. My friends get panties thrown at them. I get cookies. Women don't like me because I'm sexy, they like me because I'm friendly and safe and food-motivated.

So I give Joss a moment to see what she's getting from me, see my soft bits and the chest I don't get professionally waxed because I'm not Merrick and my utter lack of visible abs because I don't dehydrate myself before photoshoots like Blaise does. I've got a weird scar from falling off my bike when I was seven and my chest is just as freckled as my face is, and I'm just big ole me.

Joss does take me in. She's not subtle about it. She studies me with heavily lashed eyes that glitter like sapphires. Her lips part, and my nerves are soothed by the way her tongue daintily swipes over her bottom lip.

She uses her toes to tug my pants down an inch, but I finish the job. Her grin is enough to prove she's plenty satisfied with the rest of me.

And then the clever little minx drags those toes down my stiff, sensitive cock. I in no way have a foot fetish, but I nearly lose it at that alone.

I need to take control of the situation. I gave her what she wanted, and now it really is my turn. I take hold of her panties and tug them off. She does me a solid and shimmies out of her bra.

My brain breaks for a second. I've only gotten to see her tits in a half-second flash and from the aerial view in her bra and that top she had at the gala. They're barely a handful for me, but her nipples are taut, begging for my attention. Then the scent of her arousal hits me, and when I look down to the apex of her slightly parted thighs and see the blonde curls, glossy in the lamplight, tidily trimmed now but every bit as shameless as in the truck, I know where I have to go.

She's close enough to the edge of my bed that I could drop to my knees, but I want to watch her. I want to touch her everywhere, I want to lock her down. So I once again grab her by the ankles, this time forcing her knees back to her shoulders and her spine to curl. Her slick, reddened pussy unfolds beneath me as my hands grip her hips and her heels naturally fall on my shoulders, holding her in place as I swipe my tongue up the distance from her pussy to her clit.

She shivers in response.

I groan quietly against her core and dive in again, lazily lapping at her, making her go soft and breathy beneath me. I tease at her, nipping at her labia, prodding her clit with the tip of my tongue. I know she won't come like this, and that's not my goal. I haven't had the opportunity to take my time with her.

She frustrates quickly, and no wonder. She was already soaked when I took those panties off her. She hid it well, but she must have been thinking about this all night, too. I bet she had to keep herself from squirming in her seat the whole drive home. So I'm only a couple minutes into my feast when she starts rubbing one of her breasts.

It's a pretty sight, I won't lie. And I know they'll be tiny in my palms, but they more than fill hers. She spreads her fingers wide and gives it a squeeze, and the flesh bubbles up, begging me to lick there, too. I'm going to lick every inch of her tonight.

I let go of her hip, using my arm to brace her as I slide my hand under hers, knocking it away so I can play with that pretty tit. She may think I'm messing with her, but I've planned this night for a week. I engulf the impossibly soft flesh in my palm, curling my fingers to pinch her nipple between my thumb and forefinger just enough that I can tug it up and up.

And up.

Pinching hard to stretch it even further.

Until I hit the snapping point, timing it just right as I spear my tongue into her tight, hot pussy.

Joss cries out, her spine attempting to flex in all directions, her fleshy inner walls pushing in on my tongue. She covers her mouth, muffling her sounds, so I pin that hand and lash her clit.

She has the audacity to tug some of my blanket over her face.

I pull it out of her grip, struggling to bring both her wrists together so I can hold them in one hand. This time, it's two fingers I stab into her pussy as I continue the assault on her clit. I've already figured out where her most sensitive spot inside her is, and I go right for that. She twists and turns beneath me, pushing with all the tiny might she has with her feet on my shoulders, and I can tell I've got the spot right and she's going to come undone at any moment, but she's fighting me.

She's a screamer. I know this. She probably doesn't even realize she practically deafened me in the truck as she rode my cock. I don't know why she's suddenly holding back.

To finish her off, I wiggle my fingers, double-tapping inside her as I twist my wrist to dig at her rim. She tips her chin to her shoulder to bury her face against her delicate arm. I can barely hear anything.

"Why are you fighting me?"

She scowls. "Why are you not fucking me?"

I slam my mouth against hers, kissing that tasty little profanity right out of it. "You gonna scream for me when I pump my cock into you?"

She shakes her head with a teasing pout.

I scrape my teeth down her jaw and then dip my head enough to swipe my tongue over her nipple. "No? What about when I bite this little titty of yours?"

Another quick shake of her head, but she's got her lips turned in between her teeth now to mute herself.

I do bite, not too hard, just enough for her to blow out a gust of air and wail a quick, laughing, "Stop!"

I grin and kiss her nipple better. "Never. I'm going to fuck you until you can't do anything but scream."

She's so fucking beautiful, her body flushed and dewy all over, her hair mussed beneath her, her lips already kiss swollen. The way she slithers beneath me proves how needy and unabashed she is. But she screws on a serious face and shakes her head. The sincerity when she whispers, "Please don't," gives me pause.

"Are you okay?"

"Yes, of course." An enthusiastic nod to assure me. "I just don't want everyone hearing us."

My stupid lizard brain has me glaring right at the wall dividing mine and Blaise's room. I've heard him fuck dozens of chicks. Merrick? He makes it a point to fuck in common rooms, like he's establishing his dominance over the rest of us.

This is my chance to prove myself.

I look back down at Joss, at her pleading eyes and faint frown, at the flush in her cheeks that might not be purely pleasure.

This is my chance to prove myself, but not to my teammates. To her.

I kiss her gently as I slide into her, my mouth absorbing her quiet whimper. If this is what she wants, this is what I'll gladly give her. I'll give her the entire world.

On the other side of the wall, Blaise yells, "You guys want gyros? I'm ordering gyros!"

Chapter Fourteen
JOSS

Every spring, I plant early-blooming annuals along the walkway to the barn, and in the fall, I replace them with mums. In December, I uproot them and move them back behind my barn. The field attracts bees from the apiary a few blocks away and showcases a whole array of colors and varieties, whatever I can get from the local nurseries and hardware stores. Many have been gifted to me from patrons who love my mum field as much as I do.

This year, I left the relative safety of Camden to visit Wilmington shops and even took a day trip out to Wren in Salem to hit up the nurseries there for mums in Juggernauts ruby and saffron. Not just to show my support for Gabe, either. Foolishly, I thought this was an opportunity to show Wilmington I still love it.

But Wilmington does not love me. I was plagued by vandals the first few years after Brian's self-deletion, and they've returned with my return to Wilmington.

The lush gold mum in my hand is an easy fix. It lays next to the hole I carved into the earth a week ago for it, and all it takes is righting it, packing soil around it, and patting dirt off its petals. But the nearly-ruby neighbor isn't so lucky, split in half, its flowers stomped on, so I pass it off to Rose.

She sets it in the wheelbarrow that's getting stacked high with destroyed mums while Iris hands me a fresh pumpkin-colored one to replace it with. I pinch my lips tightly closed and chastise myself for threatening to shed a tear over a wrong-colored mum.

"My son was telling me about these nets they've been putting over their winter squashes to keep the deer off them," Iris says. "I could ask him to throw some over the flowers? Maybe he could rig something that you could put over them at night."

I look up from where I'm scooping out the hole to make room for the bigger mum and offer her a helpless chuckle. When I first started my quilting streams out of the barn, it wasn't anything but a way to pass the time and make friends with people outside of Wilmington. Instead of Jocelyn Page, Miss Alabama, or Jocelyn Edgars, wife of the devil himself, I could be Joss Page, just some girl. I made funny, trendy patterns, made enough money selling them online that I wouldn't starve to death. That would have been my future if Rose hadn't recognized me and emailed me to ask if, since we were in the same town, I'd be willing to teach her best friend to quilt.

Cora talked me into monetizing my tutorials, but Iris and Rose are the reason I was brave enough to open a shop and offer my space for classes. And they've been dodging church for the last five years by claiming they're busy doing charity work, but really? They have the keys to the barn and show up with the sun to quilt. This was the first Sunday in a long time they had to wake me with the unfortunate news I'd been vandalized.

"I think the culprits are smarter than deer," I tell Iris.

Rose runs her eyes down the row. Sixty mums ripped out of the earth. Some tossed to the side but others torn apart. There's one thrown far enough away that the cheeky, self-effacing side of me wants to give Blaise one of the casualties to see if he could throw it that far.

"Doesn't look that way to me," Rose says with a huff.

I want to say something to calm the situation, a reminder that we've been through this enough times and always survived or that it's never gotten worse than this or kids are going to be kids, but I don't have it in me this morning. It's a cool October morning, but I'm sweating my butt off. I was actually looking forward to going to today's game after the last two were away.

I didn't even have the heart to tell Gabe I'm bailing on the game. I texted Blaise instead, with the thought that I didn't want to upset Gabe before the game but didn't want to worry him if he notices I'm not with the other wives and girlfriends. They're having a bonfire at the Jug House tonight; I'm just going to shower up after I finish this and head over there early, maybe crawl into his bed to make up for missing the game.

If I finish. By ten a.m., I'm not even halfway down one side, and already I'm exhausted.

Iris squeezes my shoulder with deceptively strong fingers. She's the frailer of the duo, but she throws around king-sized high-loft quilts with the best of them. She's also far more even-tempered than Rose. She gets it. I just want to fix my mums, curl up in my room for a couple hours, hand stitch some binding so I feel productive, and then have a quiet night with Gabe.

A quiet night of sex. He's gotten really good at that.

"Why don't I get the next one, dear?" Iris offers, and I have to lunge up to stop her from kneeling down. I don't know if we'd ever get her up again.

"No, no, it's okay. At least I'm off today."

"You certainly are not off today!"

I groan, not needing to look to know Cora's barreling down the path. Now that fall's here, she's traded out her sandals for ankle boots, stylish even in jeans and the Briggs jersey.

I make skirts out of scrap material with ten extra inches on the waistband to prepare for my inevitable future.

"Were you going to hide this from me?" she shouts.

I only turn around then because I can hear both anger and fear in her voice, and I immediately feel guilty. It's to Cora that I need to say, "It's just kids being kids. But it's Sunday, not like I can get someone else to come out and clean—"

"It's not kids being kids, you know this!" Cora rakes her fingers through her hair, but she pays four figures to fly up to New York for the perfect layered, wavy balayage, so it lands itself right back where it was. "Did you call the police?"

I roll my eyes, same as I do every time we have this conversation. She was still living in Milan when the vandalism started. She didn't see the cops taking photos with their personal cellphones to spam the desecration across social media. They hated me like everyone else did. They didn't care that it was impossible for me to leave with my assets tangled up in the house and a baby on the way.

They didn't care when I lost the baby, either.

"I just need to fix this."

Cora hates this. She always has. She glares at the soft grass as she steps onto it, like her boots have depreciated, but she keeps going, heading toward one of the thrown plants. I ignore her, resuming my gardening, until she yells, "You can't hide forever, Joss."

"I feel like I was doing a bang-up job of it before!" I fire right back.

She picks up the mum, and thankfully it's already wrecked because she flings it right back into the ground with a furious snarl. "Then get the fuck out of Wilmington!"

Iris and Rose gasp.

"You know I can't."

She flicks an angry finger at the second story, at the corner room with its windows facing both north and west, the room I demanded we make the nursery because I thought it was the perfect amount of sun.

"Because of that?" Cora yells across the lawn.

I swallow the stone in my throat. "It's not just that anymore."

Cora finally relents and returns to me, her irritation melting into concern. "The shop can be rebuilt anywhere," she says, but I hear the hesitation, the finesse.

"You know it's not just that either."

"Is it fucking Jerry?"

I roll my eyes at her even though yeah, if I did leave Wilmington, I'd probably have to figure out if there was a way to transport a feral raccoon with me.

C. B. Alice

Cora blows out a gust of air that fluffs her bangs. "You know Gabe might not be here forever, either, right? He could get transferred."

He might also not get signed at the end of the season. They're two and two right now, and the losses have been to teams ranked high enough that Gabe says they're actually doing well. From what I hear from others, they're doing great, no reason for him to worry. But he does. And I'm not about to jinx it by saying it's a possibility, so I shrug and resume planting the next mum. "We'll cross that bridge when we get to it. But I'm not uprooting my whole life and wrecking things with Gabe over some mums."

Cora's lips pull to the side as she drums her nails on her thigh. "Maybe he can say something to the press," she says thoughtfully. "Wilmington likes him. If he asks people to leave you alone or remind them that you had no idea what Fuckhead was doing or–"

"He doesn't know about Brian."

Cora shakes a surprised jolt off. "You haven't told him? You know there's some locker room beef happening between him and Allore because of this?"

I do know this, but Gabe says it's not a big deal, he was never that close with the Allores.

But I've stalked Keira's social media. Tons of pictures of him with her baby, and he doesn't even like kids.

"He told me he doesn't want to know, and I respect that."

"He can't pretend that—what happens when he finds this shit in the morn—what about the nurs—gahh!" Cora flops down onto her knees next to me.

"What are you doing?" I gasp as Iris and Rose crowd around her, likely thinking she's petite enough they could pick her up if she's fallen.

"Give me some damn gloves. If you're gonna be this stupid about this stupid man and his stupid heart of gold nonsense and how seriously perfect he is for you, you don't get to hide from the public anymore. We're gonna fix these stupid flowers, and then we're going to go to that stupid game and you're going to hold your stupid head high."

"Here you go, dear," Iris says as Rose gives her a set of gloves.

Chapter Fifteen
GABE

The locker room is abuzz with good vibes after the game. A win is always a good thing, but it feels especially nice coming off a loss last week, a late game on the west coast, so we didn't get home until past midnight. Tonight, we get to celebrate our win all night.

Blaise slaps my ass as he strolls by in nothing but his shorts, but that's typical for Blaise after a win. He's gotta preen. We'd expect nothing less from him. "You and Jossy-girl planning yourselves a hot, sweaty bible study tonight, big guy?" he laughs.

I respond by shouldering him hard enough he stumbles into his neighboring locker, but he's a fool. His shit-eating grin splits wider at my manhandling.

"I'm about over that joke. You do not need to know or talk about our sex life."

C. B. Alice

When Joss first insisted on keeping quiet, I was bummed but went along with it. But now that I've had a month of curling up with her, rocking into her for what seems like hours, tormenting her by bringing her to the edge over and over again, sharing her space, her breaths, her every soft inch, pumping her pussy full of cum and keeping her plugged with my cock until I'm hard enough to add another load, letting it soak into her for hours, slowly spilling into her womb—

It's fucking hot. Just thinking about it has me glad my equipment buddy hasn't come by to help me out of my jersey yet, so I'm still fully suited up.

"I like her," Blaise says unexpectedly. The two of them do get along well. She gets along with everyone in the house except Merrick, and that's entirely on Merrick. She's unfailingly friendly and doesn't take offense when he gives her the cold shoulder.

I know Blaise likes her. But Blaise is also big on bro code. He hated my girlfriend in college even before she cheated on me, and he usually gets pissed whenever any of his friends get girls. Pulls the whole ball-and-chain nonsense. Even though he clearly likes Joss, I didn't expect him to admit it.

And because he's admitting it, I feel the need to return the favor, mumbling under my breath, "I want her to be the one," so no one else will hear.

But I don't have a quiet voice. That was made abundantly clear at breakfast the first night Joss stayed over and Blaise asked me — right in front of her — if I'd whacked off while she was in the bathroom or if I needed lessons on how to make my girl come. Apparently, Joss's attempt to come quietly was way more effective than mine was.

GOOD GUY GABE

Joss's face went beet-red, but she held her own with a casual "Nah, I just couldn't scream when I was face down, ass up like that."

Her words, so casually spoken as she licked her spoon clean of yogurt — Merrick's stupidly expensive imported yogurt that I gave her because he called her my 'slut' when I mentioned she'd be staying the night — was enough to make Blaise's jaw drop and earn a nod of respect out of him.

So I don't have a quiet voice, and when a locker slams hard across the bench from us, I know it's in response to my words. I glance over my shoulder quickly enough that I catch Allore's glare before he has a chance to hurry off.

He tries it anyway and gets pegged with a water bottle by Blaise. The only thing that prevents warfare is the fact it was empty and bounced off Evan's shoulder. If Blaise had truly meant it, it would have been the full water bottle that was right there in his locker, and it would have smashed Evan in the back of his head.

"Sup, bro?" Blaise says as he takes a step toward Evan, who's inadvertently cornered himself by moving toward the showers as well as Merrick's locker. "You two are besties, right? Remember when he blew off my party for your stupid shit?"

The 'stupid shit' was the birth of Evan's daughter, Shelby, almost exactly a year ago, but Blaise doesn't have a concrete concept of time.

Evan's got that deer-in-the-headlights look on his face. He glances around nervously, but Merrick's on one side, Vedder on the other. Vedder gets puppy dog eyes when he sees Joss ever since she sewed a button back onto his jacket. Which was silly, even I could have done that, but it made him happy. It's fine.

"You gonna congratulate him on getting himself a girl?" Merrick asks smugly, like he suddenly does want Joss around, but that's what Merrick does. He probably likes Joss, too, but he refuses to show the slightest human emotion. "That's what you wanted, yeah? When you were introducing him to all Keira's friends, forcing them on him so he was the absolute goofiest fucker he could be, ruining his chances with any of them? You mad he found a girl on his own?"

Evan deflates at Merrick's words. Just shrivels up there before us as he looks sadly at me. "I wanted to help. You know that right? Me and Keira, we just wanted you to be happy."

I straighten up. Not to intimidate Allore. He's terrifying on the field. The distance between us? If he wanted to attack me, he's got the room to build the momentum to demolish me. I straighten up to show him that I'm not bothered by what any of them is saying about me. None of the girls Keira set me up with would have given me the time of day if she hadn't asked them to. "Well, now I have it," I say with a slam of my own locker as I head out to hunt down my equipment buddy.

"Shelby's first birthday is next Saturday," Evan yells after me. "She misses you."

She's a baby. I miss her way more than she misses me. But Keira's already sent me a text inviting me while making it clear I can't bring a plus one, and I'm not playing that game.

While Cora strips down to her underclothes to get in the hot tub with several of the guys and the girls who live across the street, Joss is happy to curl up with me by the firepit. I grab a blanket for us before lifting her up easily, causing her to erupt in giggles, and settling her on my lap. We have a quiet moment, just the two of us staring at the fire, before others filter in around us.

"Wasn't expecting to see you here," I murmur to Drew as he and Mel take the seat across from us. They're good for the occasional barbecue, but they also have a couple of kids. Usually they go straight home after games.

Joss stiffens at that. "I invited them," she says. "Was that okay?"

Beneath the blanket, I ruck up her skirt to squeeze her thigh reassuringly. The moment I touch that firm, warm expanse of skin, I'm wondering what I'll be able to get away with here. "Absolutely. You can invite anyone you want."

Eagle-eared Blaise yells from the hot tub, "Fuck Lin, though," reminding me that although he was ready to throw down with Allore today, he'll probably always hate Lin.

I shake my head. Lin's not a bad guy. He's stuffy. He's arrogant. He's pretentious. But he's not a bad guy. "You could invite him, but he won't come."

Joss frowns, her fingers swirling in tight circles at my sternum. Since she's distressed, I figure it's only reasonable to grab her from beneath her knee while my other hand rubs her arm briskly. "I really like Wren," she says. "It'd be nice to see her more."

"She had her baby on Wednesday," Mel points out. "It's going to be rough for her to do anything for a while."

Joss nods. "Yeah, I get that. I have a friend who's pregnant. No father, though, not one in the picture. We're trying to help however we can, but we're worried about what she'll need once she has the baby."

"If she needs a dick, I dig pregnant chicks," Blaise chimes in from the hot tub.

C. B. Alice

I snag an empty beer can and crush it with my fist before launching it over my shoulder at Blaise, pinging him right in the forehead. He might be the one known for his precision, but I'm the one who has to be precise when throwing the football to him from between my legs. "Don't be gross."

"Dude, I'm being respectful. Pregnant women are awesome, and if they have needs not getting satisfied, I will happily satisfy them. What's gross about that?"

I sink into my chair — and slide my hand to Joss's thigh — with a huff. She only chuckles and says, "Trust me, Tilly wants none of that. She needs new mom friends, not man whores."

"I wear that badge proudly," Blaise says before, even more horrifyingly, he says to Cora, "It's not just pregnant chicks I'm into, in case you were concerned."

"You're never going to want to bring your friends over again, are you?" I whisper.

Joss pats my chest. "Cora's a big girl. She'll take what she wants, trust me."

I take the moment to steal a kiss from Joss. Her lips are soft and yielding, and although I don't want to do anything that's going to embarrass her — like sticking my tongue in her mouth — I take the time to savor the contact. The rest of the group circled around the fire pit can put in the effort to ignore what we're doing if we can keep it from getting too inappropriate. That's fair.

Drew grabs a fire poker to stir up the embers while Kai throws some small logs into the pit, distracting everyone. I draw the kiss out with soft pecks and a tug on her bottom lip, loving the way she melts into me as her small, delicate hand wraps around the back of my neck to support her and keep her close. Her breath is heavy on my cheek.

I take her thigh in one of my hands and dig into it. A shiver races through her, and our lips part long enough for her to say, "Gabe," faintly. The tone is questioning but breathless, and her eyes glance over to the others sitting nearby. She wants me, but not publicly.

We're not excusing ourselves now. We're celebrating a victory, and she's gotten Drew and Mel to come over. Her friend's in the hot tub, and maybe she can hold her own, but I still feel like we shouldn't run off.

I lift Joss's thigh up, pushing it to her torso, which has her foot settling on my knee.

"How are your kids doing?" I casually ask Drew and Mel. No funny business visible here — because the blanket is now tented on Joss's knee. "I haven't seen them all season."

"Well, David has hit that 'too cool to hang out with his parents' phase," Mel says with a laugh, "and has boldly declared he wants nothing to do with football. He then demanded we put him in hockey."

"Hockey's great," I tell her. "Probably cooler than football."

Drew groans. "Please don't tell him that. Then he'll think it's as uncool as football and will try to get into archery or something."

"Archery's cool, too." I don't know, I've spent my entire life playing football, and I don't regret it, but there was so long that I was in school too or working full time that football took up every other second of my life. And it still demands more than a regular job would, I'm still at the training facility six days a week and spending an hour of my day off in the weight room here, but I have actual downtime now. I don't know what to do with it other than watching TV or playing video games, the same shit I do when we're traveling and there's not much else I can do.

Hobbies are cool. Archery is cool. Quilting is cool. They're skills I don't think I could ever do, not the least because my hands are so big that I don't think I could handle anything that delicate.

"Come back to me when you've got a kid that decides the only good target for his Nerf darts is your butt," Drew chuckles.

"They sting more than you'd think," Mel tacks on.

They say that like they don't think we have an entire barrel of them inside. We have a cleaning lady that comes in weekly, and I swear half her job is collecting them. With the exception of Blaise, we're all tidy enough, nothing is terrible for her, but those darts get everywhere.

"Just tell him quilting is infinitely uncool," Joss laughs, "And I can force hexies on him until he realizes how uncool uncool things can really be."

"What's a hexie?" Mel asks, ignoring the jab Joss made at herself. It turns out Mel has a thing for sewing. The rest of us sit back and enjoy the cool evening, the warm fire, and the feminine chatter that's all but a foreign language but still soothing to the ear.

It also gives me the opportunity to focus on working my hand between Joss's thighs. Her eyes widen when I reach her panties and skim my thumb over the damp cotton. She shoots me a concerned look when I push the fabric away, but she doesn't stop me. Even when she sees the glimmer of mischief in my eye, she just takes a deep breath.

And then squeaks when I push my middle finger into her warm, inviting pussy. She's twisted some to face Mel, and at that, she grabs hold of my shirt and mangles it in her hand.

She covers her squeak with a cough like there's something in her throat, so I hand her my drink.

As she sips at it, I slide my finger in deeper and then drag it out, going slowly and carefully, savoring her slick warmth. I want her hot and limp and dopey, sex-drunk, melted fully into me. I'm going to make her come, that's a definite, but I'm going to take my time, let her have this conversation. I'm scared of losing her to someone else, someone better, but I need her fully integrated into the group. Sure, she has her own friends, and she'll keep them — ideally, I can find a way to bring at least Cora into the group, as well — but I need my world to be Joss's so she can't leave.

"You should bring Tilly to the next game," I blurt out over the conversation she's having with Mel, which has shifted to fall soup recipes. "Introduce her to Wren."

I slide my ring finger in as I say that, and her toes are already curling at those two fingers.

"Umm, yeah," she murmurs, her eyelids drooping. I'm careful to not curl my fingers inside her. I don't want to trigger anything. I can't have her a complete mess too soon. I scissor my fingers nice and slow, wishing I could lick my hand clean as her silk begins to pool in my palm. "That would . . . that would be good."

Yeah, it would. If Tilly and Wren hit it off, that'll be a new mom circle. They'll have playdates. Since Tilly's single, I'm wondering if Wren has some guy friends to hook her up with. Or, like, all the guys on the team who are single, but I'm definitely not going to hook her up with Blaise. I need a guy for her who's going to be around for the long haul. If Tilly gets something going with one of my teammates and then they break up, that could be really bad.

Oh no.

I twist to look over at the hot tub. Tilly isn't the problem; it's Cora. The hot tub is at capacity, an even mix of people in there, some couples, some other single girls, everything looks casual and friendly. But Blaise is next to Cora, and the way she's looking at him makes me think she has every intention of fucking him tonight. Everyone seems on board with it, especially Blaise, who has at least one hand on her. It's doing that *draped behind her shoulders like he's stretching but totally touching her* move, and I don't like it. Especially when I don't know what his other hand is doing.

His other hand could be doing what mine is doing, which is playing at Joss's rim to stretch it for later. Her brow crinkles, so I place a gentle kiss there, which is enough to get her to sink down into me as she murmurs, "I bet Wren will have some . . . some good ideas for things Tilly needs. And Mel? Would you be able to help her? Tilly doesn't have much for family, so she's flying blind."

"Sure thing," Mel says happily. "I gave you my number, right?"

"Yep. I'll get something organized."

"That sounds great." She yawns and pats Drew's chest. "You about ready to go, big guy?"

Drew nods and finishes off his beer before they say their farewells. It's enough to get some others to leave as well, leaving just Joss and me at the fire.

I add a third finger, and Joss clenches down on me. I don't think she means for her body to move, but her hips begin to rock, taking from me as I hold my hand steady. I kiss my way up to her ear — we're just making out a little, nothing too excessive — and whisper, "Do you need this now?"

She bites down on her bottom lip and nods against my cheek.

"Can you be still, or do we need to go inside?"

"I can be still," she whispers on a heavy breath, and my dick is already rock hard enough that her heavy, smoky voice leaves a damp spot on my sweatpants.

"That's good," I grunt, finally curling my fingers to dig into the sensitive patch inside her that has her digging her forehead into my neck.

Her entire body goes taut in my lap, her forehead pushing hard against me and her nails digging into my chest and thigh, her back straining against my arm and her thigh rippling in my hand. She's at the very brink.

"Are you fucking serious right now?" Cora shrieks.

Oh fuck.

But when I glance back, I see she's not yelling at us.

It wasn't intentional, but her outburst covers for Joss, who lets out a soft whimper as she jolts under the blanket, her pussy fluttering rapidly around my fingers as more of her cum gathers in my palm.

"Is, um," Joss starts, but she's still panting as quietly as possible. "Is she . . . is . . . ?"

I ease my fingers out of her so I can cradle her head. "She's fine."

I'm not sure if that's true, but I give Joss my undivided attention for another few seconds until her eyes droop.

It was Merrick who Cora was screaming at — and still is as she pulls her bra together in the front. It doesn't take a genius to figure out that Merrick must have unhooked the front clasp, exposing her to everyone in the hot tub.

He couldn't have been out here more than a couple minutes; after the game, he went for a drive. It's not unusual for him to dodge parties, even quiet ones. He must have just gotten home, so I have no idea what possessed him to harass Joss's friend.

Cora hoists herself out of the tub, shoves Merrick with all the might she has, and announces she's leaving. She's rushing about, collecting her stuff and hurrying into the house, and Merrick is stalking after her.

It's like a horror movie scene. She's running all over the place, but Merrick walks in slow, measured paces, no doubt catching up to her inside, where I hear her screaming at him again.

Not scared. Not crying for help. She's spitting teeth.

Jesus. I know where this is going. Nowhere good unless Cora likes being a notch on an extremely well-notched headboard.

I push Joss's bangs back to kiss her forehead. "So listen, we should probably go to your place tonight." She hasn't offered it and I haven't pushed. I'm guessing something about her place embarrasses her, but I don't care what it is.

"Mmm, why?" she murmurs.

"Because Merrick's about to fuck your friend in every room in the house."

She straightens up so quickly she chokes on a breath. "No!"

From the hot tub, Blaise calls, "Looks like he's already bent her over the island."

As Joss groans and sinks back down in my lap, we hear Cora's shrieks of pleasure only partially muffled through the glass doors.

Chapter Sixteen
JOSS

"You okay?" Gabe asks, taking my hand and drawing it to the console as we drive through Camden Square.

I nod, worried if I talk, I'll barf. He has no idea there's a nursery in my apartment, and I don't know how I'm going to explain it to him without having that conversation I've been avoiding about wanting kids.

"You, uh, need me to sit in the car for a few minutes while you clean or something? I get it if you do. No judgment."

I squeeze his hand. "Nah, it's fine. I'm just worried about Cora." I'm about to make up a lot of stupid white lies; why not start with one that's believable?

I'm stressed enough that I forget the other big issue I'm dealing with until I'm unlocking my door and Gabe says, "What happened to your mums?"

Damn, he's not going to like that I was vandalized last night. "What?" I gasp, padding my time to come up with something.

"You got different mums. Those aren't the mums you had before."

"Oh. Right. Died. Just up and died."

He frowns and, to my horror, says, "Strange. They were healthy a couple days ago. Call me next time something like that happens, okay? My dad's a landscape architect. I used to work for him when I had the time in the summers. I'm pretty good with plants."

He drops it at that. Or I force him to drop it by opening the door to my apartment and tromping up the stairs without another word. I give him a quick tour, pointing out the kitchen, living room, and dining room on one side, coming back to the converted dinette that we came in through, then pointing at the guest bath and the guest room. At the nursery, the only closed door in the apartment aside from the pantry and laundry room off the kitchen, I stammer through, "That-that's storage," and Gabe's gaze lingers only a moment too long on the door before I have him distracted with my bedroom.

It's a gigantic room. The apartment was originally designed to be two separate small apartments, and when they were combined, the rooms ended up being strange sizes. There used to be a nook by the window with two chairs and a table between them, but I sold that set. After everything went down with the civil suits, I was penniless. I sold most of the nice stuff and replaced it with basic flat-packed furniture. I've done my best to fill the space, hanging several quilts and a giant rug I wove myself, bringing in the bookshelves that had been in the living room and the rocking chair that had been in the nursery, but it feels empty. I'm used to Gabe's

Good Guy Gabe

presence consuming a room; now I have a space that's ample for him.

He studies it thoughtfully, his lips tugging up at one of the quilts, his toes nudging at the rug. He seems satisfied with it, but then he frowns at the bed.

"It's not big enough, is it?" I ask, realizing it's way smaller than his.

He heads toward the bathroom and tests the towels neatly folded and tucked into the cubby built into the wall there. "Nah, it's fine. It's what we get in the hotels usually." He lays the towel out on it, a habit he's gotten into at his place for easy clean-up. Despite it being excruciatingly banal, it's become the most domestic of foreplay. "It's just . . ." He pushes down on the bed, gives it a wiggle, makes it squeak. Like despite the less-than-romantic overture of the towel, he's having second thoughts.

"Yeah, okay, it's going to be squeaking tonight," I mutter defensively. "Unless you're going to be a jerk, and then there won't be any squeaking at all and you can head right back home."

The look he shoots me isn't of concern or apology. It's purely wicked. He's been cool and collected since we left his place, but I can see now that he's plotting. He stalks back to me, using his size to loom over me in what would be threatening if I didn't know what the nature of his plotting has been.

Although now that we're standing like this, my head craned back to meet his eyes, reminding me that I've talked him into being gentle but he's a brute when he chooses to be? I should be intimidated.

"Ma'am, it's not that frame that's going to be making the noises tonight," he growls. He grabs me by the thighs, hoists

C. B. Alice

me up, and tosses me on the bed like I'm a ragdoll. And yeah, I do let out a shocked squeak and do need to catch my breath and do find myself immediately wanting whatever he's going to do to me, but then I yelp as he grabs the mattress and drags it — and me — straight to the floor.

"What are you doing?" I shriek, laughing, my heart pounding, stunned I wasn't injured, but mattresses are sturdy enough I was never in any danger.

"Not breaking your bed." He nods to the frame. "That didn't feel sturdy enough for me." I'm sure he's wrong; he's a giant, but my bed is definitely built for two, and it's not like I'm massive, too. But then he pulls down my leggings and panties in one rough move, flips me over, and slaps my ass. "Not with what I'm planning on doing."

He doesn't even take my leggings off, just leaves them clinging to my calves. The way he's looking at me makes me think he's planning on keeping me that way for at least a few minutes. And when he tugs my shirt and bralette over my head but doesn't pull them off my arms either, instead snagging them over my head, I get that he's serious.

I could take everything fully off. It's not like I don't know how to undress myself or that anything is so restrictive I wouldn't be able wiggle free. But I let him have this. I'm curious what he intends.

He lifts my hips, bringing my ass into the air and dropping my knees to the mattress, but he keeps me face-planted. "That's it," he murmurs with a gleam in his eye and yet another smack, this time right on my slit. The sound is sharp, damp, and with the lights on, I'm sure his groan is over the sight of my muscles contracting.

I silently study him as he rubs my thighs and ass, massaging the flesh deliberately to spread me for his gaze. I'm not embarrassed by the way he manipulates me to see every slick, swollen inch from my clit all the way back to my ass, but I can't help thinking about how I've taken so much control from him.

"I'm sorry I'm weird about things at your place."

He kisses my ass cheek. "Nah, I love it. I love the challenge. And I love when you pass out still filled with my cock and my cum and I get to spend hours inside you. You're perfect."

But then he smacks that ass cheek he just lovingly kissed.

"And that's going to make this feel so much better, isn't it, ma'am?" He jabs two thick fingers inside me, pushing all the way to the knuckles. I moan into the pillow, out of habit, and he grabs my hair and yanks my ponytail back to lift my head.

"Fuck!" I hiss, although the pain of a couple broken strands isn't nearly as voice-worthy as Gabe's sudden dominance roaring forward.

"You need me to hold your head up, or are you going to behave?"

His fingers curl into my inner walls, and my back arches. I'm robbed of coherent words until he releases my hair to apply pressure to my spine, warping my body into the exact shape he wants.

"Gabe," I whimper, my head dropping back to the pillow, but I lay my cheek on it this time. "What are you doing?"

He gives me that sly grin of his as the pushing within me turns into a rough pound. He's not thrusting his fingers like he usually does, making sure to handle the sensitive patch within in a firm but cautious way to build me up slowly. No, tonight, he holds back nothing. Instead of in and out, his wrist goes up and down, stretching the back edge of my rim as his knuckles dig into my G-spot.

Sparkles dance in my eyes as I rear back, attempting to change the motion. It earns me another firm smack on my ass. My jaw drops, releasing loud, nonsensical sounds, a string of *no*s, a high keen as he attacks my pussy with total disregard for my comfort.

"Keep making that sound," he purrs. "You scream it out. Scream it right out. And think about what's going to happen after you come and it's my cock destroying this pussy."

"Fuck!" I wail as every neuron lights up, every muscle goes wild, every sense overloads.

Except that sensation. That unnaturally strong sensation in my diaphragm, that tingle that signals that my body's tipped too far past the edge.

The sounds Gabe's hand makes goes from damp to drenched, and suddenly, I feel my own slick splashing on my belly as the release pumps out uncontrollably.

"Ma'am," Gabe whispers, his voice awestruck. "Did you just squirt?"

Chapter Seventeen
GABE

I've never seen this happen before outside of porn. I wasn't even sure it was real. I always kind of thought it was a prank, girls peeing themselves to get more views.

I am awestruck. I can't believe I made Joss come this hard. Even when she stops, her body keeps popping, like when I try to keep up with the guys while we're doing laps and my thighs end up spasming for the next day, practically crippling me. And I wouldn't say Joss is crippled, but she's definitely incapacitated.

I need more. I need to feel this.

I scramble to get my pants down enough to free my cock. With her leggings still tangled around her knees, I have no choice but to straddle her calves and spread her thighs apart to make room for my cock to slide in. I notch the head on her rim, spread her cheeks wide, and slam into her.

"Oh fuck, ma'am," I groan. Oh fuck. I can *feel* it inside her. I can feel her entire body quivering around my cock as her legs kick within their confines and her hands tear at the pretty quilt on her bed.

Mattress. Not sure if this counts as a bed since I deconstructed it.

"Gabe, Gabe, Gabe, Gabe!" she mewls, going wild beneath me, every inch of her begging me to use her.

I do my best not to hurt her as I pound into her with the energy she demands of me. The harder I go, the more she begs, until I'm sweating like crazy and so worked up I've managed to edge myself. My entire body feels locked up by the need to consume her, to impale her, to merge into her. To fill her in every way I can.

I hate the position we're in. I'm fucking her with everything I've got, but I'm not touching her, not the way I need to. We're not just a cock and a pussy, two hands and this soft, lush ass of hers. I need all of her.

There's a strange sense of claustrophobia that sets my teeth grinding when I realize her stupid fucking leggings have doomed us. I manage to keep pounding into her hard enough she starts making that crazy warbling sound and then soaks my pants while I reach behind and grab her leggings by the crotch, pulling so hard I hear a ripping sound.

Not sure if I actually tore them in half, don't care. Suddenly her legs are no longer bound together, and in two quick moves, I grab her by the knees, lifting them off the mattress and pushing them up to her chest so I can get her feet around my legs to straddle me.

Finally, she's split as wide as I need her to be.

I lay my body over hers, mindful to not crush her with my weight as I anchor my hands on either side of her head. I lean down and bite her shoulder.

Good Guy Gabe

She throws her head back so fast I have to dodge her to keep from getting my nose broken and screams my name. She's leaking so much that it's heating up, a strange new friction that feels like a fire that can only be put out by pushing harder. I'm starting to feel like a wild animal, too, and I'm loving every second of it. Our sweat and voices mingle together, the sounds and smells of sex filling the room, a haze cloaking the rest of the world from us. It's just me and Joss forever. Nothing else matters.

She's my everything.

The L word almost pops out of my mouth, but I have enough brain cell left to hold it back. I need to save it for the right moment. The big moment. But I love her. Fuck. I love her so much. She's my other half. She's my whole.

"I can't," she whimpers as another orgasm crushes my cock. "Please, Gabe, I—I—"

"I've got you," I moan as the familiar tension in my balls finally reaches its cusp and I lose myself within her, pumping my seed into her, making another attempt at filling her with my baby, locking her down, ensuring she's mine forever.

I love her too fucking much to let her go.

I collapse to my elbows when it all hits me, and Joss curls as much as she can beneath me, grabbing my biceps in her tiny hands, hugging me close.

She loves me too. I know she does.

My brain is as groggy as my body, but I finally muster what I need to dig my hand under her stomach and roll us to the dry side of the bed. I ask, "Have you done that before?" but my voice is so hoarse from excursion I'm shocked she understands me.

"Hmm? Yeah. It's been years, but it's happened a couple times before. Sorry."

"Why the hell are you apologizing?"

She sighs and snuggles in more, pushing my softening cock deeper inside her, locking me in the way I like, making sure nothing leaks out. "That mess. It got everywhere, didn't it?"

"Ma'am, I don't know how you didn't notice this already, but you *always* make a mess. We'll just have to start putting two towels down. Because that was not the last time I'm making you squirt."

It's at least an hour before I get my ass in gear to actually do the necessary clean-up. Joss is passed out cold. It takes some effort moving her around without waking her, but I get us both cleaned up, toss the towel in the hamper, wiggle the quilt out from beneath her, and find another quilt to tuck her in with.

I'm awake after that. Not unusual for me. I've always had weird sleeping habits, and usually I push them on Joss, waking her up in the wee hours to make love again, but not tonight. I kiss the top of her head, tuck an extra pillow between her arms so she doesn't feel so alone, and pad out to the kitchen to see if I can scare up a cup of coffee.

I'm planning on going back to sleep, but this is part of the process. Some people need a cigarette; I need coffee.

Technically, I prefer hot cocoa, but that feels like a big ask right now.

I find a standard, bargain brand single-cup coffee maker, make a mental note to replace it with something fancier because nothing in my life is single-serving, and set it to brew. While I let it do its thing, I peek out the windows.

Good Guy Gabe

This isn't the north side of the house. I can't see that trail where the mums randomly died on her. I'm curious about that and have only my thoughts to entertain me, and I know it's way too dark to get a sense of what happened — I don't know if even broad daylight would help, but there could be something obvious — but I need to look. And there are tons of rooms on the north side of the apartment I could look out. Plenty close to where I stand.

But she was weird about that storage room. Something about it hit me strangely, just like those mums, and now it's in my brain.

She's keeping secrets from me. That's nothing unusual. Not knowing things about her, like whatever the hell her former husband did, assuages the guilt I have over knowing I'll be lying to her about one critical thing for the rest of our lives. It's no way to start a relationship. I know this. But because of that, this little voice in my head says I should go into that storage room and learn her secret. I'll keep it to myself, but I'll hold it as a reminder that this is normal. Even good people keep secrets.

I half expect an alarm to go off when I turn the knob and push the door open. It doesn't even squeak. I swear it's the only thing in the apartment that doesn't need a WD-40 bath. I peek over my shoulder to make sure Joss isn't behind me, but her place is so quiet that I can hear her breathing from across the hall. I take a big breath and push the door open.

There's a moment of confusion. The room is too dark to see much with just the kitchen light from down the hall, but I was expecting it to be some form of storage, either a hoarding nightmare or a fabric stash to rival the shop itself or shelves of doomsday prep. My imagination went wild on what might have been stored here when she stumbled over her words and quickly pivoted to her bedroom.

Nothing's stored here. Or, that's certainly not the primary function of the room. It's a bedroom. A dresser, a stocked bookshelf, a table with a lamp on it.

A crib.

It's a nursery.

Her friend is pregnant. Tilly. Joss is worried about her. What I know of the woman, I get it. I've only met her the one time in person because she works in the film industry. If what she does requires her to be there, if her skill set doesn't translate to something she can do here, that could be a big problem.

When I met her, I didn't suspect she was pregnant. She was wearing a snug tank and leggings, and nothing about her shape made me think about it. That was a month ago, so I doubt she's far along, but now I'm wondering if Joss is adopting the baby. Or taking some sort of guardianship so when Tilly is traveling, the baby can stay here?

It wouldn't surprise me. I can see why she wouldn't want to tell me or show me this room. But thinking about how far off it is, this looks like a lot of work has already gone into it.

I close the door behind me and turn the light on.

Tilly's expecting a boy, that much is obvious. Everything's blue and masculine, pushing a vehicular theme. I like cars and trucks and bulldozers. I've been to a Monster Truck rally and spent more money than I should have on a truck bigger than I need. But this is surprising to me, too. Watching Joss's streams has given me unique insights about her. She doesn't usually push the hard gender stuff. When viewers ask for suggestions for baby quilts, she goes for more neutral themes. When they ask for recommendations on specifically pink or blue fabrics, she offers soft patterns over anything princess or sports themed. She likes animals.

There's nothing animal here.

It all rubs me the wrong way. I don't know Joss as well as I want to, but either I don't know her as well as I think or this is all wrong.

Maybe I'm thinking too hard on it. There are all kinds of explanations. But then, as I wander around, checking out the changing table and the books, the small vase on the dresser, the art on the wall and the mobile, there's a stagnation that hits me. It doesn't quite click until I accidentally scuff up the corner of the rug and see the carpet beneath it. The room is carpeted in a pale, somewhat off-putting shade between seafoam and cornflower, but beneath the rug is a distinct baby blue.

The carpet's sun-faded, which means it's been here in this spot for years. And it's got a bunch of bubbly, childish cars on it, so it's not like it just happened to be here already. This nursery wasn't recently set up. Joss has had this nursery for years. Probably from a time when she did go for gendered stuff and for whatever crazy reason assumed she'd have a boy. Hell, the pageant life may have done such a number on her she didn't care what the baby would be, she'd push traditionally boy stuff on them. She's legit crazy.

Baby crazy.

Thank fuck for that.

Chapter Eighteen
JOSS

"Well, this isn't what I wanted to come home to," Tilly grumbles as she scrapes a razor up one of the windows on the front of my shop. "How long has it been going on for?"

I test the acetone on the siding, regretting the cedar facade I had done last year when I thought the vandals had finally moved on. It was an act of faith in the community, that everyone had accepted or at least forgotten me.

"Beginning of the month, what, three weeks ago? The Jags game?"

Tilly snickers. "That's how we're tracking time now?"

I admonish her with a pleading, "Stop! I just remember it because I tried to beg off from the game, but Cora refused. She actually helped me with the mums."

"No way!"

"She made me pay to get her nails fixed afterward," I laugh, feeling better. Most of the paint comes off with a little scrubbing, but the shingle looks the same when I take a few steps back, so I count that as another victory. I'm worried about the paint that's gotten into the grooves, that it might end up still showing the message — BACK OFF, spray painted in red — but if we can get most of it off, I'll feel better about the day.

"What does that even mean, *back off?*" Tilly grumbles. "Back off of what?"

I shrug. "Who knows? You sure you should be out here? Not that I don't appreciate your help just as much as I appreciate Cora's, but I don't want to hurt the baby."

She glances down at that, pats her belly. She isn't showing yet. With the medical issues she's had in the past, I'm interested to see when she does. She's home for a week before she's got a short gig in California, and then she'll be back for the month of December, but she'll be out for over two months starting in January. I worry she's going to overwork herself, but she doesn't have much choice. She's a contractor; no maternity leave.

"Nah, doc said that as long as I'm using a fume hood or working outside, I'm good with most things. And it's so warm today that I'd rather be outside doing this than inside fussing about it."

Indian summer. Wilmington always gets a good one. It's one of the reasons I fell in love with the city when I was first brought here from the gulf coast of Alabama. I was worried I was going to hate the cold season — and when I have to leave my property in February, I very much do — but I love the way it gets frosty, scaring me into thinking we're going to have six months of frigid temps, only to kick back in time for Halloween.

Good Guy Gabe

Which is approaching more rapidly than ever now that I've started counting by Game Days.

"Gabe took me on a picnic yesterday, down at the square. I don't know why I don't visit it more often. It's a ten-minute walk."

I glance over at Tilly when I don't get a response. Her arm's fallen to her side, and she's staring at the window in front of her. At the glass, at the graffiti, at the shelves within, at her own reflection? I couldn't say. But she's not the type to sit still for any length of time. Cora likes her quiet contemplation. I'm always moving, but it's typically at the speed of a sloth. My lifestyle works well for that. I will gleefully slow down to help a student see that I'm doing.

Tilly's a pinball. It's what makes her so good at her job. Yeah, she'll sit there and hand stitch a seam for an hour, but she's doing a million other things at the same time. A precise hand, a loud mouth.

"You okay?" I ask.

Her eyes narrow to the point I'm sure she's now glaring at her reflection. She anchors her hands at her sides, fluffing herself up to face me, but she's got her wig in twin flaming-red pigtails high up on the sides of her head and she picked a glittery lipstick for today. Plus, despite the weight she lost last year, she's maintained her chipmunk cheeks. "Do you think this is happening because of Gabe?"

I shrug helplessly at the sloppy letters. It's not like it's a new thought, but it is another to throw in the pile of stuff I can't talk to him about. "My face is popping back up around town again. Gabe, he tells off anyone who tries to start stuff when he's with me, but I'm guessing it's fuel for the fire. And this?" My eyes run along the four-foot-tall letters again, B CK O F now that the two windows are mostly cleaned. "What else could it be referring to? It's not like I'm suddenly popping up in places for any other reason."

"Oh no. Again?" someone calls from behind us, out on the street.

They're not the first passerby to comment in the handful of minutes we've been out here, and no, I don't want to talk about this with rubberneckers who I know happily agreed with hateful words spoken behind my back while offering me performative comfort to my face. Still, I screw on my customer service face to greet and accept their histrionics.

I soften immediately upon seeing Rachel, the Angel who makes Gabe's favorite cookies. She never quilted a day in her life but said she saw the one I made for the fundraiser and thought it'd be a good hobby now that her kids are more self-reliant. I've known her less than two months and feel like she's a bit of an oversharer and expects everyone else to share equally, but she's nice. "Oh, hey. Yeah. It happens sometimes. It's safe here, I promise. It's always overnight."

"Don't you live right there, though?" she asks. "Would you be safer if you stayed somewhere else?"

"No one's ever broken in or threatened me here before, so I'm not too worried, but I'll think about going elsewhere if it gets any worse," I promise her as she heads into the shop.

"Do you think it is someone from before?" Tilly asks. "One of the kids, grown up now, came back to town and saw you were still here or something."

"Maybe."

I stare hard at the bottom corner of the B as I scrub it. It's strange, but it happened so many times before and I've caught so many in the act — or at least seen them running away, in hoodies or masks so I couldn't see their faces but could see their body shapes well enough — that I get the impression this is a woman. The toilet paper and mailboxes, the smashed windows, those were always boys. Slow, thought-out acts, the things that took the most time and were the most irritating to fix were always girls. A girl would pull out every single mum. And these letters are meticulous, someone that was thoughtful about the space they were filling and painted them a height they could be consistent at. A girl who has experience painting giant letters, like on a sign.

Like on those signs the cheerleaders hold up.

"The way you say *maybe* makes me think you've got some other idea in your brain," Tilly observes as she sets the scraper down, replaces it with a bag of salt and vinegar potato chips, and plops down on the step.

I sit down next to her and steal one of her chips. I don't even like salt and vinegar chips, and the look Tilly gives me tells me she's fully aware of this and I've lost my mind. I just want the salt. I'm a stress eater. It's fine. "I have a *bad* idea in my brain. One of the players on the Jugs is local, Evan—"

"Allore? I do pay attention to things, you know. Even if I don't get to go to all the games for free."

"If you were in town when they were, you'd be the one going with me! Cora even bought a Briggs jersey for you."

Not that I think she's giving up that jersey now, even if she refuses to talk about what happened that night.

Tilly pushes me with her shoulder. "Just messing with you. I'm going to *all* the December games. But what about Evan? You think it's him?"

I shake my head. "And I really don't think it's his wife, either, but . . . she's been a problem. She's . . . I don't know who she is, but it sounded like one of her friends might have been a patient here. She was really upset when Gabe brought me to the gala, and then at the first game, one of the other wives had the Allores' daughter in the stands a couple rows in front of us, and she made them move. So she really doesn't like me, and I'm not going to be super mad about that, and it would be nuts for her to be doing this, but . . ."

"But what if she's been talking shit and it's driven someone else to do this?"

"It sounds even crazier when you say it."

"Not really. This is something a crazy person does. Football people can be crazy. Could be one of Allore's megafans, even." Tilly shrugs and eats another chip. Halfway through chewing, she frowns, looks in the bag, crinkles her nose, and hands them to me, her face taking on a sickly pallor. "These are gross. Finish them."

I understand enough to get up and take them to the end of the porch to finish this unexpected treat. I should set them out for Jerry, but I can't believe how good they are. I'm half ready to dump the whole bag in my mouth.

"You need one of those camera doorbells," Tilly suggests as a middle-aged woman and her husband exit the store.

The husband is laden down with a giant bag of fabric while she holds a single specialty ruler like it's her most prized possession. She's less than polite to Tilly, giving her a huffy "excuse me" and passing by before Tilly has the chance to get out of the way fully.

Tilly makes a face at her back, but Tilly's never worked customer service. She's not used to rude women who plow through the world with complete disregard for anyone deemed lower than them. Since Tilly's in denim overalls, a paint-crusted tee shirt, and chunky work boots, the lady probably thinks I hired her to clean up.

It's only when they reach their car parked on the street does she turn and notice I've been standing here the entire time. "Morning, Joss!" she yells, her voice sweet as tea. "Let Gabe know I'm rooting for him tomorrow!"

"Is that normal?" Tilly asks once they're both in the car.

"Which part—never mind, yes. Yes, customers constantly forget that they were awful ten seconds ago, yes, everyone in town thinks that knowing me means Gabe cares about them now, and yes, apparently people who don't actually know enough about the Jugs to know it's a bye week still feel the need to involve themselves."

Tilly shakes her head. "Wild."

Chapter Nineteen
GABE

The last time I was on this field, the stands felt like they reached to the sky. Down on the field, I felt like a god. Center's never been a glamorous position, but Coach Gregorson said I was going places. Didn't have a football scholarship, but none of us did in this little backwoods corner of Minnesota on the North Shore of Lake Superior, practically Canada. When I told Gregorson I'd gotten on the team at Iowa State as a walk-on, he said that was it, everyone would see how amazing I was, how much I deserved it. And then every year when the mini-camps came and went, fewer and fewer people thought I had a chance, but Coach was always there cheering me on, telling me I was so close.

I was.

C. B. Alice

And now I'm back on this field that's absolutely the tiniest fucking thing ever, its scoreboard still a wall of lightbulbs, its announcers' deck not even roofed, just six flights of bleachers and then a platform for a local sports reporter to man, and I'm over the moon at the opportunity I've been given to present a plaque to Coach Gregorson honoring his years of hard work and congratulate him on retirement.

I was a god here twelve years ago. The way the crowd cheers for me at halftime, a sea of not just the local colors of purple and white but also a ton of Jugs ruby and saffron brought out when the clock ran down, makes me realize I'm a god again.

"And it's all because of you, Coach!" I yell, and everyone cheers even more loudly. "You're an absolute legend. To Coach Gregorson!"

Gregorson is ancient, at least seventy. The last decade has not been kind to him. The team is down by twenty points at the half. They won't win their own Homecoming. A shame. But the Homecoming King gives Gregorson his crown, the Queen gives him her roses, and the feeble old man looks every bit as proud as he did the day I let him know I'd been recruited.

"You ready to settle down, old man?" I laugh, clapping him on the shoulder, the gesture broad but the touch light.

He beams up at me, and I can't help wondering if I've gotten taller, if he's gotten shorter, or if he was just larger than life in my mind until my own world became larger than life. "I got seven grandkids now," he says proudly. "That's one of 'em right there." He points to a kid on the sideline, smaller than Merrick or even Lin, but he's offensive line, holding his own. I'm literally twice his size. "Gonna have great-grandkids soon. Definitely seems about time to settle down. Maybe you should think about doing the same," he adds with a wink.

I lean over to him to conspiratorially whisper, "You know, I've got someone in mind to do the settling down with."

I didn't think Gregorson could have been happier than he was a moment ago, but he lets out a whoop, claps me on the back hard enough I jolt, and says, "It's about time, boy!"

"Dana Cambridge says Maycee Luzonn overheard Devyn Brown talking to Kayla Duncroft, and she said her little brother heard you tell Coach Gregorson you have a girlfriend."

I grew up with three sisters. One older, two younger. So I don't have issues working through what's spewed out of Leah's mouth the moment I walk into the kitchen of my childhood home. But it does take me a minute to orient myself to the fact that she's not a baby anymore and at 22, she could be off and married and pregnant like Abby was two years ago. Instead, she chose to skip out on college, pull espresso shots at the local coffee shop down the street, and figure herself out. And since she *is* the baby, my parents agreed to it far more readily than they did when Phoebe attempted it, a constant bone of contention at holidays, but Ma swears Leah's paying rent.

I have my doubts, but Phoebe got the last laugh there. She's recently divorced, 'transitioning' to single life in her childhood bedroom, and currently sprawled across the velvet rose-print sofa in the living room while Dad Netflix-surfs in his old chocolate-brown recliner and nurses a beer. At the stove, Ma is stirring a vat of chili.

But then Leah makes that comment, and two of three heads spin to me, like women possessed.

C. B. Alice

Dad belches, which might actually be his acknowledgment of what she said. I'm not saying he's inattentive at all, but he's always been a pro at letting Ma and the girls lead the fact-finding mission while he quietly absorbs and processes.

Phoebe scrambles to her feet, nearly six feet herself and still like a newborn fawn on her gangly legs despite being two years my senior. "You didn't tell us you had a girlfriend!" she shouts too loudly for the four yards of open air between us.

Ma, barely five feet, her hair a salt-and-pepper she has no interest in coloring, the red-headed stepchild despite being Ma and genetically brunette in a sea of blond and ginger giants, dumps a giant ladle of chili into one of the Thanksgiving serving bowls and thrusts it and a sleeve of saltines at me. "When are we going to meet her?"

Soon, definitely. I know I can't expect pregnancy to just happen, it might never happen, but I have a good feeling. And as soon as Joss is expecting, Ma will literally drive half a day from Duluth to Wilmington to meet her if I don't bring her out. But I'm not going to say all that — I don't want the bowl of chili thrown at me — so I'm about to play it off like it's no big deal.

And then Big-Mouth Leah tacks on, "Ryder Duncroft told Kayla Gabe told Coach he was 'settling down'." She even throws air quotes on it.

Oh shit.

I take the chili that yes, I very much want, as Ma lets out a shriek. Phoebe snorts and says, "You have the most sedentary life of any football player in the history of football players. You settled down years ago."

Ma swats her with a kitchen towel. "Oh, hush you. My boy's in love!"

Phoebe and Leah both give me a horrified look that I throw back at Ma. "Jesus, slow down."

That earns me a swat from the towel, and I lumber over to the kitchen table to shrink away from her as well as any of us can. I crunch up half the sleeve of saltines and dump them into the bowl, which is enough to keep her from terrorizing me further. Physically, at least. In Ma's eyes, I'll always be her growing boy. Since I've tracked my weight basically my entire life, I know that's not entirely false.

"Well, tell us about her," Phoebe says, crossing her arms over her chest like she's planning on destroying Joss. Understandable, after that high school girlfriend I carried through college until I found out she was sleeping with pretty much everyone on both my high school and college teams, apart from Blaise.

"Is she pretty?" Ma asks. "I bet she's pretty."

"She is very pretty," I confirm, considering and then deciding against announcing that she has pageant sashes to attest to how pretty she is. I don't want them to get the wrong idea about her, and Leah in particular has had some stellar rants about the blatant misogyny of beauty pageants.

"Is she tall?"

"Taller than you." I nod to Phoebe. "Not so tall as you."

This earns no points from her. "Hot and average height isn't a personality. Sounds like one of the pro athlete chasers. The . . . bunnies, or whatever they're called."

I swallow a big spoonful of chili — the best chili, oh my god, the harassment is so worth it for Ma's chili — and wipe a dribble out of my beard. "No one's chasing me, Phoebe. Fuck."

Ma spins her towel so she doesn't forget to swat me for cursing once I'm done eating.

"You're just too dumb to see those bimbos throwing themselves at you, you stupid shit," Leah mutters. Does she get a swat or a threatening glare? Of course not. "What's she do? She got a job?"

"What the—of course she has a job! She has her own business!"

"Doing what?" Leah and Phoebe ask in surround sound.

"She's an influencer," I say, and at the rolls of their eyes, I add, "Quilting. She does quilting tutorials. She's very successful. Don't look at me like that." I point to Ma. "You don't look at me like that, either."

While my sisters remain skeptical, Ma's eyes have gone watery, her lip trembling, her hands balled up at her chin. "Just like your great-gran."

"Great-gran was a bank teller," Phoebe says.

Leah adds, "It was a hobby for her," as her fingers fly over the keyboard of her laptop.

Ma ignores them. "I can't wait to show her great-gran's old quilts. Do you think she'll want them?"

"You saved them?" we all yell, even Dad. Those things are fucking cursed, swear to god.

Phoebe gets the swat on that one. She blocks it deftly. "She got a name? Can we prove her existence? 'Cause it's starting to sound like you're making her up to keep Ma from setting you up with one of her friends' daughters while you're in town."

"Drat, I gotta call Patty and tell her lunch tomorrow isn't happening now." Ma scurries off into the living room to find her phone.

I should thank Phoebe for shutting that nonsense down, but I refuse. Thanking my sister is akin to showing weakness.

Instead, I cop a further attitude. "What kind of question is that? Of course she's real and has a name and *everybody* has known we've been dating for over a month now, but it's good to see my own family doesn't pay attention to my life."

Yes, I'm thankful they're not following gossip rags. Again, can't show weakness.

To that end, Phoebe says, "Nobody gives a shit about your life. Everyone's probably worried that quilt lady is going to end up with your stupid gassy ass. Why do you smell like that?"

Basically, she just told me she loves me. It's sweet.

"I smell great." I accidentally dribble more chili, so I have to wipe that out of my beard, too. "I'm totally famous now, and everyone loves me. You're jealous because your—"

"Gabriel Michael Josiah Shaunessy, don't you dare say it!" Ma shrieks from the living room.

"I was just going to say her ass is where her face should be, you banshee!" I shout right back.

"Oh, I thought you were going to say something about her div—never mind."

And now I'm mad Ma thought I'd go there. That jackass cheated on Phoebe with a girl a decade younger than him and then claimed it was because Phoebe wasn't as hot as she used to be. Like 31 is absolutely ancient. Only I'm allowed to make jokes like that, and only because there are only two years between us. And the fact that Phoebe's ex slept with a chick Leah graduated high school with is gross, but Phoebe's definitely taken it to mean she's ugly now.

She's ugly. She's my sister. She's ugly. And my bud-dies are not allowed to disagree with that statement to my face, but behind my back? They always have and still do.

"Want me to drive over to his place and punch him in the balls?" I offer so she knows I love her.

C. B. Alice

"No, it's fine." She flops down in the seat next to me and snatches my bowl of chili away. Ten gallons of it on the stove, but she takes mine, and I let her. "Ma's been setting me up with her friends' sons, and it's not been—"

"Did she kill her husband?" Leah suddenly gasps.

My attention snaps to her, confused.

"I should've killed him," Phoebe mutters around a mouthful of chili and then wipes her chin off.

"Jocelyn Edgars, right? Owner of the Quilted Flower? Oh, she *is* pretty."

"Joss Page," I spit out instantly even though I already know she used to go by Jocelyn Edgars. Leah may not have gone to college, but she's the smartest one out of all of us. I shouldn't be shocked that she figured it out while Phoebe and I bickered. "And no, she didn't kill her husband."

"Well, what is all this? Did they murder someone together or—?"

"Fuuuuuuuuck." I scrub my face. *Murder?* It's like a floodgate has opened. I know too much to keep stuffing it away, like that damn nursery door.

I feel the chili rising back up in my throat at the thought of that door. Has Joss *already* had a baby? Where's that baby now?

"Oooh, no," Leah mumbles to herself, the initial look of disgust fading into something far more distressed. "Do you . . . do you know about this? About her husband?"

I shake my head miserably. "I knew there was something bad, but that she wasn't involved, and I decided I didn't want to know. She's a good woman. I know she doesn't deserve everything that's gotten thrown at her."

Leah gives me a pained but sympathetic smile. "None of this says she isn't a good person, but this is bad. Her husband was a pediatric oral surgeon, did you know that, at least?"

I close my eyes, feeling reassured by what Leah's said while simultaneously sicker about what he did for a living. He worked with children, and there's murder involved.

"You need to know this." Her hand lands on mine, and if there's one thing we all know about Leah, she doesn't like touching or being touched. The fact that she's done this to comfort me is my worst nightmare. "He raped his patients. Looks like at least four of them. Teenage girls. One of them died during the assault."

Chapter Twenty
JOSS

When Gabe returns to bed after his typical early-morning wander, curls around me, and guides his cock into me, it soothes the ache of a particularly rough Round One.

I hum in pleasure as he slides one arm beneath my waist to reach around and lazily circle my clit while the other hand massages my breast. My thoughts go silken, like if I tried to grasp one, it would slide from my hold.

"You love having your pussy plugged up by my cock, don't you?" His voice is deep and rough, barely human.

My response is another hum and a squirm of my ass deeper into the seat of his lap.

"That's it. Take it all the way in, leave no space." He bottoms out, hits the sensitive upper wall, backs out only an inch or so before nudging at it again. "Is that the spot? If I come right there, will I fill you here?" His hand lowers from my breast to my belly, below my navel. He spreads his hand wide and digs into the soft flesh there.

In the twilight of my sleep- and lust-fogged mind, his meaning is clear. But the delicate dance I've played with him ever since he told me about his vasectomy wounds me, the sting that much more poignant since he started talking like this in these ethereal half-asleep rounds. "Yes," I moan.

"Will you grow here? Will you get bigger and bigger?"

"Yes! Come inside me, Gabe."

"Yeah? You want that? You want the whole world to know you let me fuck you raw over and over? That I pumped my cum into you so many times I took root here?"

That part of me that knows only instincts, that id, that voice that's forced to be silent in polite society but quietly waits for the most base, primal moment to speak, wails a desperate "Yes!" I want it so badly, and I can be nothing less than honest now even if he doesn't mean it, if it's his way of talking kinky.

His hands draw away from me, but his cock continues to pump rhythmically in that scant inch, driving himself ever forward to make good on his promise. A hand on my shoulder pushes me back onto the mattress, and even the twist in my spine, the lock he's got on my position feels good.

He looms over me, a Viking warrior with his giant body, his rosy complexion, his copper beard, and takes hold of my breast, more roughly this time. "These are gonna get big and firm and sore, and you're going to love that too, aren't you?"

I toss my head back, pushing into his hand, wanting to ache everywhere.

"Fuck, baby. They'll leak just as much as your pussy, won't they? You're going to make the biggest mess every time we

Good Guy Gabe

fuck, and I bet you'll beg for it again . . . and again . . . and again."

He punctuates it with a hard thrust each time. Tears pool in my eyes, but all I can say is, "More."

He laughs, darkly and knowingly. Possessively. "As many as you want, Joss. I'll keep you full forever if that's what you need. Is that what you need?"

My spine begins to rebel, my entire body driven to take from him the one thing only he can give me, mindless to the fact he's made sure he can't. I reach between my legs, ignoring my own pleasure to grab hold of his balls. "Now, give it to me now."

He groans long and low, his head dropping down, his crown of copper hair dusting over my chest, making even the least sensitive spots go electric. Still, he manages to say, "What do you want me to do?"

He may be able to talk pretty and deep and playful, but I'm little more than an animal rutting. The best I can say is, "Give me a baby!"

He flips me onto my stomach and brings us on our knees long enough for him to get a few hard thrusts in before he leans his whole weight into my ass to go as deep as he can, making sure I can feel every hot, liquid jet blasting against my inner seal. And before either of us has a chance to cool down, he puts me back on my side, a hand on my clit and his mouth on my nipple.

He's so tightly curled around me there's no escape. His suckling is bruising, sure to leave both an ache and a dark, lasting mark as he forces me to come more, even as my pussy milks his cock for every drop until it softens within me, sealing everything inside.

It's the perfect moment, this fantasy that he means everything he just said, he wants everything I want, far too soon for our relationship, but we're both old enough for it. Stable and comfortable, too. I don't begrudge Tilly for what she's got, not when it's an inconvenient miracle, but it's going to be a struggle for her. If the impossible happened tonight and if Gabe really did mean the words he said, it would be the happiest of surprises.

I hold that fantasy.

I cleave to it.

And then Gabe makes a sound so faint I would have missed the distress in it if he didn't also flop onto his back and groan in frustration at the ceiling.

I roll over into him. "Are you okay?"

"No. Yes. No. Fuck." He sits up, moving way too fast for this hour, only to slump forward. "I know. My sister told me."

"You know what?"

"About you. About . . . about him."

A chill settles over me as I put space between us. The way he says that? The rejection is swift and heavy.

And painful.

I tell myself to hold my tongue, to accept the rejection as I have countless times, but I'm raw. He *made* me raw for this exact moment.

"So, what? This was a goodbye fuck?" I seethe. "Fuck Miss Alabama one last time before you kick her to the curb?"

"What? Shit, no! Fuck, I'm doing this wrong. I'm—"

He reaches for me, but I skitter out of his reach, backing myself in the corner, immediately feeling naked and exposed in a way I've never felt with him before, not even in that bathroom at the gala. I squat down and wrap my arms around myself to cover up as I best as I can.

I've spent years humiliated by the fact that I had no idea what my husband was doing directly below my feet as I mindlessly went about my days. None of the accusations that I knew could match the fact that I didn't know. But none of the humiliation has ever been as acute as the string of Gabe's semen leaking out of me onto the floor. It's enough to knock the stupidest, most indulgent sob out of me.

Gabe is on me in a blink of an eye, scooping me up and holding me in his arms. "I know you're innocent, I swear. I promise you, if anything, you're even more amazing than you were already. It was just a lot, and I don't understand a bunch of it. There were so many articles, and none of the time lines make sense, and you were missing from so much of it, and—fuck. I shouldn't have sprung this on you now. Forgive me?"

I hiccup like a toddler and hug him tightly, burying my face in his shoulder as my teeth grind. A shiver races up my spine. "Don't scare me like that, okay?"

"Never again. Let's get you tucked back in and talk about it in the morning."

"I'd rather talk about it now, if it's all the same."

"It is wild how small this is."

Gabe chuckles softly as he gets two giant mugs out of the cupboard.

I tug at the hem of his jersey. It seemed like a fun idea when I picked it from his closet before he scooped me up and carried me to the kitchen, a neutral area for me to explain about Brian. I have the jersey Cora got me, of course, but that doesn't smell like Gabe. He's never worn that. He would never fit into it. So when I saw this hanging in there, I expected it to be a tent and then didn't pay attention when he pulled it out.

On me, it's a comfortable but very short and slim-fit dress. Long enough to cover my butt but nothing left to the imagination. And he sat me down atop the island, so there's nothing but my thankfully full-coverage panties between my flesh and the cold marble surface.

"There's no way you fit into this. This has to be Merrick's. He's tiny."

"Don't you ever say that to his face," Gabe warns me, but he laughs as he says it. "And nope, that's my number. That's my name. That's last year's away jersey."

I tug it out from my chest. There's a bit of extra space, and if I was Cora, I'd be able to quantify it better, but I don't make garments. I would call this a ladies' large. And not a busty ladies' large. "How on earth did you get it on?"

The electric kettle beeps, and Gabe pours a cup for each of us. Mine is chamomile mint tea. Gabe's hot chocolate bomb fizzes and pops open in an explosion of rainbow mini-marshmallows.

"I have a guy for that," Gabe says as he pours too much honey into my tea, not that I would ever correct it.

"You have . . . a guy?"

"Yep." He grabs a couple ice cubes from the freezer and tosses them into my tea. "Between the jerseys and the shoulder pads, you can, you know, get trapped."

I do my best to hide my smirk, but my lip is twitching. "Does everybody have a guy?"

"Well, no. Not everyone. And it's not like it's *my* guy. He helps Jennings, too. And Thompson. Rydell Thompson, not Donnie Thompson. I think Bodley."

I bite my lip. "What's his name?"

"It's Steve. He's—you're making fun of me, aren't you?"

It's enough to break me. Laughter bubbles out of me, and only Gabe shimmying between my legs and kissing me gets me to stop. "You're going to wake the entire house, and then you're gonna have to tell Rydell you were laughing at him. Now here, drink this."

He stays in my space as I sip my tea, his hands absently wandering under the hem of the jersey but not going too far. It's just touch. Just contact. I savor my sip for a moment longer than I need to before I say, "I was 20 years old when I met Brian Edgars. He was 32. In retrospect, I should have known something was up then, but what girl ever realizes she's being groomed until after the fact?"

Gabe hums, just a single note, and then those hands travel further up the jersey. To my waist, to pull me closer.

This is good. This is safe. In his arms, I don't have to be scared of the story.

"He seemed amazing. He was kind and understanding and so incredibly smart. You expect someone like him to be controlling, but he wasn't. Not in any obvious way. I was still in college, and he encouraged me to finish. He liked that I was a pageant contestant but also a business major, said it proved that I was motivated. He was finishing up his residency and planning to start his own practice. Said he'd need someone who could run the administrative side of the practice. That could be me.

"I ate it up. Every word of it. My mom had died the year before. Scholarship money from the pageants was the only thing that kept me in school, and my grades were slipping because I was working so much to cover expenses. Brian helped with all that."

Gabe smiles reassuringly. "I don't know how anyone in that situation could have been thinking clearly enough to see someone like that for what he was."

C. B. Alice

I want to point out that he has no idea what Brian was, but he would have gotten only the absolute worst of it from those news articles. Instead, I take the moment to breathe in his scent. We both need a shower, but his musk blended with the sandalwood in his bodywash is a comfort.

"I married him straight out of college. I finished in May, moved to Wilmington in June, married in July, bought the house in August. He gifted it to me. He told me since I owned the house free and clear but his practice was in it, I could trust he'd never leave me, and I actually thought it was romantic. Turned out, that's the only reason it survived the civil suits. I . . ." I shake my head. "I don't know why he gifted me the house. I don't know why he did anything. One day, life was normal, happy, perfect, exactly what I thought I wanted, and the next day, one of his patients is dead. And it was awful, right, but he's a surgeon. An oral surgeon, but his patients are still getting anesthesia; it's always a risk. I must have spent a week terrified that he was going to lose his license, and what was going to happen then?

"And then they did the autopsy. She was fourteen years old. A flautist, and she was getting corrective surgery for her jaw and was scared she wouldn't be able to play anymore. They discovered she'd been raped. Brian raped her while she was sedated. According to him, she came to in the middle of it, so he, um, he gave her more anesthetic. Too much more."

"Come here," Gabe murmurs even though I'm already pressed against him, but he sinks enough that I can throw my arms around him and dry my damp eyes on his shoulder as he kisses my neck. "You didn't do it. You didn't hurt that girl. You didn't know."

"I should have!" I sniffle to clear my thoughts. "She wasn't the only victim. No one knows how many there were. Four that we know of. They all came forward while we were waiting for the trial. He was charged with assault and second-degree murder for the one girl, but it was taking forever to start. There were both criminal and civil trials happening, and since they went with second-degree, he was able to make bail. He was still living at home, sharing a bed with me. I didn't believe his lies, that he was at fault for the girl's death but not the assaults, he'd just made a terrible mistake, but I . . . I . . ."

I let it happen because I didn't have a choice.

"It must have been terrifying for you," Gabe says, but he has to think I'm one of those women who believe their criminal husbands are innocent to the point of embarrassing themselves.

"One of the girls who came forward, she was sixteen, and she wasn't a virgin. But she swore she didn't know how she could have been pregnant, that she hadn't been active at the time. Everyone thought she was lying. The other kids bullied her. Her parents thought they could force her to admit who the father was if they pushed hard enough. No one believed her that she truly didn't know — because she was raped by my husband and had no idea. They put the kid up for adoption when they were born. I tried to take the baby in, but my lawyers wouldn't let me. Said it would look bad if I embraced anything related to Brian. But it was a baby. They needed someone who would have loved and protected them, and that could have been me. I could have—!"

I cut myself off once I realize I've gotten hysterical. I couldn't get any information about that baby. I didn't have any right to it. They weren't mine, no genetic relation, only a horrific connection. I don't even know if it was a girl or a boy or if the adopted parents are local or not. I still think about them frequently, whenever I see a kid about that age who looks at all like Brian. I've lost nights of sleep wondering if Keira Allore's friend is the one who had the kid, if that's why she hates me so much.

And now I'm blabbering about how much I wanted that kid to Gabe. Not only am I spilling the nightmare of Brian's crimes out on him, I'm bordering on forcing the baby conversation on him.

"I'm sorry," I whisper as evenly as I can, fiercely swiping more tears away. "It's . . . never mind, it's dumb."

Gabe kisses my forehead and says, "I've seen your nursery."

"Shit." I shouldn't be surprised about it. He's been over there enough that he probably didn't realize when I told him not to go in there, I meant it was off-limits. And off-limits purely because of my own insanity that refuses to let go of the past or even have this one critical conversation with him.

"You wanted to adopt that baby so badly you set up your home to welcome them."

My brain shuts down at that, at the idea that I would have done something like that, that the truth of why I really wanted to adopt that baby wasn't so incredibly pathetic. I peel away from him, and he lets me. He even looks hopeful, like we've gotten over the worst of it and I'll be happy for his support and understanding here.

I grab my cup and hold it between my hands, a crucial barrier.

"A lot of people didn't believe me that I didn't know, that I wasn't in on it in some way. I was working in the office, I set up appointments, I knew these girls. And he liked to brag about how I was a pageant queen, and you know there's all kinds of nasty stuff behind the scenes there." I take a sip of my tea, frown down at it, and wrinkle my nose. The first couple of sips were fine, but this one's off. Probably my rapidly souring mood. "They think we're all nasty in the pageant world. That's why Emily Hess tried to get me removed from the fundraiser. Why Keira Allore hates me so much."

"I'm going to talk to them," Gabe insists for the millionth time.

"You won't. They're entitled to their feelings, and they're not hurting me."

"You were crushed!"

I look him in the eye, needing him to see me and not his idea of me or the world around me. Not what a perfect world should be like but what it actually is. "Gabe, I lost everything in the civil suits. Everything except that house. I didn't have anything going into the marriage. I narrowly avoided bankruptcy. And on the day the judge decided that everything was done properly so the house could not be seized, I was leaving the courthouse, and someone threw a rock at me. I don't think they meant to seriously hurt—Gabe!" I shriek as he backs out of my space, only to punch a hole through the drywall next to the fridge.

He stands there for several seconds, taking deep breaths and staring hard at where his fist has just vanished, before he reclaims it from the void between the studs. "Are they in jail now?"

I shrug. "I don't know who did it. I was knocked out and—stop!" I whimper as he puts yet another hole in that wall.

"This was six years ago, yeah? And you were leaving a courthouse, where you've got cops and security guards and reporters and cameras and—"

"Nobody was covering it that day. The newsworthy stuff was over. It was just me." I draw my feet up onto the counter to rest my cheek on my knees and vanish. Gabe comes back to me, but the way I turn my face away from him is enough to halt his footfalls. "I woke up in an ambulance. Whether anyone saw it or not, no one cared. You have no idea how much they hated me during the trial. I was paraded in front of everyone. I was the one trying to keep the money, you know? I think that day at the courthouse, that was my penance. The rock hit me in the forehead, and I fell down the stairs and was knocked unconscious. They got me to the hospital as quick as they could, but that night, I delivered and lost my baby."

I accept Gabe's embrace this time, not that I think I could push him away, but I don't need it. Honestly, I'm just cold.

"The nursery?" he asks.

"I had a son. Aiden James Page. Was supposed to be Aiden Brian Edgars, but I couldn't name him that, and the doctor who was so kind to me when no one else was, who let me hold him and didn't insist on life support when we all knew he wasn't going to make it, his name was James." The numbness allows me to speak clearly even as it reminds me why I should never have agreed to go out with Gabe in the first place, why the world outside my walls, even the world on my lawn, is so awful. "His heart beat for an hour, but he never opened his eyes. Never cried, never suckled. He lay there in my arms sleeping, but he was pink, and he was warm, and he breathed in and out, sleeping like any baby, and I took him home in—" my voice cracks, my jaw aches, my sinuses burn— "I took him home in an urn, and he's—"

"Stop, stop, stop," Gabe begs, his own voice unsteady, his hold on me so tight he might be trying to silence me by forcing the air out of me. "You can stop."

I can't, though.

"He's been in his room ever since."

Chapter Twenty-One
GABE

"Great practice, guys. Really looking good out there," Coach Keenan says as we file into the locker room. "Really great. This rate, we're looking at a division championship. Proud of you boys. Looking good, Huang. That was a great catch, Merrick. Good scramble, Vedder."

We're all exchanging looks. Keenan is a good coach. No faults there. But this is weird. Something's up, and since I'm at the back of the line, I have the entire team to see if he's about to lock us in and flip his shit over some shenanigans — we've been good, but not stellar, and media likes to take nothing and turn it into something on slow days — or if one of us is about to get whisked off to his office.

The anxious part of me is going wild, taking the most absurd, impossible, devastating thing and running with it.

C. B. Alice

Three weeks ago, it would have been that I was getting cut. It's that time of year when teams, even winning ones, start to reconsider their lineup and replace the weakest links. I've done well overall, but I've also had my share of mistakes like anyone, and mine are more obvious than some other positions. I love being a center, it's obviously a position I do well at or I wouldn't be playing in the NFL, but I'm forever stressing about it. It's my natural state. And I don't know yet if I'm getting signed on again. This could be my last season.

That's what I should be stressing about.

But my brain's got its own ideas about what's the most critical issue, and it's spent over two weeks now fixating on Joss.

I fucked up.

I fucked up so bad.

And I don't know how to fix it.

I keep bailing on overnights. The last two games were away, so that helped. I made up early practices and then actually did haul my ass down to the training facility at four in the morning to send her selfies of me working out with Merrick so I didn't look like a liar. Then I had to lie to Merrick about wanting to get in better shape.

And then ate my shame with a dozen donuts before regular practice started. I nearly barfed on the field the second time I attempted it.

Dinner dates. Movie nights. Hanging around in her studio. I'm trying to act normal, but every time I come up with another reason why we can't share a bed, she looks more and more rejected.

The worst part is she's gotta be thinking it's because of what she told me, and it's the opposite of that. Or, it's not what happened six years ago but what it's forced me to consider about myself.

I am not a good guy.

It never once crossed my mind that she might have been pregnant before. I certainly didn't consider that she might be grieving over a child. This whole time, I've been thinking that the way she reacts to anything baby related comes from a place of yearning, and it turns out it's heartache.

And I never should have made that assumption to begin with.

I don't know how to fix this. A vow of celibacy isn't going to cut it, and not just because no matter how hard I try, I can't avoid our physical needs. I've been skirting around them with oral sex, hand jobs, even pulling out. She actually sounded distressed when I did that, which made me feel awful. This is not sustainable, and it's cruel to Joss, who's just shared something so important and personal with me.

But I don't know how to fix this without losing her.

So the dread that fills me as I near Coach Keenan and he continues with his bland platitudes isn't of whether I'm about to get cut. It's that somehow everyone knows about my lie and there are cops in his office waiting to arrest me for lying to my girlfriend.

My stomach flips as it hits me what I've been doing might actually be illegal. The more I think about it, the more I feel like it should be illegal. I'm going to jail. I'll have to admit this to everyone and most importantly, lose Joss, but nearly as importantly, lose everyone else. And go to jail.

I don't think I can handle jail. Sure, I'm a giant and strong as an ox, but I'm soft. I have fancy pillows for my sleep apnea. The cleaning lady has to wash my clothes in the expensive dye-free stuff or I get hives. I'm not cut out for jail.

C. B. Alice

When Keenan nods at me and casually says, "Shaunessy, got time for a quick chat in my office?" I nearly jut my hands out for him to arrest me.

I give him my biggest, dumbest smile in the hopes that he doesn't sense my fear. "Sure thing, coach!"

Everyone watches from the locker room — most attempt subtlety, but Blaise peeks out, bug-eyed, until Merrick grabs him by the shoulder and yanks him back — as I follow Keenan past the locker room and into his office. He motions for me to take a seat and closes the door behind me, and I feel like my heart is going to leap out of my chest.

The way Keenan leans back in his chair should be of some comfort. He's casual. Relaxed. Like someone about to have an easy conversation. But now I'm thinking he's hated me this whole time and he's relaxed because he knows he's never going to talk to me again.

I have to be green. He has to see that I've turned green. His grin proves that he wants to be rid of me and he's going to laugh when I barf all over everything.

"Good season so far, yeah?" he asks as he reaches under his desk.

Irrationally, absurdly irrationally, I think he's about to pull a gun on me. I really need to get some sleep. I'm a mess. "Six and two," I reply, my tone lacking the depth that would convey any sort of joy.

Keenan doesn't seem to notice this. "Yeah, that's great. We're already a shoo-in for the play-offs. And you're a big part of that. You know that, yeah?"

"Thank you, sir," I reply mechanically.

"I hope Sinclair appreciates how much of his load you take on. ESPN's talking about how he's finally matured enough for the Super Bowl, but I don't think they see that you're the reason for that."

"It's an honor, sir." I taste bile. There are only two ways I can imagine this conversation going, and that's him handing over a contract for the next three seasons or him saying that's why he's so mad at me that he has to fire me for being a criminal and then letting the cops in.

And that contract doesn't come from him.

"You know I've been doing this a long time. Both pro and college. I never felt I was coaching children when I was at SC. But it's different when you've got a team that's just out of high school and no longer in their parents' houses, living on their own for the first time and figuring themselves out. Someone said something they shouldn't have. Someone got drunk and broke someone else's Xbox. Someone slept with someone else's girlfriend. You got me?"

I nod, wondering if these are universals or if he knows my life that well. I did have a habit of saying things the wrong way, and I did break my buddy's Xbox on accident and it was my girlfriend that half the team slept with.

"I had to deal with those issues. That's part of life with college kids. But I don't usually deal with stuff like this at the pro level. You guys are adults. You've got families, mortgages, your own group of friends instead of just your teammates."

I've got none of those things. He has to know that.

"So I'm going to make this simple. When things are going this well, it doesn't make too much sense for me to rock the boat. This is not a rocking of the boat."

That sounds like I'm not getting fired or going to jail. People in jail don't get to play pro football. That's not how *The Longest Yard* worked out.

C. B. Alice

"But I'm concerned about this thing between you and Allore."

Shit.

"I wasn't at first. You two are never on the field together. I was happy you guys were buddies, and then you weren't, and it didn't matter too much. But I'm now starting to think there's beef between you and Morales, too, and—"

"There isn't!" I blurt out. "Absolutely not. Morales is great. I promise I will do just as well if he has to step in for Blaise."

"I'm sure." Keenan nods, but his smile is weak. "But Morales and Allore are friends. You were part of that group. And it seems like you're the one who's not willing to work with Allore anymore, and since Allore and Morales have so much in common—"

"Dom is a decade older than Evan."

"And their babies practically share a crib."

Now his tone has a bite to it. That's my fault. I shouldn't have thrown that at him like that.

"I've had Pruitt working with Morales to be his center. I can pull you when I pull Sinclair. Do you want that?"

I'd noticed Pruitt was going over a playbook with Morales recently but didn't think anything of it. Of course I can't be the only center. I'm as prone to injury as anyone else. More so, in fact. I take bad hits in every game because of the position I'm in when I hike the ball. But I'm not Blaise's center, I'm the Jugs' center, and I can't rely on Blaise to carry me. He's incredible, but at the end of the day, he was expendable enough for the Colts to donate him to the expansion even with me in tow. "No, absolutely not."

"That's not a threat, it's an offer. I need to know how to keep this team running this smoothly."

"You do not need to worry about this," I insist.

"Then you need to let go of whatever's set you off with Allore. I know you, Shaunessy. I know you're not the guy to beef with others. Even if I didn't know you personally, I can see it clearly throughout your career. This isn't you, and you need to stop this."

I sigh, the sound unintentionally frustrated as it rumbles over my vocal cords. I've fucked up just about every way I can with Joss, but the one thing I know I got right was pushing Allore out of my life, no matter how much that hurt. "I can't. You don't get it. What you're saying, you're telling me I have to pick my teammate over my girlfriend, and I'm not doing that."

Keenan's sigh mirrors mine. "So that's what this is about, huh? I've gotten quite the earful about her. Emily Hess is not happy."

"Emily Hess can choke on a dick."

I immediately regret saying that, but Keenan only laughs. "I have certainly thought that my fair share of times. Game used to not be like this. You play well, you don't commit any crimes, you don't say anything too dumb in front of reporters, you're good. Now we have to have social media specialists babysitting your accounts in case you accidentally drink a Coke five years after Pepsi ran an ad in the stadium of a team you weren't even playing for at the time or wear a shirt that's . . . too short, I guess."

That's Blaise, who's gotten himself in enough hot water over inappropriate conduct that they had to add a clause into his contract saying he can't do product endorsements in cropped shirts. After the Monster nipple incident this past July, he's not even allowed in wet shirts anymore.

"Time was, as long as you weren't openly fooling around with a married woman, no one cared who you were dating.

And I want that to still be the world, and believe me when I say I've been going to bat for you. But this is affecting not just you and Allore and Emily Hess. We have hotshot contributors who are squeamish about seeing Ms. Page on the jumbotron."

I scrub my beard, hating where this is going. Hating that Keenan is making it clear he truly does not want it to go this way. Hating what I have to say. "There isn't a scenario where I don't choose her."

He stares me hard in the eye, but I don't waver. I refuse to shrink and back off. I don't need time to think about this or to reconsider. I'm not going to take back my words.

With a nod of his head, Keenan finally says, "That's good. I like that. And I hope that means you'll get it when I tell you she can't sit by the sidelines or the tunnel anymore. I'm not saying nosebleeds, but lower visibility. And keep this thing between you and Allore off the field and out of the locker room. Now go on, get out of here. And keep up the good work."

Chapter Twenty Two
JOSS

My kitchen distresses me. I don't know. All my favorite foods are in here, but none of them look right. My stomach's been off all morning.

I bypass my usuals of yogurt, eggs, and cheese. Even the orange juice isn't appealing to me today. I shuffle over to my pantry, poking around the sealed bags of flour and out-of-date spices, finally stumbling upon a dusty can of black olives.

Yes, this is what I want.

I wipe it down, pop it open, drain it, and toss the olives into a bowl before I make my way downstairs to the barn. I let out a sigh of relief when I see no vandalism has happened. My mums, my siding, my windows. Everything's intact. Jerry ate the half burger I set out for him after my appetite turned last night.

Rose and Iris haven't gotten in for the day yet, which surprises me until I realize it's Thursday. They don't come on

C. B. Alice

Thursdays. Never have. Weird that I would have even thought that.

I'm just being absent-minded, I guess, because when I enter my studio, I realize I have no idea what I said I was going to work on today. I don't usually forget things like that, but I've been distracted lately. I stand there at my desk, scanning the partial projects, the pile of half square triangles and the beginner's foundation paper piecing flowers and the bargello on my longarm. Nothing clicks.

Silly. This is silly.

A flutter of irritation shakes my olive-filled belly. I've been a mess for weeks. Forgetting my schedule, misplacing my phone, walking into a room just to look around and realize I have no idea what I've gone in there for. It's like telling Gabe what happened has sent me right back to how I was when it was actually happening.

I should have expected this. This is why my love life has always been disastrous, after all. They ultimately break under the weight of the reality of what all truly happened. I should have expected nothing else from Gabe.

But I did.

And bless his heart because he's trying. But sud-denly he's too busy to see me most nights, or he makes sure we're only in public places with limited time. He doesn't hold me anymore, not like he used to, not in the middle of the night like he's claiming every mote of me.

The bargello, I decide after sitting for too long contemplating. I'm scheduled to start in five minutes. Most days, that means I'm already logged in and going, but I can't seem to get myself moving. If I'm working on that bargello, the camera doesn't need to be on my face so much.

I fire up my computer, get all my monitors going, and check my progress on the quilt. It's one of my favorite bargellos, a blend of tans and blues and greens, gender-neutral and giant, wide enough for a king-sized bed. It's also an ancient one, a quilt that I started long before I ever had a show, when I was trying to make something more appealing for a masculine aesthetic because Brian complained about how the quilt I'd put on our bed was girly.

Six years, this quilt was jammed in a drawer, unfinished, a top I'd spent months on, and I finally thought I had it in me to finish it. Now, it's what's easiest for me.

The stream goes live. I have a camera on my face to open the show, but that's fine. I can get my introduction out and then move on. It's easy. No problem. Just have that game face on to say hello and then hyperfocus on the quilt. I can do this.

"Good morning, everyone!" I sing-song, selling my energy as best as I can. "And good afternoon, Sandy and Ingmar," I tack on with a wink when I catch their names among the list of thirty-seven people who have logged on already. I have quite a few international subscribers, which I love. Not just because it's super cool that I'm overseas but because they both pose an extra challenge and provide additional insight. They don't have access to a lot of products I use, so I've had to get innovative in our one-on-one and small group sessions, but they've also clued me into some hacks that they've done because of it. I love this part of my job.

I see Cora and Gabe in the roster, but they don't say anything in chat. They'll both tune in if they're working — or working out — but can let my show run in the background. I tell myself not to be bothered by Gabe's silence, not when

Cora's also silent, but I can't help lumping it into our recent distance.

"So unless there are any protests, I thought we'd have a casual day of free motion quilting. Just that good Zen vibe. How's that sound to everyone?"

Several thumbs-ups, enthusiastic yesses, and a cheers emoji. One viewer asks if I can demonstrate how to use one of my free motion templates, which is perfect. I haven't done that in a while, and the way I've got this quilt laid out, I have plenty of panel space to switch to different methods. I can go wild on one corner, and it won't be anything strange for the quilt.

"Yes, absolutely! I got this new one in stock. It's a different brand I haven't tried before, so we can all see if it's worth the price tag—"

I stop speaking there as my stomach does something weird. Just a twinge, a hiccup, but it's like a red flag. I take a deep breath to push through it, lifting a hand up so everyone knows I'm fine, just having a moment.

I exhale through rounded lips, and my brain goes a little fuzzy, light-headed, but it's okay.

"Ha! Weird," I laugh. "I swear I'm fine, just a blurp. Let me grab that ruler so you can all see it before I put it on the machine."

I lean down to open the bottom drawer where the ruler is stashed. The fact that I'm leaning over is the only reason no one sees my face suddenly go green and my cheeks puff out, giving me a three-second warning for me to dump the contents of a Ziploc bag before I barf in it.

I take a couple of ragged breaths. I don't even feel sick. Not the sort of sick that would result in my holding a bag of vomit. And once my throat does the thing so I can breathe properly again, I feel like I could eat an entire steak.

I wipe my face off, sit back up, and stare stupidly at the camera, not sure how to respond to the rapidly scrolling inquiries on my screen.

I don't know if I'm okay.

But I feel okay, so I say, "Wow, lesson learned about having canned olives for breakfast!" and continue.

It's all of twenty minutes before Cora comes bustling through my door, waving furiously at me to turn the longarm off and end the stream. I roll my eyes and shoo her off, having insisted no less than a dozen times that I'm fine, I had a stupid craving for olives, and they were probably bad. I felt fine thirty seconds later and even ate a protein bar to prove my point.

You did not need to come here, I mouth back at Cora, gesturing at the door she just walked through.

Come here, she mouths back, pointing at the floor next to her.

I respond by pointing with one hand at the camera that's facing her while dangling the pointer finger of my other hand threateningly over the keyboard where I'm one button away from turning that camera on and outing Cora to the Quilted Flower fandom. She got famous through a televised sewing competition. My viewers *will* recognize her and *will* make it impossible for her to continue to participate in my streams. Gabe gets enough good-natured harassment for Cora to know she'll suffer a far worse fate if everyone finds out CP2468 is world-famous fashion designer Cora Prasad.

She lifts a grocery bag up in front of her face. It would be a good way to block herself from the camera, but that's not her intention. She reaches right into that bag and pulls out a far greater threat to my stream.

A selection of pregnancy tests.

My stomach goes wobbly at that, the remnants of the protein bar churning within.

I'm not pregnant, I mouth, but damn, that feels like a lie.

Cora holds up one finger and mouths *oversleeping*. A second finger is *olives*. A third is *barfing*. For the fourth, she points at her brain, which I don't understand until she marches over to my workbench and moves the half-square triangles out of the way, revealing a kit for a felt applique nativity calendar.

What I absolutely said I was going to work on today because they got over-ordered but are easy enough for people to finish it for December if they order it today.

I totally forgot.

"Hey everyone, I'm starting to feel sick again, so I'm going to sign out for the day, but I promise I'm going to make it up to you tomorrow with an advent calendar project. Have a great day!"

"What am I going to do?" I moan as the second line appears on yet another test.

Cora squats down in front of me on the bathroom rug and takes hold of my knees. "You're going to have a baby. You're going to have the baby you've wanted and deserved for so long."

She says it gently, more gently than she's said anything to me in a long time because I usually have thicker skin than this and I don't like being coddled. Life is hard. I have a soft life, but I got this through years of shoveling the worst sort of muck.

Cora thinks she gets it, and I love her for thinking that what I need right now is a gentle reality check with enough firmness in it to make me think I can do this despite the nightmare that happened last time.

I shake my head. "It's not that. It's — well, it should be that, but . . ." I scrunch my nose in hopes I can get my emotions under control now that I know why I've been a wreck lately. I was a leaky faucet last time I was pregnant. I'm actually proud of myself for keeping it together as well as I have. I take that deep breath, shift my weight on the edge of the bathtub, and straighten my spine. "Gabe had a vasectomy."

"You slept with someone else?" In a flash, her wide eyes go slitted into a scowl. "Was it Merrick? Because I will cut his balls—"

"It wasn't Merrick! It wasn't anyone. I haven't had sex with anyone else. Think about it, did *I* have sex with anyone else?"

Cora stares at me for another half second and then snorts. "No, definitely not. So he's the dad. That's what paternity tests are for."

"I know, but how is he going to believe me? And he doesn't want kids."

That's enough to get Cora to scowl and stand back up, planting her fists at her waist. "Well, he's going to be a fucking dad now, and you're not going to let him bully you—"

She's cut off by the sound of a bull stampeding up my stairs. We don't need an announcement to know who it is, although Gabe's bellow of "Joss? Are you up here?" falls only a second behind the stampede.

Cora storms out of the bathroom, ready to face off with Gabe. "You better take care of her. I will hunt you down and cut off your dick if you don't."

"I will take care of her until the day I die," Gabe says.

And that's it. That's all the time I have, that's all the conviction I need.

Gabe appears in the doorway to the bathroom, still dressed in his workout gear, clearly stressed, a bottle of ginger beer in hand, and I burst into tears and lift my arms to him. There's no hesitation from him. I ask him to hold me, and he scoops me right up.

"I'm here," he promises. "I'm here for you."

"I'm pregnant," I sob, unable to hold it back for even a second as I flop my weight onto him, so ridiculously thankful he's this big and strong, that he's going to hold me like this while I have this meltdown, positive that no matter what tomorrow looks like, he's going to hold me today.

"I'm going to take care of you," he assures me again.

"It's yours, I swear, I would never ever sleep with anyone else. I—oh god, I'm going to barf."

"Because of morning sickness or because you think I would ever doubt for a second this baby is mine? Because I will put you down if it's morning sickness."

I sniffle and reach up from the shoulder I'm gripping to rub my eyes. "But not if I'm barfing because I'm worried that you won't think it's yours?"

"Nope, I figure if I hold you through that and you barf all over me, it'll prove my point better. If you're pregnant, it's with my baby."

"But your vasectomy?"

"Well, I've still got nuts, and they're still doing their job, so I'm guessing sometimes, things don't work the way they're supposed to."

He says it so calmly and rationally when I'm feeling anything but, and it seems so strange that he can be calm in a moment like this. Then again, I've had to stay calm in the face of absolute nightmares. When I found out about what Brian had done, once the medical examiner's report dropped, I *knew*. I didn't question it for a second. But I stayed calm because I had to. Because of my baby.

"You should talk to a doctor about it," I tell Gabe. "See if it's something they can test. How often this happens. And we'll schedule a paternity test as soon as possible. I know they can do them in vitro now."

"I don't need a paternity test. I know that baby's mine."

"We should get it anyway. Peace of mind."

"Hey." Gabe takes me by the jaw and tilts my head up so I have to meet him in the eye when I don't immediately look at him.

The way he looks at me, his eyes wild, his pupils blown slightly, his complexion off and forehead creased, sets my heart pounding. I'm so spun it's hard to think. And then his thumb traces over my lip, so light and thoughtless, a gentle caress.

"Hey," he says more gently, maneuvering us out of the bathroom and into the bedroom with slow, careful steps. Herding me with a soft look and a soft touch until we reach the bed. He sits there on the box spring, barren since he pulled the mattress off of it and left it on the floor, a promise he'd always come back. He sits on that box spring and sets me on my feet in front of him, and he's low enough that we have a rare moment of leveled eyes.

"I don't need that test," he says as I continue to resist him. "I definitely don't want you to do anything while the baby's in here." He brings one palm to my belly and smiles. He actually smiles, like he's totally fine with this. "But do you need peace of mind?"

I frown and shake my head. "What? No. *I* know you're the father." My balance wavers as it hits me what he said, what I said. Gabe's knees go to my hips to support me, and I brace myself on his thighs. "Oh god, no. Gabe, I don't—I didn't mean *I'm* questioning that. Not at all."

"I know. I only meant if you're scared that I'm going to ghost you, I won't. So if you need that test, I'll take it. And whatever else you need. Whatever you need to do, whatever you need me to do, anything." He moves that hand away from my belly, instead covering my hands with his. His eyes stay firmly on mine. "And if you're not okay with this, I'll support whatever you need there, too."

I blink a couple times to figure out if what he's saying makes sense and I'm just struggling, if he's saying if I don't want him to father my child or support me or . . . I don't even know what. I have no idea what he's saying.

He finally looks away from me, his eyes shifting meaningfully toward the doorway that leads to the hallway and the room across the way.

The nursery.

But then he sweeps my knees out from under me and scoops me up onto his lap. His lips go to mine, and his kiss is every bit as gentle as his thumb was, but it's long and deep, his hands spearing my hair to massage my scalp. When his lips part, he tilts so that our foreheads are together, and we share the air between us for several breaths.

"I love you, Joss. I want to marry you and spend my life with you and raise a family with you. I want it all. Whatever you want, I want more. But if you don't want this baby, either because you don't want the risk of another pregnancy or you're not interested in having kids anymore, I respect that. This is your body, and I would never expect you to do something you don't want to do with it."

I can't believe he just said that.

I can't believe I'm this lucky this time around.

Here I go crying again.

"I said that wrong, didn't I?" Gabe mutters. "Dammit. I was saving the love thing for the right moment, and I thought this was it."

I hug him as best as I can even though his shoulders are too broad for me to ever hope of getting around him. I'm gross and wet and snotty. My head hurts from crying out all my hydration, and I'm starving. I don't know what I'm doing, and there's so much that needs to be done — I remember exactly how long eight months felt last time, and it was simultaneously an eternity and a blink of an eye — but in the moment, I laugh and say, "I want it all, too. And even though I've only known this baby for three seconds, I'm so much in love with them. And you. I love you so much."

"Well, that's great then. That's perfect."

Chapter Twenty Three
GABE

JOSS

> Do you need a Cohen Special on the way home?

I don't understand it at first, but then I glance over and see that despite this being our worst loss of the season so far, Drew Cohen's got an absent grin on his face. I remember what Joss told me Mel does to make him feel better after losses.

Joss just offered to give me a blow job on the drive home tonight. Not going to happen, because I'll be stressing way too much to enjoy it, but that means she's feeling okay. I can't see her from the field anymore, not in the new seats she's in, and Cora's out of town, so I got tickets for Rose and Iris. I'm sure they had a blast, but they aren't quite Cora. This gives me some breathing room.

We've got an away game for Thanksgiving next week and then another home game before we're both going to Minnesota for the game there and my family's holiday party. By the time we're back, Tilly will be in town and able to go to the games. I wish there was someone younger and more able-bodied to hang out with Joss during the first December game, but Joss keeps reminding me that I stress too much.

I stress about whether my truck with its extended cab is good for a baby or if I need to trade it in for an SUV. I stress that Joss wasn't taking folic acid before she got pregnant. I stress over whether she'll like the engagement ring I'm picking out. I stress she's going to miscarry. I stress about my fears and greed and stupid lies hurting her all over again.

I stress about the ghost of Brian Edgars haunting her to this day and how little control I have over that.

But I do have a little control.

I glance over my shoulder.

Evan's staring right at me.

I quickly look away, only to remember he's literally the guy I was going to talk to. I look at him again, and he shoots me an uncomfortable smile.

"Joss is pregnant," I tell him.

We're in this great big locker room, and yeah, everyone's shuffling in and out of clothes, slamming their doors, talking to each other. The showers are running full blast around the corner from us. But Evan and I are a couple yards away from each other, and I just kind of blurted that out.

To the entire team.

The room goes still. Plenty of the guys around me are married with kids. Or divorced with kids. Or never married with kids with three different women and child support so high that he didn't have a choice but to move into what Joss described, accurately enough, as a frat house. Pregnancy announcements aren't all that unusual, unless they are. Unless there's a reason to think this might not be a happy announcement.

Everyone turns to me, assessing me with scrutinizing eyes.

And then on one side of me, Blaise slaps my shoulder and says, "You *have* been banging her, rock on!" while Merrick rolls his eyes with, "There are condoms *everywhere* in the house."

I shove them both off with a laugh that gets the team moving again, several guys giving me congratulations and praising Joss, plenty grabbing their phones to fire off texts to make sure no one else has a bun in their partner's oven. This is the sort of thing that spreads like wildfire with the WAGs. Morales and Allore both had babies last season, Huang's newborn is absolutely the chunkiest of monkeys and made his debut at Monday night team dinner last week, now I've got one on the way? Men are scared.

Once everything quiets back down, I look back to Allore. He's the first to take a step forward, but I meet him in the middle.

"Congratulations," he says after a beat, nodding to himself like he's satisfied with how it felt saying that. "You deserve it, man. You're great with kids."

"I don't deserve it." I shake my head to clear the thoughts that come with that. I didn't earn anything; I lied and manipulated and got so fucking lucky that it worked. I could never admit to Evan what I did, so I clarify with, "I don't deserve Joss. She's amazing. *Amazing.*"

Evan frowns and glances around the room nervously. "Look, I don't know her. What her husband did—"

"Her husband. Not her."

Evan holds his hands up for peace. "I know. If she had left Wilmington, I'm sure that she'd be the most popular person wherever she landed—"

"She couldn't." Whether it was because she'd lost everything else and couldn't sell the house or if she couldn't let go of that nursery, it's all the same.

"I know. I'm trying to tell you I'm glad you two found each other. I'm sure she's a real nice lady because you wouldn't be with her otherwise, so I'm glad she has you to protect her."

"She's not allowed to sit with the other wives."

"Aw, man." Evan scratches his head helplessly, fluffing up his red-tipped mohawk. We all thought he'd grow out of that after joining the NFL and having a kid, but he just changed the color from Wilm State navy to Jugs red. "I didn't ask for that. I know Keira didn't either." But the way his face reddens to a shade closer to his hair makes me think they had a hand in it.

I've been catching on to the fact that Joss hides stuff from me. I get it, she's her own person and has dealt with so much on her own already. But I'm going to need to talk with her about transparency. It's not just us now; it's a baby, too. And not that she wasn't more justified in keeping stuff from me before, but now I've got the best reason ever for why I need to know these things.

So now I'm wondering what Keira has done. I believe Evan that neither of them asked for Joss to get kicked out of the section, but I've got three sisters. I've seen Mean Girls. I know how skilled women can be at manipulating situations to ostracize others.

But I'm not going to make accusations.

"I know you didn't. This came from upstairs. Joss is bad PR. But she's all alone right now, and her friends travel a lot.

She had to bring two grannies with her today. And obviously I'm not going to expect Keira to be friends with her, but I need Keira to *not* be driving the other wives away from her, okay?"

There's no way for me to say this without it being an attack on Keira. Keira's a mama bear. She's telling the other wives because she thinks she's protecting them.

I don't care.

I push harder. "I can't watch her every second of the day, and I'm scared. You get that, yeah? You get that I need to protect her. She's carrying my child, and I need her here so I can protect her. But I can't protect her if I can't see her, and I can't go against Coach, so I need everyone else watching out for her, just checking in. And that's not going to happen if everyone thinks they're picking a side simply by walking down a couple sections and saying a couple of nice words to my girl."

Evan sighs. He swallows a lump in his throat, thinks on it a moment longer, and nods. "I'll talk to Keira."

December rolls in with a frigid snap that leaves the morning lawn frosted in white. I pour myself a cup of coffee from the coffeemaker I upgraded Joss to after her obstetrician assured us she could continue to have her morning and late-morning coffee. Joss is still asleep, but I set up the espresso pod and pour milk into the little pitcher for her to make her cappuccino when she wakes up.

I yawn and stretch as I stare out her kitchen window at her crystallized back lawn, glittering in the scant dawn sunlight. It seems darker than it should be, but that's December.

C. B. Alice

I frown, though, when I realize that it is darker than it should be. Across the lawn, the barn is dark in a way I can't immediately put my finger on. I can barely read the words painted on the window inviting people to come on in, words I've stared at in the dark on so many nights.

It must be reflective paint, but there's no light for the paint to reflect. There should be, even in the middle of the night. Joss has a soft light over that window. The bulb must have blown.

I know Joss has no plans on going downstairs until at least midday. She's changed her schedule to make sure we have Tuesdays off together, and the first trimester is kicking her butt. She assures me that by the New Year, she should be vomiting way less and back to full energy, but in the meantime, she doesn't argue over the chores I've quietly taken over for her.

I wedge my feet into the pair of boots I have stashed in the closet at the top of the stairs, warily eyeing the lack of door there for the millionth time. I throw on my hoodie, grab a box of lightbulbs, and shuffle down the stairs.

Harsh winds hit me as I step outside. The buildings make a wind tunnel. This place needs so many renovations — like that missing door — to make it what I'd consider baby safe that I wonder if it's worth it when there are perfectly good houses nearby we could buy. But the more I think about it, the more I know deep down in my gut that Joss is going to want to stay here. She's a phoenix; this is the site of her demise, but it's also the site of her resurrection.

Around the corner from the current entrance to the house is the footprint of a demolished deck, the rectangle of out-of-place wall marking where an exterior door once was on Joss's apartment. We could rebuild the deck and add that door back in, make safer stairs or even a ramp. A little cubby for the raccoon to nest in since Joss promises me it's had a rabies vaccine.

I flip the collar up on my flannel and pause there next to her house, sending a quick text over to Merrick telling him he needs to come help me clean up the mums that are going to wilt now that winter's hit. He'll piss and moan and refuse, but he'll make everyone else come over, and then he'll get lonely and show up an hour later.

I nudge at the mum next to me with the toe of my boot, shaking the surprisingly heavy frost off it, except a bit of it shatters loudly when it hits the concrete path. It's not frost at all.

I glance back at the house, at the light fixture next to the door. It's been smashed.

It's outdoors and not well protected; a bird could have flown up into it and accidentally shattered it. A lot of people pass by here with tools of the quilting trade stuffed in bags, and some of that stuff is big and unwieldy. It wouldn't surprise me if a particularly clumsy customer accidentally shattered it. With the wind tunnel, it wouldn't even be so outlandish for some bit of debris to get kicked up and hit it just right.

But this isn't the only light that's out.

I jog down the path to the barn and find another pile of glass beneath the light fixture. Around to the front of the shop, the two lights next to the front door and even the lamppost in the lawn have all been shattered. The worst damage is that post, the entire fixture having been knocked off.

Light is security. Criminals knock lightbulbs out before they commit far worse crimes, sometimes well in advance so it's not so obvious. This could be the preamble to a big problem, one I might not be around for. I can't take her with me on trips, not other than the upcoming Minnesota game because of the special clearance I got for it since we're staying in town, so I won't be able to protect her.

Just like that, my heart's pounding again. I'll stay here every night I can. Start those renovations, finally replace her bed so we're not sleeping on the floor on that tiny mattress anymore. When I'm not here, she'll have sleepovers with Tilly. She could stay at my place, but no one will be there, and I'd rather she have someone with her.

I'm rounding the corner of the house to head over to the shed to get a thick pair of gloves and some pliers when I hear, "Gabe? Are you out here?"

"Don't come out!" I yell, hustling to stop her, but by the time I reach her, she's already stepped outside, right into that glass.

She yelps and hops back on one foot. She's got slippers on, but I know they don't have anything except a bunch of padding and some rubber anti-slip nubs on them. I'm on her in two seconds, carefully scooping her up even with the box of bulbs in my one hand, flipping her over my shoulder to navigate the narrow, awful stairwell.

"Was that glass?" she asks, her voice watery. The way she's leaned over me with her knees bent, I can see the bottom of her slippers, dusty from picking up the usual detritus off the floor. Blood is already blooming around the large sliver of glass skewering it.

"Lightbulb. Someone's smashed all your lightbulbs. Let's get you bandaged up and call the cops. Get a report filed."

Joss's huff isn't one of fear so much as irritation. Maybe even resignation. "We don't need to do that."

I set her down on that platform that's where a dining room table should be. More work to be done if we're going to have a baby here. "We absolutely do. You've got tens of thousands of dollars of merchandise."

She sighs and leans forward, attempting to take hold of her slipper. "They didn't take anything, right? The store wasn't broken into or anything?"

I slap her hand away more firmly than I should, but she's going to end up doing more damage and seriously hurting herself. It's in her heel, so she's probably not feeling too much right now, but she's about to slice her foot open. "No, but that's—"

"It's a prank, then."

I grip the sole of her slipper on either side of the glass and give it a sharp tug to split it wide open.

"Gabe!" she gasps in irritation.

Not apologizing for that, either. I'm angry she's acting so calmly about this. "It's not a prank. This is what home invaders do when they have actual marks. Whoever did this wants to hurt you."

"They don't!" She's the one slapping now, knocking my arm back and pulling her foot in, lifting herself up on the other foot.

"Where the hell do you think you're going?"

"Oh my god, I'm just getting tweezers," she huffs. "So you don't cut yourself, too. And trust me, they're not going to break in. They never break in."

"What do you mean by that?" I keep my voice low, as passive as I can, knowing that I'm going to lose my temper in about half a second if I'm not careful. I let her hop down the hall to the bathroom, but I wrap an arm around her rib cage.

She gives in enough to lean into me until we can get her butt onto the closed toilet lid and I can dig out the first aid kit. "It means . . . this happens sometimes."

I clench my fist and release it a few times, carefully take hold of that first aid kit. "What exactly happens sometimes?"

"Just stuff. Vandalism. They'll knock down my mail-box or throw garbage in the lawn, mess with my plants."

I select the tweezers from the kit, find a disinfecting wipe and some antibacterial ointment. I breathe. I clutch the edge of the counter and breathe again. I think about her replacement mums.

I sit down on the edge of the tub and take her foot, waiting to say anything until I've already got the glass pinched in the tweezers. I know I won't do anything to hurt Joss, so I'll be steady with this. "How often does this happen?"

Joss's toes curl minutely, tensing up. She makes a humming sound she tries to pass off as casual. "Sometimes," she says lamely.

Sometimes. Hell. "When did it happen last?" Her immediate silence has me adding, "And I noticed when you redid the mums, so please don't say you don't remember when."

She's still silent. I ease the shard out from her foot, pressing a wad of cotton against it to staunch the bleeding, but it only trickles. Not too big, not too deep. She won't need stitches. She'll just need to be careful going up and down the stairs.

Which means she's moving in with me for the next week.

I glance back up then, and she's chewing up her bottom lip. I'll be absolutely shocked if she doesn't break skin. "How often, Joss?" I ask more gently.

"Last week was the trash. There have been a couple incidents, but it started in September. It happened a lot the first couple years after Brian and then again when I opened the shop. And now . . ."

"Because of me."

She attempts half a smile, her eyes damp but hopeful, filled with love. She loves me. I love her. That's the most important thing. I need to figure out how to stop this for my own sanity, but that's the most important thing. "It's worth it, though."

I get her foot situated in my hand so that when I lean forward, I don't hurt her. Her soft blonde hair is loose, falling in gentle waves, the ponytail bump prominent. Fatigue from the pregnancy has made her forget to put her hair up first thing in the morning, and I love it that right now, I can dig my fingers into the warm, silky strands and kiss her as gently as possible, lingering there, savoring the moment, knowing that I will protect her.

Chapter Twenty Four
JOSS

"Geez Louise, what's she doing in a Jugs jersey way over here?"

It's not the first time I've heard that since walking into the U.S. Bank Stadium in Minneapolis this afternoon, and I doubt it will be the last. I can't even be mad about it, any more than I could be mad when I ordered a drink at concessions and got ribbed for calling it a soda instead of a pop and for wearing red instead of purple. The Minnesota accent is too fun to get mad at their mildest of insults, and I'm mostly upset at how well Gabe has apparently squashed his own accent.

I haven't seen him since yesterday morning when he dropped me off at the airport, and he's been in a state over the fact that I had to go solo on the first two days of the trip. He's on the clock, after all. Team protocol.

C. B. Alice

But I'm loving this. I've spent the last six years on my own. There are some days I don't have another human being in reaching distance for the entire day. I love Gabe, I'd rather him smother me than not be in my life at all, but Minneapolis is a new adventure for me. I'm having a blast.

I visited four local fabric shops in the area yesterday and this morning. I called them in advance, casually dropped my name in the conversation, and three of the four ladies asked me to do a meet and greet. I graciously accepted — graciously to them, but it was really the purpose of the call.

I don't know, maybe it's petty and self-indulgent, but I bask in those meet and greets. I absorb the adoration from the quilters who come by like I'd absorb sunlight. And that fourth shop? The moment I walked in, the lady at the cutting table looked up, got halfway through her rote greeting, and wrecked her cut. "Oh my word, you're Joss Page."

So yeah, I get an impromptu meet and greet there, too. It's the guiltiest of pleasures, filling me with all those happy good feelings from back in my pageant days, when I was routinely getting Miss Congeniality if I wasn't winning the tiara itself.

I've just sat down in the sea of purple when the lady two seats down comments on the jersey. I'm ready to ignore it, but then a heavy hand lands on my shoulder and a friendly voice behind me says, "Yeah, no, it's Shaunessy's jersey. You come down from Duluth for the game?"

The man behind me looks as friendly as he sounds, wearing a silly Viking helmet with fake — hopefully — fishing lures dangling from it and a Vikings tee, but also the biggest grin and a bushy white Santa beard. I want to say yes, I'm from Duluth, to hide the fact that I'm on a first-name basis with half the team, but there's no way I'd be able to pass with my voice. My mother put me in diction classes for years so I wouldn't sound like a Southern hillbilly, but I can only pull off neutral.

"I'm Gabe's girlfriend," I admit, feeling better about that than lying, even if it's going to make me a spectacle.

The guy on my other side slaps my back too hard. "Well then, you're family!" he yells, obviously drunk but happy.

I make fast friends with my neighbors after that, trading friendly jabs but grudgingly complimenting each other's teams. They're as stressed as I am when Merrick has to be helped off the field at the beginning of the first quarter, but they have him iced down, taped up, and back on the sideline halfway through the second quarter.

By then, the Vikings have pulled ahead of the Jugs and are leading by nine at the half. They're taking the field again and we're speculating about whether Merrick is going to be put back in when I hear, "Joss? Oh my god, Joss, it is you!" from down the way.

I lean forward to look past the rest of the spectators to see Rachel in her Gabriel's Angels halo on the stairs. "What on earth are you doing here?" I yell back with an incredulous laugh.

"I'm at a conference in Minneapolis this weekend!" She pushes her way to me, but everyone's happy to get out of her way. No one ever claimed the seat next to me, so there's room for her. "Came in a day early to see the boys."

I nearly ask her why call center workers would need to have a conference, but then it hits me I don't know all that much about her and there are all sorts of conferences for hobbies, including hobbies I really don't need to know my students are into. Instead I go with, "How did you find me in fifty thousand people?"

She points at the gigantic screen showing everyone getting set up for the kick-off. We're the receivers, and Merrick still isn't on the field. Crud.

"You were on the jumbotron, and the section number was visible. Thought I'd come investigate. This isn't crazy, is it?"

I laugh. "It's a crazy coincidence, but I'm glad you're here." As she sits, I notice she's got a container of the cookies she always makes for Gabe in her bag, but this time, there's a letter taped to the top of it, folded so I can't see what it says. "Did you want me to give those to Gabe?"

She looks down at her bag and closes it quickly. "Oops! No, those aren't for Gabe. I'm . . . meeting coworkers after the game. It's for them." She sounds flustered, so I'm betting they're not coworkers at all.

She's here for some weird sex convention, I just know it.

Merrick does eventually make it back onto the field, but we still end up losing in a nail-biter. My neighbors and I exchange encouraging *good games* as we file out of the stadium, and I have Rachel to commiserate with until Gabe texts me where to meet him and the rental car.

"You wanna get a room for the night?" I ask him the moment he intercepts me at the closest section of the path that keeps him out of Viking fan traffic. He looks tired, bummed out from the loss. I know he's wearing a boring black hoodie and navy sweatpants to avoid attention, but the lack of pink Party Animal cat makes him look that much sadder. He brightens up when I'm close enough for him to snag me and reel me in, but he's slumped and he holds me for too long.

"Nah, I'd rather get home."

"Are you sure? It's going to be one a.m. by the time we get there."

"Yeah. Ma's gonna have a breakfast casserole for us. She'll be bummed if we're not there for it."

I feel really bad that they lost this one. I never played sports, but I can imagine this was a big deal, going back to where he grew up — roughly — and losing. Still, I peel back so I can look him in the eye and say, "Oh, sweetheart. It's called hotdish. Get it right."

"Well, now, you are just the prettiest girlfriend Gabriel has ever had," Mrs. Shaunessy says, looking me up and down. "Isn't she absolutely beautiful, Hank? Way prettier than that hussy Megan."

"Ma," Gabe groans, his expression horrified as I mouth *Megan?* and Mr. Shaunessy grunts in agreement.

"Ma has Joss's picture as her lockscreen," Leah tattles as she breezes by her mom in her barista's uniform, splattered in coffee, having already returned from her shift despite it being after ten. Meanwhile, Gabe and I are just now getting up for the day.

Okay, we woke up hours ago, the time zone wreaking havoc on us, but Gabe talked me into utilizing our quiet time skills from the Jug house in his childhood bedroom, and that was enough to put me back to sleep.

No one's judging us openly about it, and Gabe has already assured me his parents are used to enough shenanigans already that a lazy morning isn't going to get a reaction out of them. Leah grabs a big scoop of the breakfast casserole but adds a packet of toaster pastries, which she eats frozen. Since no one reacts to that either, I'm guessing Gabe is right about the level of shenanigans.

Gabe snatches his mom's phone off the counter and scowls when he sees the photo there. "I'm not even in it."

I take a peek and am pleasantly surprised to see it's one of my professional headshots done last year, not anything from my pageant years. I wasn't sure what they were going to expect of me since they knew my past.

Mrs. Shaunessy shrugs. "She looks prettier without you."

I'm immediately in love with Gabe's whole family.

His dad seems to be attempting the role of cliche TV surfer dad but straining at the seams to leap into the eternal fray. Half the time, he's mumbling about the game being on — even when he's watching reruns of X-Files — but the other half the time, he's giving me advice on how to pull my hair back without a hair tie or settling arguments with obscure facts that negate the whole discussion. His mom clearly has ADHD but is in her fifties and rolling with it.

I'd love to see Phoebe get into an argument with Merrick, just to see who would win, and Gabe begs me to retract that because that's Merrick's foreplay, but I have a sneaking suspicion that Phoebe wouldn't be seduced nearly as easily as other people.

Like Cora.

Leah, meanwhile, is reckless and brazen and grossly underestimated. I get why she's underestimated, she's the baby of the family and she's a comparatively late bloomer, but she's also a different generation than Gabe, Phoebe, and me, and she's quietly biding her time. I'm not surprised to learn she was the one who figured out my past with nothing but my first name and my profession.

On Friday after breakfast, Hank takes Gabe ice fishing while Liza, Phoebe, and I work on food and decorations for the holiday party. Liza and Phoebe insist on make-up and frilly aprons. They put on one of the radio stations on the lower end of the dial and plot out which pies the men will prefer. I don't get a chance to make an opinion of it and talk myself into deciding it's quaint and not misogynist before Leah pitches a fit about that exact issue and takes off. It's at that moment that Liza and Phoebe exchange a satisfied nod and crack open a bottle of whiskey.

"I thought she'd never leave," Phoebe groans and takes a swig directly from the bottle and passes it to Liza.

Liza makes herself a whiskey ginger. "You want some, Joss? Or a margarita? I've got some wine stashed?"

I turn her down as politely as I can. "Not a big drinker these days, but I'd love one of those ginger beers." It's all nice and fizzy in my belly, which has mostly gotten over morning sickness but still has its moments. "I feel like I'm missing something, though."

"Hank and Leah love to cook," Liza says.

"Horribly," Phoebe further explains. "They love to cook horribly, and the worst part is they *like* what they cook."

"He made her like that," Liza humphs. "Babied her. Turned her off from flavor. He saw how busy I was with you heathens and took advantage of it."

Phoebe nods in agreement, no offense taken. "And Gabe hates ice fishing, but he knows Dad won't miss an opportunity to take him, even though Dad also secretly hates ice fishing."

My eyes go damp, my knees go wobbly.

"No, don't do that. They're my biological relatives. They've both absolutely wrecked the bathroom and then let me walk in without warning me. Do not go all googly-eyed over them. They're gross."

I bite down on my bottom lip and nod, but the way she rolls her eyes tells me I wasn't convincing enough.

I'm bummed I don't get to spend much time with Abigail, the middle sister, but she doesn't arrive until the party's already going, and there's a houseful of friends and family buzzing around me. She shows up with two toddlers, an infant, and what I quickly figure out is a man-child of a husband. She's tall and beautiful as her sisters, but she's exhausted. The infant's no more than six months old and colicky, so she has no choice but to hold them the entire time while Dwayne, her husband, acts like he's doing the lion's work watching the toddlers.

He cracks open a beer and plops down next to Hank to watch hockey. The toddlers terrorize the guests, who seem used to it but uninterested or ill-equipped to handle their energy for more than a couple minutes.

Liza drags me around to all of Gabe's aunts, uncles, and cousins while he gets dragged into the same football conversation over and over again. "Have you met Gabriel's fiancée?" Liza says to every single one of them even though she knows darn well they haven't and we're not engaged. "Isn't she beautiful? She's a quilter, just like Granny Bernie!"

I'm not about to correct her on the fact that I'm not Gabe's fiancée. Partly because it's rude, but mostly because I don't want anyone to get the wrong idea — well, right idea, technically — about me when we make our announcement.

Gabe keeps making meaningful eye contact with me, as though asking if it's time yet, but Abigail excuses herself early on to take care of the baby and doesn't come back. The extended family, I'm not so worried about, but she's his sister. I don't think he realizes she's not here, and I know he wanted to tell everyone together. That was why he pushed for me to come with him when I'd rather wait on announcements for the second trimester.

This is the night.

I end up getting dragged back to the master bedroom with Liza and her sister Sally so they can show me their grandmother's quilts. They're rustic, mostly handstitched, made from traditional prints.

I have a laugh when they show me the traditionally pieced Cathedral Window. "This is what I was making when I first met Gabe. I make it a different way than this, but plenty of quilters will say this is the only right way." I look up to Liza and notice she and her sister are both holding their breath in anticipation. I'm not sure what for, though. "Have you shown these to Gabe recently? He'll know some of these patterns now."

"Tell us the whole story!" Sally coos.

Liza asks, "Was he romantic?"

"What? Oh." I can't hold back my giant grin. "He was, actually. The first thing he told me was that he thought I was a marry."

They seem satisfied with this answer, albeit confused. By the time we head back to the party — Sally stopping in Leah's room to rouse Abigail, who's asleep with a very-much awake infant crawling on her — there's no way I'd be able to convince them I'm anything less than a fiancée.

C. B. Alice

I scan the den when we return, lamenting that as an average height woman, I'm no match for Gabe's family's genetics, but he's still been easy to spot all night. I frown, concerned he might have joined the men who went out earlier to smoke cigars. That smell is definitely going to turn my stomach after an evening of highly suspicious dishes brought in by the relatives. But no, everyone is accounted for other than Gabe.

Phoebe solves the mystery for me when she points at the monster eight-foot Christmas tree. I peek around everyone until I see that sitting criss-cross applesauce, Gabe is playing mountain for his niece and nephew. Oliver is attempting to scale him while Luna is pushing a toy train up his arm.

Gabe, bless him, looks pleased as anything keeping the little ones contained while the adults mingle around him.

He doesn't even like kids, but he's putting the effort in.

Something catches his attention, I'm not sure what, but his eyes are suddenly on me and looking concerned. Liza nudges my arm, discreetly passing me a paper napkin, and I realize I'm crying. *I love you*, I mouth to Gabe so he doesn't think these are sad or angry or frustrated or *I remembered a commercial with dogs in it* or *why won't this peanut butter jar open* tears.

He makes a roaring sound, getting everyone's attention and making the kids squeal, but really, he's just standing dramatically, the mountain coming to life as a dragon with a kid under each arm. It's as good a way as any to start, I guess, and he yells, "We got an announcement!" as he makes his way through the crowd to me.

Dwayne grumbles, "They actually sign your ass again?" behind me.

I turn to glare because wow, this is not the time, and Gabe's actually been really stressed about it even though I've assured him a million times that what we have saved between us is plenty if he's not. Hank smacks Dwayne upside the head and winks at me.

Pretty sure Hank's my new hero.

"I knew it, I knew it."

"You didn't know it," Phoebe scoffs.

Liza swats her daughter with her towel, wielding it with expert precision. "I did, too. I knew it the moment I set eyes on her. She's got that expectant mama glow."

Phoebe rolls her eyes and dunks another of the endless stack of plates in the sink. There was a whole fight this morning about whether this was a fine china or paper plate event, Liza championing china while everyone else told her she'd be frustrated when it came to cleanup time.

I mentioned the risk of her nice plates breaking, and she said she had more plates in the set than she'd ever need, so I offered to help wash them if she wanted to use them. Now, though, she isn't having any of that. Not with the next grandbaby in here. Phoebe isn't putting up a fuss about taking over my task while Liza dries them, and I've been keeping myself helpful packing up stacks of tupperware, so it's worked out.

"It's not mama glow, it's frostbite," Phoebe argues. "She's from Alabama. She's probably never been this cold in her life."

Alabama has its cold moments and Wilmington has a decent winter — nothing like this, but plenty of snow — but I'm not going to argue. It *is* cold.

"It's mama glow. And then she confirmed it when she didn't have a drink with us yesterday."

"It was eleven in the morning, and we were doing shots of whiskey."

Liza sniffs indignantly. "I was *not* drinking shots."

"Pfft. We both saw the splash of soda you used."

"I knew she was pregnant! Why do you think I told everyone they're engaged?"

"Because you're clearly a lunatic who needs to be tossed in an asylum."

I seal up another container and add it to the stack, quietly smiling as they trade jabs. It was always mom and me growing up. No siblings, no dad in the picture. Supposedly he died before I was born, but the older I got, the more I suspected she was never in a relationship with him. I've spent a lot of time with Cora's family, and Brian and I visited his family on holidays, but every family is different. Watching Liza and Phoebe bicker makes me happier than it should. There's so much love.

I peek back into the den. Most of the guests have gone, but Abigail and her family are staying the night. She was shooed right out of the kitchen with that towel when she offered to help on clean-up, so she's sitting in the rocker with the baby, chatting with Gabe while he lies on the floor performing calisthenics — which I know he hates — while the toddlers hold onto his limbs and go for rides.

"He's gonna be such a good dad," I whisper, blushing when I realize I've spoken loud enough Liza and Phoebe heard me.

Neither of them even glance my way, though. "Of course he will," Phoebe says as Liza says, "Why wouldn't he be?" at the same time.

"Oh, you know, because he didn't want kids." I shoot a nervous look his way, worried I'm betraying a secret he was keeping from his family.

Phoebe grips the edge of the sink to keep herself upright as she laughs. Liza's whole body shakes. "Did he tell you that because of Suzie doll?"

I shake my head, not understanding.

Liza waves her towel at a photo collage on the wall. They're all over the house, and I've looked at every one of them, mostly hunting Gabe down and then speculating what our baby will look like based on the pictures. He's in most of the pics in this spread, not surprising since he's the second of four, and since he's the only boy, it didn't stick out before that he's holding a doll in a lot of them. They're all holding dolls. It would make sense he'd end up with dolls as well.

Only now that it's been said do I realize that from toddler up to the youngest pics with Leah, he's holding the same doll, which seems to be getting progressively smaller but that's how much he's growing. That must be Suzie doll.

"Aww, that's sweet that he had a baby doll growing up."

"It wasn't sweet," Phoebe says. "It was creepy."

That feels strong. Just because he was a boy, that doesn't mean it was creepy for him to have a doll. He was probably copying his big sister. He was happy. It's sweet.

But then Liza says, "We weren't sure if we were going to have more kids after these two. But then Gabe got obsessed about having a little sibling. Would cry, throw tantrums about it. And then even after Abigail, he begged for another. The only reason we put him in peewee football was to get the other boys to bully him for being baby crazy."

Phoebe nods like she agrees this was a sane and logical solution. "Baby crazy. His whole life."

I'm telling myself it hasn't been his whole life, it was a phase he eventually grew out of. There was a time in my life when I secretly wanted to be an anti-pageant activist, but looking back on my childhood now, I would never want to lose those experiences.

Gabe's having the time of his life. He's been playing with those kids for hours. Now that the crowd has thinned down, the party over, he could easily pop in a movie for them and join the adults again, but he's shown no interest in that. It's obvious he's missed them, too.

"That ex-girlfriend of his, the one he had in college, was she anti-kid?"

"Totally!" Phoebe blurts out, putting me at ease. He got the vasectomy for her, then. Dumb, but I'm not surprised with Gabe.

Only, Liza then adds, "Not to his face, though."

"She couldn't be. He'd have dumped her." Phoebe gives her mom a nudge. "I showed you his profile I found on that dating site, right? His whole *big family, ready to settle down and have kids with the right woman* thing?"

"When did you see that?" I ask.

"A couple years ago."

My final thread of hope is it might have been an old, long-forgotten profile.

And then Phoebe says, "He took it down right after he moved to Wilmington, though, since it was a local service."

Chapter Twenty-Five
GABE

Something's wrong.

Joss was already asleep by the time I made it to bed after the party. The next morning was a whirlwind, two hours of Minnesota goodbyes that resulted in a pile of leftovers and a case of ginger beer I had to cram into our luggage. Joss was quiet on the drive to the airport, but there was a fresh coat of snow covering every surface. It's hypnotic. Soft and quiet. I can see why she'd be focused on the world outside.

We barely made our flight. Joss took the window seat and curled up in a ball to stare out at the clouds, giving her back to me, but I've never flown with her before. We all have our quirks. I've had teammates near to brawling because of overhead lights.

C. B. Alice

It bothered me. I shouldn't have let it, but we've spent more time together the past two days than we've gotten a chance to before or will again until the season ends, and it felt like she was putting as much space between us as possible.

My breaking point is when we're back in my truck, cruising up from Wilmington to Camden, and I reach over the console to take her hand. Yet again, she's staring out the window, yet again, all I see is her shoulder when I look her way, and when I touch her hand, she pulls it away, tucking it into her lap.

"You feeling okay, ma'am?" I ask, figuring it's the safest question to ask. She's been sick a lot. Nothing of concern to her doctor, but that doesn't mean I don't want to take care of her however I can. "You've been quiet today."

"Just tired," she says, but there's a prickle in her voice.

Outside of when she first took that test, she's been in high spirits, but I know not to expect that every day. All those physical things lead to grouchy days. Hormones lead to grouchy days.

"We'll be home soon," I murmur, moving my hand to her lower back, rubbing her there. She's hunched over a lot with quilting, no matter how often she corrects her posture. Her back is in constant need of a rub.

I swear I feel her skin crawl under my touch, but I shake my head, assuming I'm imagining it or she had an involuntary shiver.

"You wanna come over to my place?" I ask.

"I've got a lot of work to do."

"Okay. We can hang out at your place then. I'll cook us—"

"It's a lot of work. You should drop me off."

She just took a lot of days off, and she's the type to work every single day, if only for an hour or two. She's a workaholic, but I don't think it's bad for her. It makes her happy. Calms her. It's not surprising if she feels behind. It's not even surprising that she doesn't want me around to distract her.

But the way she says it is short and flat, her words coming out on a single breath with no break or inflection. It's dark enough that I can see her reflection in the window when I glance over, and her brow is tight, her lips pinched into a scowl.

I take a second to think about what I want to say. I'm glad I take it because I'd be using nasty tones if I didn't, accusing her of lying or holding back when I know her well enough to know that if she's upset, she's internalizing it, likely blaming herself for whatever it is. It doesn't take long before I realize that she's scared to tell me what's bothering her.

"It's okay if you don't like my family."

That finally has her looking at me. "Your family is great," she says, but even that feels like an attack.

"Did Leah say something? She can get really inappropriate at times. I'm not going to defend her if you didn't like her."

"I like her. I like your family. They were great."

"Look, something's bothering you. And I don't want to drop you off if we haven't resolved it. I don't like us not being on the same page."

"They told me about the doll. Suzie?"

Blood rushes to my cheeks. I swear my mother destroyed every picture of me *without* Suzie doll just to make sure I look as weird as possible to everyone who steps into my parents' house. Phoebe says no, I just never let go of that doll, I even washed her and changed her clothes, but that's insane. "I wasn't a weirdo, I swear. And it's not like I had the doll forever."

Even though my teammates through middle school and high school never let me live it down after one of them saw it in my room. I claimed it was my sisters', but they didn't believe me.

"You liked babies."

A fact, but another one that hits wrong. Dread settles like coal in my stomach even though it shouldn't. Isn't this better? I'm going to be a good dad. There's no way Joss missed how frustrated Abigail was with Dwayne. She won't have to worry a second about that.

But the way she says it doesn't sound very happy.

"I did, yeah. My sisters would have driven me crazy if I didn't."

There's another lull in the conversation. Joss brings her hand to her mouth and nibbles on her nail. It's such a normal thing, but not for Joss. She's not a frivolous person by any means, but her nails are impeccable, her salon appointments twice monthly, one of the few times she leaves her property. Cameras are constantly zoomed in on her hands, after all, and although she gets subtle designs on her nails, they're always intricate and perfectly shined and shaped. She absolutely does not chew on her nails.

When I try once again to take her hand, her head spins around to pin me with a glare and then return to that window. "Phoebe found your profile on a dating site."

Blood heats my cheeks. "Well, that's embarrassing."

"It was from two years ago, when you were in Indiana."

"Yeah, we were politely asked to not be on dating sites when we came to Wilmington. Not until the PR team had a good feel for how everyone was going to respond to us. Didn't stop Blaise from using one of those, uhh, fetish sites, but—"

"You really wanted kids two years ago."

It's like a house of cards proving how much I've always wanted kids. Rows and rows of evidence balanced just so. That Suzie doll at the top, my dating profile toward the bottom, but there are plenty of layers in between. Girlfriends I didn't have for more than a couple weeks because they didn't know when they'd be ready for kids, the one who hurt me as much for telling me she'd lied about it as she did for cheating on me. All the kids' charities I've volunteered for, the pee-wee football I coached before the Colts picked me up. But even more concrete than all of that is the time I spent with my niece and nephew and, most importantly, every single thing I've said to Joss since her pregnancy test.

It should be a good, strong house. It should withstand the stiffest winds.

Except there at the bottom is a single card, that fucking vasectomy lie.

I told myself it didn't matter anymore. She's happy. She wants this baby. She wants me to raise this baby with her, and she wants to spend the rest of her life with me. In my mind, that vasectomy card gently laid itself down while the house of cards stayed intact.

Joss's tone tells me this is not the case.

I signal to the drivers behind me that I'm pulling over to the side of the road. I can't have this conversation at fifty miles per hour, eyes ahead.

"If you stop this car now," Joss says, her tone far too even and deliberate, "I will get out and walk the rest of the way. Do not test me."

God help me, but for a moment there, I consider testing it. Even if she does get out, I'm so much stronger than her, so much better equipped to handle whatever fight she throws at me. Unless she sprints and happens to be a faster runner than me — not a difficult feat for my teammates, but they're professional athletes, and Joss's favorite sin is definitely sloth — it won't be difficult to wrangle her and keep her contained so we can have this conversation the way I want to.

But she doesn't have to say, "I will call 911 and end you," for me to know how bad of an idea this is.

Oh, she does say it, but she doesn't have to.

"I love you," I say helplessly. "I love you so much. Everything I did was out of love."

"What did you do, Gabe." There's no question. She already has her answer.

I swallow hard. "I know this is bad, but—"

"Tell me what you did. You need to say it."

Ironically, we're roughly where we were when it all started. It feels symbolic, in a way, that the little service road I found for us is only a mile ahead. I drive this road every day going to the sports complex. That turn-off frequently gets my attention. And as happy as I get whenever it catches my attention, a twinge of guilt always hits me. It's faded as the months have passed, become less of a serious fuck-up and more of a necessary evil. I think I'd almost convinced myself I did the right thing.

"I didn't mean to hurt you, I swear. It was stupid and reckless, but it wasn't—"

"Tell me . . . what you . . . did."

I have to focus on the road. I have to keep us all safe. This is my entire life. This is the only thing that matters. The lines blur in front of me, a solid white streak on either side of my hood guiding me forward. Guiding me to my doom.

If I stop the truck, she'll get out. She's gone.

If I keep the truck between these two white lines, she stays with me. I only lose her if I get off this road. I can keep her forever if I can keep driving.

I have a quarter tank of gas.

This is impossible.

So I turn off the main road and onto the one that will take us to Joss's place.

"I never got a vasectomy."

I want it to feel good to get it off my chest, but that's stupid. It would have felt good if I'd confessed it without it being forced out of me. It would have been terrifying, but I would have known then.

"No, that's not what you did. Not to me."

I can't play dumb here. There's no point in pretending like the vasectomy is the real issue when she wants kids so badly. "I lied to you."

I expect a tirade from her. This is her chance to lay into me, and honestly, I'm down for it. When I dislocate my shoulder, I don't want to walk all the way to the locker room to deal with it, and I don't want a ride there on the golfcart while they make a spectacle of me. I don't want the medics to do gentle rotations to ease it back into place or a countdown while three people hold me to pop it back in.

I want Vedder to put his cleat on my chest, grab my arm, and yank.

That's what I want Joss to do.

She doesn't. She hums, brief and low, and looks back out that fucking window.

"I'm sorry. I know it was stupid. I was ridiculously irresponsible. I didn't know if I had a condom in the truck, and I just said the first thing that popped into my head. I was going to tell you, I swear, but then I got all up in my head about how you were perfect for me. You *are* perfect."

I should stop talking, I know this. I need to let her talk even if she doesn't want to. But the words keep coming out of me the second I pause and silence fills the cab again.

"I got scared that you were going to realize how much better you are than me, how much more you deserve, and I . . . I didn't want to hurt you, but then I saw the nursery and got it in my head that you wanted a kid and would be as happy with a surprise pregnancy as I would be. If we talked about it, we'd end up getting bogged down in waiting a year to get engaged and then waiting another year to get married and then waiting still another year to start having kids, and why do that if we could have a kid now? This was for us."

Dead silence. Absolute silence.

This wasn't for us. I told myself it was, I calmed myself with that, but it wasn't.

"I'm an asshole."

I'm so relieved when Joss finally responds that it lessens the blow of her words. "You were supposed to be the good guy. I felt terrible letting you into my life without telling you why I'm so hated in Wilmington, and it was so hard to respect your opinion that you didn't want to know when you really needed to know, but I did respect your opinion. I respected you. And I told myself that you're a good guy. I didn't have to worry about you doing something so horrible because you're a *good guy*.

"The lie should have been the worst part. Or . . . how massive the fallout from it would be. This isn't just a lie, this is my entire life. This is a human being, their whole life too. Like, lying about a crime and someone else going to jail for it."

I taste vomit in my throat at that. I've never done anything worse than throwing back beers in high school or driving a little over the speed limit.

If one of my sisters came crying to me that a man she'd had sex with lied about a vasectomy and got her pregnant, what would I do? I don't know, but I'd be pissed. I'd probably beat the guy up, and I can count on two hands the number of physical fights I've gotten into off the field and outside of the usual scuffles with teammates.

"The worst part isn't the lying, and it's not the fact that you've taken it upon yourself to rewrite my life or that you're forcing me to bring a child into the world based on some ridiculous assumption about why there's a nursery in my home."

"That's why I stopped having sex with you after—"

Joss interrupts me with a voice dripping with venom. "I know that."

It has me wanting to shrink away. I have this ridiculous urge to curl up at her feet like a bad dog who's being punished for doing what he knew was going to upset his master but did it anyway. I want to whimper on the floor until she caves and remembers that she loves me.

Because that's what you do with dogs. Because they're dogs.

I am not a dog.

"Do you understand how much that hurt me?" she continues after a harsh breath, the hatred breaking into something more raw and far more devastating. "I had just bared my soul to you. I told you what my husband had done, how ashamed I was for not knowing anything about it, how badly the town shunned me, how I *lost my baby,* and then you refuse to touch me again? Do you have any concept of how dirty you made me feel?"

It's a sucker punch. My heart constricts in my chest as I white-knuckle the steering wheel. I don't know how I can apologize for that. I don't think I can. But I can't let her feel like that. "Can I hold your hand?" I ask, my voice reedy.

She pans her head, tilting slowly. "Are you for real right now? No, Gabe, you cannot hold my hand. You cannot touch me. You are going to drop me off at my place and get very far away from me for a long time."

Silence falls between us as I hyper-fixate on the traffic light we're sitting at, only three blocks away from her doorstep. I have three blocks to fix this. I can't possibly do that. I wasn't ready. I should have been, I know that, but I got so comfortable that I lost sight of this possibility. It was never going to be in the car, driving home from the airport, after she just met the entire family and every single one of them, even dad, made it very clear I could not fuck this up, that Joss is too good for me to throw away with something stupid.

It was never going to be while she was pregnant with my child.

That's where my brain sticks as I navigate through the intersection. I can't leave her. No matter what happens between us, we're going to have a kid together. I'll be devastated if I lose her, but she can't remove me from her life entirely. "You need me. The baby—"

"There was a moment when I was flat broke in a way that's practically inconceivable now. I was scared that even if I earned money on my own, it would still get taken away from me. And at that moment, I would have done anything, *anything,* to raise two babies by myself. I did do everything I could. So if you think that it would be an issue for me now, you are sorely mistaken."

I tell myself to keep my frustration bottled up inside. I'll be back home soon with people and weight room equipment I can beat the crap out of. Joss has every right to be upset, and we say things we don't mean when we're upset all the time. This is a conversation we can revisit tomorrow.

But I can't do it. I can't keep my mouth from moving. "If you think you're keeping me from my child, you have lost your goddamn mind."

Joss doesn't say another word. She doesn't have to. It's fifteen seconds before I'm pulling the truck up to the side door. She hops out before I even have it in park. I start to open my door, and she says, "I will call the cops if you get out."

"I'm getting your bag for you!" I snap at her.

She slams the door hard enough that I keep my ass in the seat, glowering at her reflection in the rearview as she drops the tailgate, half-climbs into the bed, and yanks her bag out. She doesn't bother to close the tailgate before marching to her door and letting herself inside.

I sit there, waiting to make sure she gets up the stairs okay before I pull out and park on the side of the road to close the tailgate plus sneak around her property to make sure there wasn't any vandalism while we were gone. Before I can do anything, though, she throws her door open and yells, "Hey Gabe?"

I roll the window down, hoping she's backing down, hoping there's damage inside, even. Some excuse for me to stand next to her on solid ground and work this shit out. To say things right the second time around.

"The worst part is I wanted this baby. Desperately. If you'd only asked me, I would have said yes."

Chapter Twenty-Six
JOSS

A single gift remains under the Christmas tree in the barn. Most were doled out at the annual Quilted Flower Christmas party, both the personal gifts to my closest friends and the White Elephant gifts that had amassed in the weeks leading up to the event. There were gifts for the Jug House, Mel Cohen, and Lin and Wren, which Cora distributed for me when she returned from her trip on Christmas Eve.

She insisted it wasn't an excuse to see Merrick, but since I didn't ask if it was an excuse to see Merrick, I have my doubts.

That leaves a single gift under the tree on January second.

"You could auction it off," Tilly suggests as she reaches up to take the first ornament off the tree and her shirt rides up slightly, revealing her baby bump. Because of everything her body's been through the last couple years, it's hard to tell she's pregnant even at six months. The shape of her belly is slightly unusual, but it mostly looks like she's just filled back in what she already had. Most people think she's put the old weight back on.

Good for her. Everything's going smoothly for her, which she deserves after almost dying last year. She's got one more job to get through. The longer she doesn't show, the better.

Meanwhile, I'm already grouchy about people touching my distended tummy, which the doctor has promised me isn't gigantor baby at all but bloating. I'm bloated, and people are touching me.

So I'm justifiably crabby with my response of "That's stupid."

Cora chokes down a laugh as she packs the ornaments Tilly hands her. "I can still take it over to the Jug House."

Tilly waggles an eyebrow at her. "And ride that Merrick train?"

Cora throws a wad of bubble wrap at her, but it gets caught on the air and sinks long before it closes the distance. "It was one time, oh my god."

"Two times, minimum. Did you think Joss and I weren't going to compare notes and realize you were telling us about two different days?"

"I didn't tell Joss about anything," she bristles, but the argument falls as flat as that bubble wrap. "This is so lame without mimosas."

Tilly grins like this is the greatest moment she's ever experienced and not the fifth time Cora has complained about having to break tradition this year. "Go make yourself a mimosa, then!"

"I'm not drinking by myself, that's even lamer."

"Then take the gift over to the Jug House and ride the Merrick train until you're knocked up, and then we'll all be in this together."

Cora gags, legitimately gags, at that. "That is disgusting. I don't want a kid at all, let alone one with that asshole. I'm gonna drop this off on the doorstep. It says 'Gabe' on it, they'll figure it out."

"I don't want to do that." I stoop down to pick it up, get it out of the way. My usual instinct to squeeze it, knowing there's a fluffy quilt inside, fleece lined for warmth and big enough to properly cover his bed, is absent. I don't even want to touch it.

I thought he was going to be the one to save me. To protect me. To breathe life into me.

Cora shuffles toward me reflexively, unendingly reliable to lend a shoulder for me to cry on, but it's become rote since it's all I do anymore when I'm out of the public eye.

"I have to stop this," I grumble into her shoulder, irritated with myself. I ended things, not him. I outed him for the bastard he is, and I freed myself before my life was ruined by a man for a second time. This is a time of celebration, not of grief.

Cora hugs me fiercely, no doubt realizing she was half-assing the support I didn't deserve anyway. "You don't. What Gabe did is disgusting. It's caveman shit. And we all fell for it. So you have every right to be upset. I'm upset."

"Men are trash," Tilly says cheerily. Coming from someone who's never dated seriously, I'm not surprised. She dodged a bullet getting knocked up by a stranger, I swear.

That's it. I'm over it. I let this ruin the holidays, but that's enough. "You know what else is trash?" I say, giving the gift that squeeze I didn't give it before. "This." I push it toward Tilly. "Throw this out. It's trash."

Cora and Tilly gasp together, horrified. "It's a quilt!" Cora squeals.

"You could sell it!" Tilly adds.

"It didn't do anything wrong."

"You spent days on it!"

"It's a quilt!"

The way Cora says it the second time makes it sound like I'm talking about a baby, but I shake my head firmly. "No, I make quilts every day of my life. I've given away more than I've kept, and if I throw out exactly one quilt in my life, that sounds like a good record. I don't want it, And I don't want it to be some shitty symbolic thing for Gabe. Whether he thinks it's a peace offering or a petty tease, I don't want that. And it meant too much as I was making it to sell it or give it away."

"But . . . homeless people?" Tilly attempts, which has me reaching over to a storage cupboard. It's giant, an old wardrobe that I pulled the rod from and filled with shelves. I open it, revealing a stash of quilts from my streaming classes that are so tightly packed in that one shelf explodes, spewing half a dozen small quilts at my feet.

"Jesus," Cora whispers.

"Donate those," I tell Tilly. "Every single one of them can go to the homeless. I've already donated an entire truckload to the women's shelter. I've been worried that if a bunch of homeless people are seen with my quilts, people are gonna come at me for encouraging panhandlers to come out to the suburbs, but honestly, they come at me for everything I do. Bring it on. But that quilt needs to be thrown out."

Tilly's sunny disposition dims through my rant until tears are pooling in her eyes at my final command. I should feel bad, but I don't. Misery loves company and all that. She nods and squeezes that gift-wrapped quilt to her body as she heads toward the door.

Cora taps her foot angrily, and I stare her down. I'm not apologizing, I'm not easing back. I'm taking my life back. We're going to angrily break down this tree, we're going to go get lunch, and then we're going to come back and get work done. One of us is going to have a silly thought and share it with the group, and then we're all going to have a laugh, and life will be good again.

I'm sure of it.

We hear Tilly yelp outside. She darts back in a second later, hands empty.

I tilt to look around Tilly's shoulder, confused about why, if she's scared, she's left the door open behind her. "What was that?"

Cora anchors her fists at her waist. "Is it that stupid raccoon?"

I frown and head toward the door. "Please don't throw quilts at Jerry."

Tilly half-heartedly attempts to block me from passing her. No less than twenty feet away, on the lawn between the barn and the back of the house, Gabe bends down to pick up the Christmas present that was just hurled at him.

There's another man with him, and they're both dressed in jeans, steel-toed boots, work gloves, and duck cloth jackets. The stranger has a leather tool belt on his hips and a tablet and stylus in his hand. Usually, I'd consider him to be a big guy, but then Gabe straightens up and dwarfs him by about half a foot and a hundred pounds.

I got used to how big he was when we were together. He seemed like the perfect fit for me, like we were made for each other. It hardly ever crossed my mind that my eyes hit his chest, because he was so natural at keeping us level in every way that mattered. And it took not even a month for him to be impossibly big again, a whole other evolution of man. The next step in those charts where every iteration of humanity is larger than the last.

And that patch I sewed over my heart? The one that was supposed to be my next evolution? Gabe rips the seams right out of it by simply meeting my eyes.

We're too far apart for me to see the pretty hazel that so captivated me when he hovered over me in the studio that first day, but I can see the longing. I can feel it within myself because my heart doesn't care that he is not what he seems. My heart doesn't get that he might not be the monster Brian was, but Brian at least recognized me as more than a means to get what he wanted. As anathema as it is, these weeks have forced me to admit that Brian cared about me, so much so that he went to incredible lengths to make sure that I would still have something if his vile habits ruined us.

I see Gabe's lips move. I know he's saying my name, but I can't hear it.

"I told you to never come back here."

I'm not sure if my voice is any louder than his, but he jogs up to us, and bless their hearts, Cora and Tilly step in front of me to block, like they're anything more substantial than bowling pins to him. But he stops before he gets too close and nods to them both, acknowledging them. Respecting them more than he ever respected me.

"And I told you I'm going to take care of my child. So—"

"So I guess I'll see you in July," I bristle.

Gabe glances between Cora and Tilly as he formulates a response. He points at my belly. "Now. Just because they're in there doesn't mean they don't need to be taken care of."

My spine straightens as my temper flares. "Are you accusing me of not being able to take care of them? Do you think it's my fault I miscarried?"

Tilly and Cora pull in more tightly as Gabe has the audacity to roll his eyes and say, "Of course I don't," enunciating slowly like he thinks I can't understand basic English. He gestures to the man who wisely stayed behind. "That's Jeff. I'm contracting him to build a new balcony here and install a door there where it used to be."

That has me pushing right through my friends and slamming the heel of my palm into Gabe's chest. A month ago, he would have stepped back, pretending that I'm able to move him, but he stands his ground unflinchingly.

"You think you can just do what you want to my home? You lost the right—"

"I'm making it safer!" he roars, his volume enough for me to stumble back.

And that, of all things, has him flinching.

Or maybe it's the quivering in my bottom lip.

He raises his hand and levels his voice out. "I just want to help. Those stairs are going to be a nightmare for you. They're too narrow to carry a car seat up so you won't be able to bring it upstairs. You won't be able to drag a stroller up, either. If we build that balcony, we can add a ramp or even a lift, whatever you want. Please let me do this."

I want to say no. I want to scream at him and tell him I don't need his help. I definitely can't tell him that I've always hated those stairs and cursed whoever took that porch off, and I don't want to tell him I could never convince myself I needed such an expensive and extravagant renovation.

I close my eyes, wishing I could vanish from this moment.

C. B. Alice

And Tilly and Cora come to my rescue, filling the space between us again, that space that would have been so easy for me to fall into and vanish, as he's allowed me to do within his arms so many times. Tilly steps into me, gently coaxing me back inside the barn, while Cora takes Gabe's arm and accompanies him back to Jeff.

Before Tilly gets the door closed, I hear Cora say, "We'll need to work out a schedule for this. You are hurting her being here."

And I hear Gabe reply with, "And I am suffocating without her."

But I can't care about that. I can't.

Chapter Twenty-Seven
GABE

There's this moment, a fraction of a second, where I hesitate. My arms go still, my elbows locked on either side of me, my knuckles white-fisted, the bar pressed against my chest, and I stop.

A normal place to stop. It's a transition. I've brought the bar down, and now I have to push it back up. And at three hundred pounds, it's a place where most men, even others in this weight room, would struggle through the transition. They would need this time to find that oomph, that extra strength, that adrenaline that seems to come from nowhere to push through it.

But not me. This isn't easy by any means, but this is what I lift. Not even. There are two more sets of plates waiting to be added to this bar to make this a serious challenge. The last month's been rough. I've taken some bad hits on the field in recent games. I probably won't add the last set of plates today. But it's not the strain that has me pausing.

I stare up at the ceiling, the rows of neon lights, the constellation of dimples in the panels of the drop ceiling. The random note cards Blaise has jammed into some of the corners, their messages a mix of crude drawings, random insults, and highest praises. I feel the weight of the bar on my ribs, the padding of muscle, fat, and flesh doing only so much to buffer the pressure. I imagine the weight I feel in my hands transferring to that thin line across my ribs.

And I stop.

An eternity frozen in one breath, just the expansion of my chest, constricted by that cold, thin bar of steel.

The industrial overhead lights are enough to blind a man who's staring too intensely at them. When they suddenly vanish from my sight and the world goes dark, it's like an eclipse. With a glow of fiery red along the rim.

Nope, that's Allore's hair as he leans over me and grabs the bar on either side of my hands.

"I'm good," I tell him, snapping back to the moment, hating how raw my voice is and how bad my eyes burn from staring at those lights.

He keeps his hands next to mine as he says, "You're not," his voice low enough that the guys who are busy on the machines a few feet away can't hear him. But he lets me lift that bar myself, his hands merely hovering.

As soon as the bar's back in the cradle, he does take hold of it, pushing down to prevent me from attempting to lift it again.

"I'm fine," I insist. "I just . . . needed a breath."

That's dumb. That sounds really dumb. That sounds like exactly the reason why I shouldn't be bench pressing anything right now and also why I should be seeing the docs for them to work their magic so I'm upright for the game in two days.

Except I'm not sick, of course. I'm not out of breath. Not in a way that can be fixed with Vitamin C and a shot of something we don't question since it doesn't flag on drug tests. I just

I just can't

breathe.

Evan continues to stare down at me from above, his face upside-down and distorted, although with Evan, it's probably not the angle so much as the struggle of big thoughts that has his face screwed up. We test each other, playing an invisible tug-of-war with that bar, me pushing at it until he forgets and leans back enough that I can move it in the cradle, only for him to slam his weight back down on it.

"You want to talk about it?"

"Not even a little bit."

"Dude, you looked like you were about to do some unaliving nonsense, and we were going to have to rescue your ass, and then we'd all get stuck filling out incident reports, which suck."

They do. I've had to fill them out twice now, both because of shenanigans with Blaise. "I'm not talking about this shit with you."

His face morphs into one of those theater masks, the sad one. I swear I've never met a man who's so equally stupid and sensitive who can actually function like a normal human being. "Why not? I'm practically your best friend!"

He's not. He's been a good buddy since our first training camp, when he basically forced us to be friends. As a Wilmington local, he's been a useful resource. I'm not saying I've taken advantage of that at all, but it's one of his biggest selling points. That and hanging out with him and Keira, especially when Dom and Cadence are also there with their kids. That group scratched an itch Merrick and Blaise and the rest of the Jugs House crew can't.

But that group doesn't exist anymore. I'm on speaking terms with Evan again, but it's not the same.

I school my eyes on those lights, focusing slightly off from Evan so I don't have to actually look at him, see every muscle in his face shift infinitesimally when I say, "Because it's about Joss."

He takes a heavy breath, looks up at that same light, tilts his head, and reads out slowly, "'You're doing amazing.' Huh, that's a nice—is that a dick with a little hat on?"

"Blaise calls him Carl."

"Huh. We should go for a run."

"There's nothing, absolutely nothing, I wanna do less than go for a run."

"Yeah, but do it anyway."

I can't breathe.

I take one step, and then another, each one lowering me to my knees so that I can gently collapse face-first.

At Evan's prodding — his literal prodding, squatting down in a runner's lunge and pushing at my side — I roll onto my back and suck in the air that was so frigid when we got out on the track an hour ago.

"I'm gonna die," I groan.

Evan flops down on the grass next to the track and crushes a snow angel into the untouched blanket. We're the only idiots outside in the frigid temps. "Man, this is nice!" Evan yells, only a couple feet away from me but facing the sky.

I roll my head over to look at him, wondering if his stupid ass is the last thing I'll see.

His mouth is open, collecting snow.

I want to tell Keira he's eating snow. She'd chew him out right in front of me, and the whole time, I'd feel like I was getting the revenge I was owed for being forced to run five miles on a snowy track. I'd tell her why I ratted him out afterward, and we'd all laugh about it.

Except I can't tell her. Strangely, it wasn't until I lost Joss that I realized I'd lost Keira, as well. There was this hope when I smoothed things out with Evan and me that it would make Keira see that she was being unfair to Joss. Now, I don't think there's any way to move forward with Keira without Joss seeing me as siding with her bully.

I'm losing everything.

Evan waggles his tongue to collect more snow. I'm wheezing; he's having his own fun.

"If I tell you what happened, you'll side with me even though I was the one who fucked up, and then you'll say shit about Joss, and I won't be able to be your friend anymore. Because if I ever get her back, I'll remember what you said."

He contorts himself enough that he can roll his head back to look at me upside-down. It's going to be upside-down day. Upside-down life. "Nah, man. You're gonna tell me how you fucked up, and I'm going to tell you how to fix it. That's what friends do."

"Merrick's congratulated me for escaping. Blaise feeds me shots when I'm sad."

"That's why you've been playing like crap."

"Thanks, man."

"Nah, man, that's on him." Evan shrugs, adding a humpback to his snow angel. "It's his fault his sacks have doubled the last few weeks." He rolls onto his side and props his head on his elbow like a teenage girl dishing at a slumber party despite the work-out gear in three inches of snow. "Listen, you got single friends, and you got married friends, right? And right now, you're listening to single friends who want to keep you single, but that's not what you want. You want married. You want a honeymoon and married sex and joint bank accounts and debates about how many streaming services is too many and a good school district and *what do you want for dinner, I don't know, what do you want for dinner* for the rest of your life. Tell me I'm wrong."

I sigh, which at least means I've caught my breath.

"Exactly," Evan continues. "So you need to be talking to me."

"I don't."

"You fucked up, you don't deserve Joss because she would never fuck up the way you fucked up, and what you did is a deal breaker, one hundo, not coming back from, but you don't care because you need Joss back."

"Right. So I'm an asshole for trying to get her back."

"Nah, it's like that oldie. You know, that song, it's ancient, back when people still had actual cameras? And it's the two dudes, and the one got busted for cheating — you didn't cheat, did you? Because that's not cool."

"Of course not." With a groan, I roll onto my side to look at the idiot.

"Cool, cool. But that song, and the other dude's like *just fucking lie, fam?* You know the song."

I shake my head. There are no oldies about that.

Evan snaps his finger. "Shaggy! It Wasn't Me! God, it was so cringe when my parents would listen to that, but if I'm being real? It was a vibe."

I slide my pinky up to the bridge of my nose. An oldie. I was in elementary school when it came out.

"Gabe, let me be your Shaggy."

"Fuck."

Evan gives me the shit-eatingest grin.

"So, that night at the fundraiser? When everyone was being an ass to Joss, including you?"

Evan nods like I didn't just call him an ass.

"Joss and I were on the way home and ended up hooking up, but we were in my truck, and I didn't think I had any condoms."

"Sounds hot."

"So I told her I had a vasectomy."

Evan is speechless for a solid three seconds, a miracle for him, and then he says, "Fuck, that's fucking genius, bro."

I blink at him several times, daring him to take it back, but he doesn't.

"Sooooo I was going to tell her the next day, make it right, you know, see if she wanted one of those pills."

"The laxative-looking ones, yep."

I almost give up right there, just make something else up or run another five miles to escape him. I'm pretty sure that's the motivation I need. But Keira is a sane, relatively level-headed, intelligent woman. Somehow, Evan has kept her happy, so he has to know what he's doing in this one thing.

"And then when I took her to meet my family, she found out I've always wanted kids and was lying the whole time, even after finding out the shit you and Keira are pissed at her for."

"Okay, two things. First, I've never been pissed at Joss, I wanted to do you a solid, and Keira was looking out for her friends. And second, this is totally fixable. I'm your Shaggy all day."

This is my worst nightmare.

And then I get pegged in the gut with a football. I curl up, winded all over again, tipping to see Blaise and Merrick standing no more than ten feet away, close enough to have heard that conversation, which means Evan was fully aware of their approach and kept going.

"Come on, ladies," Merrick says as they both lean down, offering their hands to help us up. "I got a whole bunch of tampons and chocolate inside for you."

"Boo, misogyny," Evan grumbles in that whiny way of his. "One day, you're all gonna be girl dads, and you're gonna feel really shitty about saying stuff like that."

Chapter Twenty Eight
JOSS

It's January. It's freezing outside. Nothing's rotten, nothing smells bad. The trash strewn across my lawn is mostly from quilting. My biggest concern is Jerry might eat a spool of thread and get an intestinal blockage and have to go to a vet.

Except I won't know because he's not an actual pet, so I'm just going to walk out and find him dead on my doorstep.

I pat my knuckle against the corner of my eye. I'm okay with the trash. It's something to clean up, that's all. I'm happy I got up early this morning to crank the heat up in the barn for Barb's early class and saw this before the students did. But I don't like the thought that this might have harmed Jerry. He's an innocent raccoon. He didn't do anything wrong.

"It's just plain terrible," Rachel laments as she corrals the recycling bin's contents with a rake. The receipt paper and thinner stock we use for paper piecing didn't fare well in the snow, so I'm not sure what else to do there. "I'm starting to think this isn't ever going to stop unless you leave."

I want to tell her she's wrong, but I'm not in the mood to lie. I'm not leaving, so it doesn't matter. I do have to consider this more seriously, what with the baby on the way, but running away isn't the solution. More security lights. A fence. A proper security system. I've been dragging my heels over a security camera doorbell, but I should start there. In the meantime, I'm happy Rachel showed up half an hour early for Barb's class and offered to help clean.

I finish my coffee and tug on a set of gloves from the shed. Snow starts to fall as I bend down to pick up the first handful of trash. It muffles the world, makes the task gentler. I'm not being harassed, I'm just doing clean-up. This is fine.

"Can I help?"

I look back at the unfamiliar voice, surprised to see Keira Allore on the walkway, her toddler stumbling in front of her in a puffy snowsuit so well padded that if she actually fell, I'm pretty sure she'd bounce.

I freeze, momentarily a deer in the headlights, and then look around to see if Gabe is hiding somewhere, like this is some comedy and he's managed to tuck over 300 pounds behind the lamp post.

I take a step back, my nerves fraying. Keira's not going to attack me or anything, not physically, but she's certainly proven herself adept at hurting my feelings.

She holds her hands up in surrender. "I just want to talk, I swear." She frowns at the mess around her. "And help you clean this up. Did a raccoon get into your trash or something?"

"No, he's a good raccoon," I say automatically. Jerry's been getting a lot of bad press lately that he doesn't deserve. "I'm more worried he's going to get sick from this."

Keira finds a clean spot to lead the baby — Shelby, if I remember right — to and pulls out a collection of toys to keep her amused. Shelby immediately starts making snowballs, contained for the moment as Keira scoops up a handful of fabric clippings and brings them to me for bagging.

"I'm sorry."

I swallow, still feeling skittish, thinking now would be a good time for that flight response to kick in. I feel like I'm back in my high school days, when the movies told me that being pretty would make me popular, but I was the wrong kind of pretty. Keira's the right kind of pretty, her naturally deep auburn hair and green eyes, her slightly wide-set features just unusual enough to be exotic, her presence bold and commanding. She was a cheerleader, probably already dating local legend Evan. I bet they were prom king and queen.

The mean girls at my high school were monsters. I tried to be kind to everyone and make friends with the other kids who were ostracized for their extra-curriculars. That made the mean girls a special sort of monster with me, fake-befriending me one week just to pull humiliating pranks on me the following week.

Keira's apology sounds an awful lot like a threat.

She frowns as she deposits the scraps in the bag and immediately takes a step back. "Gabe's one of my favorite people, and he won't be my friend anymore."

I let the words sink in as I study her bright, flawless, entrancing face. Gorgeous. If pageants really were just about beauty, she would have trounced me.

"Rachel, you should go get ready for class. You don't want to be late."

She looks between us as though she's making sure I'm safe, but Keira's baby's right here. Besides, I'm sure if she was going to hurt me, she'd have someone else do it. Or she'd go right for my feelings, and my feelings have built up quite the callus. I can take what she's going to dish out.

I'm in a mood. I know it. I'm being irrational to prove that she is a mean girl, and I hate that she's prettier than me. I'm going to be petty here, and I don't need Rachel witnessing it.

At my nod of assurance, Rachel grudgingly heads off.

"You win, okay?" I stomp past Keira to scoop up the pizza box from two nights ago and use it to scrape the chicken wings accompanying it out of the snow. "I'm not going to games and he's not my boyfriend anymore, so you can have him back. Just leave me alone."

Keira trails after me with a long strip of batting I'm surprised she even spotted in the snow and a paper bag that likely contains used blades or broken glass. I snatch it from her so she doesn't try to send me to jail for letting her cut herself on my trash.

"Please, Joss. I promise I'm not here to fight. Gabe is devastated. Evan says he's actually worried that Gabe is going to hurt himself, whether it's on purpose or just being reckless on the field."

"And ruin your precious game." I stare down at a pile of dirt I'm fairly sure is the contents of one of the shop vacuums. "I've ruined everything else in Wilmington. It stands to reason I'll ruin the Jugs."

Keira shakes her head and mildly curses under her breath. "You didn't. You don't. I shouldn't have ever gotten in your business like I did. I was just scared you were going to hurt Gabe."

"Well, he hurt me, so I guess you didn't need to worry."

"I didn't have a lot of friends in high school, okay?"

With the most exhausted huff, I stomp toward a bag that looks intact, but looks can be deceiving. Mean girls can be deceiving. They can make up stupid lies like *I didn't have a lot of friends in high school.*

What a joke.

"I was new in town," Keira calls after me. "My mom had just abandoned me. My dad was an alcoholic, couldn't keep a job. I lost my chance at gymnastics and had to do cheerleading, and I was miserable. I only had a couple of friends. And then your hus—*him,* he killed one of them."

I stop at that, tilt my head up to the sky, let the snow fall on my face. My lips, my nose, even my eyes. It is unending. Maybe Rachel is right and I do need to leave Wilmington. "Danielle Marsh."

The girl who my husband killed ten feet below me on a Tuesday afternoon while I was distracting myself reading one of Aiden's books when I was supposed to be organizing the changing table.

"Mikayla Behrensen, actually. You wouldn't know about her. She never came forward. Her parents were fundamentalists. They were top-notch victim blamers, no matter the crime. I knew something was wrong, but she wouldn't talk to me, either. When I pushed, she withdrew from me completely. And then she transferred to a private school. Two months later, her mom called me, told me she died. An accident, she said, but then it turned out she overdosed on her prescription meds. She killed h—are you okay?"

"Yup." Not even a little bit. Brian destroyed lives. It's one of those things that lurks forever in the back of my thoughts. When it's right in my face like this? When I have to see this woman who doesn't know me but hates me because Brian drove her friend to overdose? When I know there's nothing I can do to amend this because the people who really need to deal with this are both long gone and we're stuck holding the pieces?

It sucks.

So I'm squatting on my front lawn in a pile of trash, with my forehead on the hands draped over my knees. I guess I get why Keira can tell I'm not okay.

"And now I'm scared I'm going to lose Gabe."

I close my eyes and breathe in this little space I've made for myself. This space that's just me and the stupid bloating that my baby's hiding under, the only safe space I really have anymore. I stare at the pooch in the winter coat that isn't even bloating, just bunched up fabric, and I think about why Keira hates me. By the time I say, "And that's going to be my fault, too," I'm angry all over again.

Stupid, asshole Gabe. Stupid, asshole men. They're all awful, and they're always going to take advantage of me in some horrible way.

"No, of course not! God, I mean it, Joss, *I'm sorry*. You brought up all these horrible memories for me, and I got all caught up in it, and I . . . dammit. I was the one who superglued your locks. I'm sorry for that, too."

I pop upright, terrified that I'm going to have to have a locksmith come out and break into my own house again. But I'm two steps forward, brushing past Keira, when it hits me that I've already been in the shop and the barn today. No one's tampered with my locks. Not in probably five years.

I laugh incredulously as it clicks what she means. "You mean back then, when you were a kid?"

"I was eighteen. And a bitch. And when you popped up at that fundraiser, with Gabe of all people, it sent my head right back here, dripping superglue into the locks, because all anyone could talk about was how you kept this great big house while all those girls were falling apart."

I'm as acutely aware as anyone that this house should have been torn down, the earth salted. But I couldn't afford that, so I remade it into something happy and peaceful and safe. "It wouldn't have healed them. Nothing would have."

"I know. I see that now, and how you couldn't have known what was happening. Gabe loves you so much, and I can't think of another man who is as good a judge of character as he is."

"Wow. Okay. Not to call you out or anything, but you have no idea what he really is."

"I know what he did. The lie."

I struggle to keep myself from scrubbing my face with my gloved hands that have been all over the trash. It shouldn't be difficult to resist, but my mind is completely blown by this. Why would he tell people what he did? "Why are you here right now? Why is—what—I don't understand what this is."

Keira nods for too long before saying, "Right, yeah. This does seem crazy. I'm sorry I didn't welcome you like I should have and like you deserved. Everything's a mess, and a lot of that is my fault."

"Did you tell him to lie to me to get me pregnant?"

At that, Keira looks flustered, and I finally feel like she's realizing how uncomfortable she's making me. "No, but . . . but he loves you, and I promise I get where you're coming from. This might come as a surprise to you, but Evan has done many incredibly stupid and irresponsible things."

"It, uhhh, it doesn't, actually."

"Right, he's an idiot. I love him to death, but . . ." She shakes her head. "Evan specifically asked me not to come here when he told me what happened, but I couldn't help it. And I'm not telling you to be okay with what Gabe did or automatically forgive and forget. I'm asking you to not force him out entirely. Give him that little bit of peace of mind that he's being a good dad and taking care of what's his."

"Counterpoint: he's not a good dad, and I'm not his."

"But you miss him terribly."

I cross my arms over my chest and purse my lips. I don't appreciate getting read by someone who doesn't know me, because by her own admittance, she shunned me when I didn't deserve it.

"You're crazy about him. I can tell. I could that night at the fundraiser. I wasn't just protecting Gabe, I was trying to hurt you the way I told myself you hurt me. So I'm coming to you as a person who was awful to you and praying that you'll see it in your heart to forgive me enough to at least help my friend—" She sighs and shakes her head again. When she looks at me, her eyes are misty. "I just realized how terribly inappropriate it is of me to be here. I'm so sorry."

With that admission, it seems like she should quietly but rapidly leave. Instead, she takes up Rachel's rake and coaxes the receipt sludge into the bag. Deciding I don't have the mental fortitude for this, I kneel down next to Shelby and help her stack her little snowballs. She gives me a big, toothy grin and then erupts in giggles when I say, "Boop!" and poke the stack, letting it fall in her lap.

"Hey, where's your kid?" Keira asks from the trash can she's smooshing the leaf bag into.

"Oh, err, I'm currently pregnant. Like, I know you can't see it now because of the coat, but—"

She chuckles. "No, your older one. I won't lie, when I glued your locks, I made myself sick thinking your baby was going to be trapped inside if something happened. Which feels even cruddier—"

"Keira—"

"—that you could have also been trapped inside—"

"No but—"

"—if there was a fire or something. You could have—"

"Keira, I miscarried. I was attacked. The day the judge ruled I could keep the house."

Her words die off as horror takes over her face. She stands there for several seconds longer before she throws her arms around me.

I know I shouldn't be comforted by this. Hell, if she's the one who glued my locks — a stupid prank, but one that cost me money I didn't have — she might know who threw that rock. But there's no way her shock isn't real, that the heartache I feel as her arms tighten is fabricated. So I sink into her as a fresh wave of grief, dulled with the passing of time but never gone, washes over me.

"Please let me help you even if you won't let Gabe," Keira begs softly. "I've hurt you so much that even if you think you don't need help, I owe it to you."

I want to say no in the hopes that it'll make her feel as bad as she's made me feel, but that's not who I am. Not really. "I'd like that."

"The division championship is this weekend. There's a ticket for you."

"Thank you, but . . . but I can't. I do love him, but what he did? I can't just go and act like everything's okay. God, I either dress normal and everyone sees and wonders why, or I wear his jersey, and . . . no. I can't."

"I get it. I guess you're probably not a sports fan to begin with."

I manage to crack a smile at that. "Not really. And, um, if you're the one who's been knocking over my trashcans and everything else, just stop and we'll call it even."

"God no, I promise I *have* grown up in the last five years, even if I haven't acted like it. But I will clean your yard as much as you want me to."

Chapter Twenty-Nine
GABE

Fourth and long.

Forty-three seconds left on the clock.

We're down by five.

If we don't get a first down, game's over. The Chargers will get the ball and run out the clock. Not the most noble win, but this isn't the time for nobility. Whoever wins this will be one game away from the Super Bowl. There's no more room for error.

Blaise pats me as I lower myself down, letting my hand hover over the ball for another second. "You got this, buddy," he says, but I don't got this. This is part of his ritual, his need to settle his own nerves by playing like someone else is nervous, but it rubs me the wrong way.

I don't got any of this.

C. B. Alice

We're going to lose, management is going to see that I was the one who hiked the ball wrong when Blaise fumbles it or let through the guy who sacks him, and I'm not going to come back next year.

Everyone in Wilmington is going to know. No one will hire me. I'll get a really nice compensation package, but it's not living-off-of-it-the-rest-of-my-life money. I'm going to have to move. Joss won't move with me, so I won't get the chance to fix this shit between us. I'll end up being a child support dad. I'll never get to bond with my kid. I'll be that weird, sad guy who shows his friends pictures of his kid being raised by some other guy.

It's going to be Blaise. She likes Blaise.

My friends will recognize him because he's a superstar, and I'll just be a big loser.

I don't got any of this at any level.

Blaise straight-up slaps my ass and yells, "You got this, buddy!" so the entire line hears.

And responds with, "We got this!"

Vedder gives me a nod, telling me this isn't as self-serving of Blaise as usual. Everyone knows I'm nervous. Fuck me.

The guy standing nearly shoulder-to-shoulder across from me, Willis Brand, is a meat wall. He's grinning at me like he doesn't want to slip past me, he wants to slam me down and stomp on my spine. He's an unnerving guy, everyone says so, but I'm not usually unnerved. The problem is he knows what we're going to do. Everyone does. The penalty we got on the last play pushed us back another five yards, making a first down only possible with a long pass.

Merrick's fucked. I'm fucked. We're all fucked.

But miracles happen.

The clock is running out. We gotta go.

Good Guy Gabe

"Alex Trebek 47!" Blaise yells. "Alex Trebek 47!" It's gibberish, everyone already got the play from me, but it makes him happy.

I count down from two and hike the ball.

It all happens in slow-motion. It's like that sometimes. Not even necessarily big plays. Sometimes, it's just another day at the office, and other days, it's every speck, every minutia, decanted into single moments.

It's the rough leather gritting along my fingertips before propelling away into Blaise's hand.

It's the head rush that comes from righting myself to brace for collision. Everyone else is prepared when that ball is snapped, but my neck's a second's delay from getting a nasty bend, a ringing of the old bell.

It's my eyes filling with white streaked by yellow and blue lightning, the Charger's jersey.

It's the sudden dark of the collision.

It's pushing back at Brand, but the next collision is with his knees as I go down and he gets over me.

The ball launches over my head. There's a moment where I actually see it from the frame of my helmet.

It's wrong. I only get a glimpse, but it's wrong. I know where Merrick is supposed to be, and that not where that ball is going. Not even close.

There's cheering in the stadium, always cheering, but it's the Chargers fans who flew out to Wilmington to root their team on. They've won.

Our season is over.

I'm over.

Definitely did one or two more shots than I should have.

No more than five shots too many.

Jeff slams a can of coffee in my hand as he hoists himself back up into the work truck. When I start to open it, he takes it back and opens it himself, keeping the tab pulled forward so he can slide a slushie straw into the hole. Then he hands it back to me.

He kiddie-cupped my coffee. He fucking kiddie-cupped my coffee.

He pats my knee as I slurp it down. "Figure you've been throwing back so much alcohol lately you might need something to keep yourself from guzzling it like an idiot."

I glare at him as I suck on the straw, not that he can see. I've chosen mirrored sunglasses for today, in the style that hugs the face to keep the sun from getting in around the sides. It seems like it hasn't stopped snowing since I blew the game a week ago. I've been able to hide inside in a cocoon of blankets and alcohol, but I told Jeff I'd help him and his crew with the deck once the season was over.

Surprise, the season's over.

I've already had two coffees, and yeah, I did shotgun the second one in the parking lot of the hardware store, so Jeff's concern is valid. Everyone was cool with me in the hardware store, even signed a couple autographs, lots of comments about better luck next season, but I know.

No one from Jugs management has talked to me about it yet, but I know.

I'm done. Everyone knows.

We pull up to Joss's place as I'm flipping the straw around to stick the spoon side in my mouth so I can make obnoxious slurping sounds in Jeff's ear. He does contract stuff at the stadium, usually constructing platforms and sign posts, the extra stuff we need for special events and the VIP tailgate village. He gets passes to a lot of the events he crafts for, so I knew him well enough I was comfortable with him working around Joss's place when I couldn't be there.

But I prefer to be here, even if I am hungover.

His crew's already arrived. Just two other guys, Sam and Dennis. Sam's his dad, Dennis is his cousin. Wilmington's like that. They're sitting in a car, engine and heat on, holding their coffees close to their faces to warm up in the pre-dawn frost.

Nah, that's not for me.

I haul myself out of the truck, toss my can in Joss's recycle bin and straw in the trash, unsure of the type of plastic it is, and pull the flag off the pile of lumber at the back of the truck. It's a massive stack of 2x8s and 6x6s, and I go straight for the thick ones, hauling two up onto my shoulder.

"Well now, don't go hurting yourself," Jeff warns, attempting to take one back.

"I'm good." Technically, I feel like I'm going to barf, but I'm good with the weight. "Why don't you get started on digging those post holes? That's going to be a bitch."

It takes me an hour to unload the truck. Or, it takes me fifteen minutes to unload the truck and forty-five minutes to shovel and salt the path after I nearly bust ass with 250 pounds of lumber on my shoulder. The guys use a propane torch to thaw the earth as they go, so we're all working at about the same pace. By the time I've got all the lumber sandwiched between tarps and join them, I'm winded and working up a sweat, but I want more. Dennis swings a pickaxe to break through the spot he's working on. It's loud as fuck, giving me a damn headache, but I wanna do that.

I strip off my winter coat and shirt, sopping sweat off with it and tossing it onto the tarps. Jeff gives me a look like I've

C. B. Alice

lost my mind, and sure, it's below freezing, but I'm Minnesotan, born and raised. My skin may have thinned out some in the more moderate climate of Wilmington, but I'm basically a polar bear.

Dennis hands me the axe, and the rest of the crew steps back as I take a swing. And another. And another.

And another.

It feels good. Just beating the shit out of the earth for a minute while drifting snow steams off my skin feels good. When I start hitting frozen earth again, Sam brings the torch over, but he's been torching another spot. I don't need to stop swinging. So I don't.

I hit a rock on the next swing, one too large for the pickaxe to break through. It bounces off the impenetrable wall, reverberating through my arms and into my body. Usually, I would hate this sensation. I've done this sort of work for my dad enough times, and it always sets my teeth on edge. It does now, but it's also one of those sensations that at the right time can scratch an itch. A deep, metaphysical, cosmic itch.

My arms go limp at my sides, the pickaxe landing with a thud against my calf as my shoulders roll back and my head tips up. I groan at the sky, loving this second where every kink in my body, not just from last night's bender or my recent stress but the whole season I'm meant to be recovering from, melts away.

The sun feels good on my face.

And there on the second floor, her coffee in her hand and her forehead pressed against the window, her jaw lax and her eyelids heavy, Joss is watching me.

Chapter Thirty
JOSS

He saw me.

Oh no.

I didn't mean to linger at the window when I heard the crew. My plan had been to glare at them for starting so early and then either go back to bed or start my coffee once I decided if I was actually getting up or not. I wasn't going to say anything, and I wasn't even that mad. This is a smart renovation, and I'd rather it be done now when I haven't started work on the inside. Once they get it set up and put the new entrance in, it's going to change the whole flow of the apartment.

There's a box in the attic Gabe will need to get down for me. It's got outlet covers, furniture bumpers, cabinet locks. No point buying fresh when I've been saving them all these years for this moment.

C. B. Alice

That's what I'm thinking about when I get to the window and look down. I see Jeff and his crew down below, attempting to dig holes in the ground, and I do feel bad for them having to do this in January, but that's on Gabe.

Gabe appears while I'm still at the mercy of the coffee maker. I want to be pissed and go down there and yell at him for hauling lumber around when he's a goddamn football player and taunt him for the loss for good measure, but I can't. When I look at him, I tell myself to feel anger, but it's only ever grief. Longing. Heartache. This desperate, self-defeating need to yell at him but only so he can hold me because the freer the people in my life have gotten with hugs, the more it's sunk in that none of them feel as good as him.

And I hate him for that, but that's not what I feel when I look at him.

That's definitely not what I feel when he throws that pile of lumber down, chugs an entire bottle of water, and tugs his shirt off.

Dammit. God freaking dammit.

He's a floor below me, but he's larger than life. In the dead of winter, his skin holds enough of a tan still to be freckled, those little flecks sprinkled across his shoulder and chest, those biceps too big for me to get my hands around and that giant torso that looks like it would be soft until the light hits just right, revealing the grooves of dense muscle.

His hair is overgrown, his beard in need of tidying, but it makes him look like a feral mountain man standing in the snow naked from the waist up. And from the waist down, he's wearing the jeans that I secretly obsessed over even when we were together because his ass is so perfectly formed in them. Yeah, his workout stuff is hot. The sweatpants are hot, that stupid pink hoodie is hot for being an inch too short on him, but these jeans?

This has to be a pregnancy hot flash I'm feeling.

I peel myself away from the window, fix my coffee, and tell myself to go to another room where I can properly hate Gabe, but damn my eyes for drifting right back to him swinging that axe.

Holy hell, it's soft-core porn.

He's shiny with sweat, every inch of him flushed, and with each swing of the axe, he grunts loudly enough I can hear it. Memories flood my mind — and elsewhere — at the sound. It's the sound of getting absolutely wrecked on that mattress on my bedroom floor, of Gabe working out the week's frustration in the most brutal, carnal way, of the knowledge there's not a chance in hell I'll be walking right the next day.

His scent, his sounds, his breath. The way he'd look up at me from between my legs or the sudden jerk when he was behind me but needing me closer, so he'd grab me by the ponytail and haul me up to him. How his cock felt pulsing inside me.

This is bad.

There's only one thing I can do now. My rose and my rabbit have been working double-time lately, but at least they're on the charger.

I give myself a pep talk to back away. My pussy clenches and tells me if I stay here long enough, she'll figure the rest out, like I'm gonna grind one out on my kitchen counter.

The idea has some merit.

And then, horror of horrors, he looks up at me.

And drops his axe.

And grins wickedly at me.

Well, crud.

C. B. Alice

It's wild how quickly we're fighting. I tell him he's not welcome inside, he grumbles about my lack of security and how the whole world can get in here, I tell him it's none of his business, and then we're screaming at each other.

"Everything you do is my business!" he roars like some monster rising from the deep.

But I'm at the top of the stairs and he's several steps down, still a head below me. It's loud, but I stand my ground. "You don't own me, asshole!"

"No, but that baby is mine."

"Through no choice of mine! You ruined everything, not me."

"Yeah, I did, and that doesn't change the fact that I'm the only one trying to keep you and the baby safe!"

He's still below, staring up at me with pure, undiluted anger in his eyes. He looks like he could murder me right now. It doesn't make any sense that he would do that, he literally just said that he's trying to keep the baby and me safe, but this irrational fear takes hold of me.

Brian never hurt me, but he hurt so many other people. Other women. Teenage girls who were already helplessly underpowered against him before being sedated.

Gabe hurts people every day. He gets hurt, too — that hit he took in the final play of their loss against the Chargers was terrible, all the sports reporters said that — but he gets up and keeps going.

He could hurt me in a blink of an eye, and there's no way I could stop him.

God help me, I shove him back.

And thank god because he doesn't fall. I *know* I'm being crazy right now, but he would seriously hurt himself if he fell down those stairs.

He surges forward, lifting me by the waist and carrying me back, back, back, until I'm pushed up against one of the mirrors set up around Cora's hemming platform. I cry out at the cold, afraid it's going to shatter, but he lets me go, gripping the frame of the mirror in his hands to box me in.

I lean against the glass, but there's no escape. He looms over me, his nostrils flared and his breath hot against my face as his chest heaves.

"You're going to be the fucking death of me," he groans.

"I'm sorry," I whisper, choking on the adrenaline surging through me. "I shouldn't have pushed you."

"You can't move me." His voice is a growl, so much anger in it. "Don't you fucking get that? You . . . can't . . . move . . . me. So when it takes four numbers to get into your apartment, and those four digits are literally your birth year and day, you should be terrified that if someone even close to my size breaks in, *you can't move them.*"

"Why are you being so mean to me?" I cry out, closing my eyes and recoiling as best as I can, but there's nowhere to go.

"Because I'm hung over!" he yells as vehemently as everything else he says. But it's enough for him to drop slightly, to lean his head down to mine and take a breath. "And because everything is falling apart, and I get why you hate me, but I can't stop loving you or worrying about you or doing what I need to do, right? I can't leave you to clean up my mess on your own."

All that adrenaline coursing through me goes straight to my heart, squeezing tight. "Gabe—"

There's a loud thud next to my head, Gabe hitting the wall behind the mirror. The room is wood paneled, so he leaves nothing but a minor dent no one will ever notice except me.

"Not a mess to clean up," he corrects himself, his hand with its now bruised knuckles sliding over my stomach. "A baby to take care of. I know you hate me, Joss, I know you do. But this is my baby, and you can't take that away from me. I have so much love to give them. You can reject my love, but it's not fair for you to make that decision for them when you know, you know, how good a father I'm going to be. You know."

I swipe away the tear that's welling in my eye, that's always there, that will never stop falling and I'm so completely exhausted with the unending tears that I'm as frustrated with myself as I am with him. "You are. But how can I possibly trust you after what you did? You're not even willing to give me space, you're constantly coming over—"

"I was outside!" he bellows as he pushes himself back to give himself the space to wave his hands wildly without hitting me. "Fuck, I've been taking care of the goddamn walkways for you *and your customers* so you don't have to. This is the first time I've been inside, and I'm sorry, but you were the one glaring at me when the fucking ground is frozen and I'm just trying to bust the dirt up so the crew can get this deck going!"

"I mean, I wasn't glaring at you," I grumble.

"I saw you!"

"But it wasn't a glare. Or, it was a glare, but because . . ." I don't think I need to explain this, but Gabe is staring me down like he genuinely doesn't understand why I was watching him when he was literally out there swinging an axe without a shirt on. I huff in irritation for caving to this level of manipulation. "You know my hormones are all over the place."

Gabe blinks and rears back. He's all over the place right now, and he's still red, his skin still damp with sweat. I don't understand what's up with him. I know he's hurt, but this is ridiculous.

Until it clicks.

It's only been five months I've known him, a blink of an eye, truncated over and over again by the demands of his schedule that has him forever traveling and keeping weird hours.

But an eternity. And as much as I hate that I know this so well and that when I've caught it in the past, it's always been endearing enough that I feel the ghost of that warm fuzzy welling within me again, I know exactly what's happened.

The big dummy's had too much coffee this morning.

"Are you okay?" he asks, panicked. "Did the morning sickness come back? Is your blood pressure okay?"

"No, I'm fine, it's fine, it's—" I roll my eyes up to the ceiling and grudgingly admit, "I mean, yeah, you elevated my blood pressure, probably, but . . ."

He sinks, dejected, before he straightens up with a playful ma'am that's absolutely unfair to me.

Because I feel it settling between my legs.

I let out an exasperated sigh. "Don't get all ma'am with me like you don't know you're a thirst trap."

The idiot actually lights up like he didn't know this. "You think I'm a thirst trap?"

"You *are* a thirst trap. Look at you."

He looks down at himself like he genuinely didn't know this. "No one thinks I'm a thirst trap."

"What are you talking about? You have a whole goddamn thirst trap club, just like Blaise and Merrick!"

"The Angels? They're just making cookies for me because they're nice ladies."

"Are you absolutely insane? Are we actually talking about this right now? They make cookies because they think you're the marrying type, so they figure it's better to get your attention with baking than boobs. Do you really think Rachel went to the game in Minnesota because of the team? She went because of how great your ass looks in the white pants!"

Gabe is quiet for several seconds as he takes this in. He's quiet for long enough that I'm thinking he truly didn't know this before and I've opened his eyes to this whole new world.

Stupid me, because when I see that grin start to form and those eyes start to twinkle with joy, I get mad. Now he knows all those women are waiting for him to sweep them off their feet. "So, you can drag your lying ass over to their houses," I grumble, turning toward my bedroom to get dressed for the day. I'm out here arguing with Gabe in an oversized tee-shirt, for god's sake.

Gabe boxes me in with his arms again. "You miss me."

"Do not," I spit out, perhaps too quickly and vehemently to be believable.

"You miss my dick."

"Get over yourself."

He smirks and drops his eyes down, blatantly checking me out. "You've got all those pregnancy hormones begging for a good fuck."

I look him dead in the eye, fully aware that I am poking a bear when I say, "If I need to get laid, I'll get laid. Plenty of guys think I'm hot." The words taste like ash on my tongue. It's an empty threat.

And Gabe doesn't even have the courtesy to act threatened. "Yeah, everyone thinks you're hot. But they're not going to fuck you. They know you're mine. And you're not going to the bars or getting one of those hookup apps. You want my cock."

He pushes his body against mine, reminding me of exactly what I want. To prove his point.

I swallow a lump in my throat. "Stop."

He brings a hand to my shoulder, tracing the path where my throat just bobbed. "Saw that," he says more softly. Darkly.

My breath hitches.

His hand travels down to my chest. "Saw that, too."

I frown, irritated with my body for craving him despite what he's done to it. "I mean it, Gabe, stop."

"Ma'am." He slides that devilish hand of his down, down, down my thigh and up the hem of my shirt, pausing at my mound to clutch the curls there between his fingers and give them a slight tug.

I whimper. My brow creases as my toes curl. "Damn you."

He leans down enough that his lips graze my ear. "Yes, damn me for giving you what you need. You're so wet it's soaked into your bush. Is that from watching me or from fighting me?"

I turn away, refusing to answer that.

His laugh is husky. "Both, then."

His fingers winnow between my labia, teasing at my clit, making my knees wobbly. I grab for what I can to balance myself, but it's all Gabe. His arm and his pants. I tell myself not to grind against those fingers, but I can't help it any more than I can help the whimper of disappointment when he abandons my clit.

He skewers my pussy with a finger, and my body pulses around him.

"You need my cock here?"

I shake my head.

"Yes, you do."

"No," I whine, but my eyelids flutter back.

He adds another finger, forcing my stance wider as he pushes his knuckles between my thighs to dig deep. "No one needs to know. This can be our little secret."

My head rolls back on my neck as my pelvis rocks forward, forcing his fingers to rub inside me. "Damn you," I hiss, refusing to say I do need this. I don't need him, but I need this. I feel like I'm about to combust internally. "You son of a bitch."

"I won't tell a soul that you let me fuck you. You won't need to forgive me. You won't need to get over your mad. Let me fuck you, Joss."

I squeeze my eyes shut, not that it does anything to block out his voice or the complete nightmare of the logic.

"Tell me to stop now," Gabe says once he begins to move his fingers rhythmically inside me, once he knows he has me snared, "and I'll walk away."

I'm going to curse him to the end of the world and back, I know this and he knows this, because I'm digging my nails into him as my pussy clenches and my pelvis digs into his palm, and he knows I can't say anything now.

He unzips his jeans, hoists me up, plasters my back to the mirror, and slams his cock into me.

I cry out in pain — sweet, succinct pain — and my mind goes quiet, the concern for the mirror the only gray thought I have as he fucks me way too hard, possessing me in the most primal way, driving into me over and over again like I'm nothing but a toy for his pleasure. Every glorious thrust has me forgetting why this is bad, why he shouldn't be doing this, why I regret every time I believed his pretty words and ignored every single filthy truth he purred while filling me with his cum and stuffing it back in when it tried to escape.

"Harder," I whimper even though I really should be concerned about the mirror. "Fuck me harder."

"You need me to come inside you, don't you?" he growls.

"Please, Gabe. Oh god, I need it. I need you. I—" I tighten up, nearing the edge of detonation.

But then Gabe stops, groans low in his throat, and pumps twice more, giving me the dopiest grin.

"Did you just come?" I whisper, attempting to keep grinding on him, to get my fix, even though the snug hold he's suddenly got on me while he peels me off the mirror makes it all but impossible.

"Yup," he says, absolutely pleased with himself. "That's not how you're going to come today."

"What? But you—I—oh my god, you're such an—"

My curse is cut off unceremoniously when he dumps me on my ass on the platform and forces me to lie down.

"What are you doing?" I shriek, although my outrage is cut with far more excitement than it should be. Whatever he's planning, I want right now. I won't later, but it's hard to be against him manhandling me when he does it oh, so well.

"Getting what I want." He takes hold of my ankles in one hand and pushes them up, folding me in half, before jamming two fingers back into my swollen, desperate core and crooking his fingertips.

Oh no.

Oh no.

"Stop!" I beg as his stroking goes from nothing to way too hard immediately and my insides twist up. He knows this too well, knows how easily it is to take me over completely with a flick of his fingertips. He digs in hard enough I swear I can feel the rough grain of his fingerprints against my G-spot.

In another second, I'm thrashing and panting, bearing down like I could possibly reject him even though if he removed his fingers from me now, I'd kick him in the nose for rejecting me.

"That's it," he croons at the growing tension in my abdomen, the tremors consuming my whole body as he claims my pussy so roughly. "Give it to me, baby. Make a mess for me."

He flicks my clit at the right moment, the moment he's spent months honing in on, timing it like it's an exact science, and I explode. I hear my release splashing on the floor next to the pedestal as the electric current rushes through me. I want it to be a quick jolt that leaves my hair standing on end and my heart pounding; instead, I get a car battery clamped to my core, sending an unending surge into my pussy that can't be stopped.

I writhe beneath the hand he settles on my pelvis to keep me from thrashing too hard as I come with the rhythm of my heartbeat, leaving my ass and everything else soaked.

"Oh fuck," I gasp on my first caught breath and the heady feeling that follows, the blessed satisfaction that makes it all worth it even if I'm going to be pissed about this later.

Gabe looks smug as he eases my knees apart, exposing me in a way that seems so much bigger than a rough fuck against the mirror or the detachment of blocking the rest of my body with my legs. As though to prove the point, he pushes my shirt up to expose my nipples to the cool air. "There we go."

I sink down, feeling done in the most glorious way. I don't even think anything of it when Gabe crawls between my legs. We already fucked, we may as well cuddle at this point.

Except he's hard again, and he's stroking his cock against my slit.

I squirm against him.

He slides himself into me and holds himself there.

I squirm more as my muscles work along his length, needing less and more and none at all and everything all at once.

"Shhh," he whispers like I've said something, but I know he's speaking to my body.

"Gabe," I whimper as claustrophobia settles into my chest.

He lowers his lips to mine, a single, gentle kiss, nothing more than a damp press and a pause to feel each other. Even when I can't resist and my lips begin to move, he doesn't insist on more.

He moves over me, staring me hard in the eye as he forces my body to rock with his. I try to look away, not wanting any of this, and he won't let me. His hands go to either side of my head, leaving my eyelids as my only escape.

It's not enough.

I keep looking at him.

At my heart.

At the one person I was willing to share my life with again.

At the man I was so damn excited to make a family with that I thought there was no way I could be fooled again.

"Shhh," he says yet again, this time talking to my mind or the tears pooling or the whole cosmic disaster this is.

And again, it teases words from me. "Why couldn't you have been the one?"

"Why can't I still be?" he counters, but it's not a challenge.

It's a release.

He leans down and kisses my neck below my ear, trailing down to nibble my shoulder, releasing me from anything but the heady sensation of our bodies joining the way they join best, deep and hot and at all points.

We come together this time, and it's enough that if this had been a decade ago and I'd never been destroyed by Brian, my foolish heart would be ready to forgive Gabe.

Maybe he gets that. Maybe I do something that makes it clear even if I don't catch myself doing it. Or maybe Gabe's a bit salty still or making good on his promise. Whatever it is, Gabe stands up, stretches, fastens his pants, and says, "You can clean up your own mess this time," before heading back downstairs.

Chapter Thirty One
GABE

"You made it!" Evan yells as I walk up to his front door, saving me the embarrassment of not knowing if I should let myself in like I always used to or if I'm back to the knock stage. It's weird losing and regaining a friend. Sure, I've reconnected with people. High school buddies when I returned to Minnesota after college, teammates from Iowa who I met again in the pros. Hell, we even had one guy, Peltham, who was with us on the Colts, got traded to the Packers my second year, and ended up with the Jugs this year.

Evan's always been right here, a couple blocks down from the intersection I drive through every time I go to Camden Square. I was seeing him six days a week all season. So I don't know.

It feels like I just saw Shelby yesterday, but it's been half a year. Crazy how time flies.

Time wouldn't have flown for her. Six months is a blink of an eye when I've got about thirty more years behind me. For Shelby, I've missed out on half of her life.

But Evan opens that door for me, hugs me like he hasn't seen me in a decade, and says, "We're about to beat the crap out of each other in Mortal Kombat. You want in?"

It's an easy out. Just drop down on his sofa, take a controller, piss away the afternoon mashing buttons. Ease myself back in and slip away from my thoughts.

But I need to get stuff handled. And in the absence of handling the stuff I truly do need to handle — specifically, Joss and my career — I'm going to get this fixed.

I luck out that Dom and Lin are in the kitchen while Keira, Cadence, and Wren are elsewhere. Seeing the chicken nuggie, mac and cheese, and applesauce explosion Dom's handling while Lin's got baby Isaiah and a bottle in one hand, dumping a can of Coke into a pressure cooker with the other, I'm guessing the ladies are dealing with bath time. Dom's baby, Valeria, and Shelby are about the same age, both born last season, so they're food bombs.

I turn the oven on and toss my tater tot hot dish in to warm it up, scoop the baby and bottle out of Lin's arm, and hazard a glance into the cooker to see what sort of dessert Lin's cooking up.

Chicken wings.

Huh.

"It's Coca Cola wings," Lin says defensively even though I haven't said anything. "They're huge in China."

"I love Chinese food," I tell him.

"Yeah, but that's not real Chinese food. This is real Chinese food."

I have to hide my smirk and look him dead in the eye to keep from looking like I'm ridiculing the ancient Chinese secret of . . . Coke. Some of the Jugs can be dicks to Lin. And they will absolutely go for low-hanging fruit like Lin's rice-heavy diet.

Merrick eats at least a cup of rice a day, usually with dry chicken and a steamed vegetable. It doesn't make any sense to criticize Lin when his fried rice is life-changing. My friends are dicks.

"I like real Chinese food, too. Really, I just wanted this baby."

He is a fucking chunk of a baby, too. Fat rolls for days. Looks like he'd fight me if I took the bottle away, and he'd probably shriek loudly enough he'd win. I want to gobble him up.

That has Dom, Lin, and Evan exchanging nods like they're on to me. I roll my eyes. "Pfft, you knew this was happening. Don't act like you didn't. Come on, Isaiah, you're mine now." Before the guys have the chance to razz me, I steal Isaiah off down the hall, following the sounds of squealing toddlers.

As predicted, bath time is in full swing in Evan and Keira's master bath, where they've half-filled the garden tub and thrown a mountain of toys in for Shelby and Valeria to splash around in. I hesitate in the doorway, watching Keira, Cadence, and Wren as they crowd around the tub, entertaining the kids while they scrub them. Maybe I shouldn't have come down here. I don't want Shelby to not recognize me. If I went straight from the kitchen to Mortal Kombat, Shelby would have eventually figured out who I was in her own time. That sounds way better.

I'm seriously considering backing out and wandering through the quieter hallways, using Isaiah as an excuse, when Shelby suddenly sees me and lunges for the wall of the tub to climb out. "Un Kay Kay!" she shrieks. "Un Kay Kay!"

Keira doesn't bother to fight her. She dumps one last cup of water on Shelby's head to rinse out any lingering wash and scoops the wriggling toddler up into a big towel.

"Is she talking now? What's she saying?" I ask as Wren plucks Isaiah out of my arms and sets to work burping him.

I could have done that, but fine.

"She's not saying a lot yet, but she's already mastered no and dada," Keira says with a self-deprecating shrug.

Cadence scoffs while she works ketchup out of Valeria's white blonde hair. "She likes the tongue sounds better than the lip sounds. At least for now you can just chuck her at Evan."

Valeria, meanwhile, is emitting a steady stream of, "Mamamamamamamama."

It's so fucking cute. I bet Dom happily answers to that. Valeria's technically his step-daughter, but you'd never know it other than the fact that that she looks nothing like him or his other two kids.

"Well, now she's saying *Uncle Gabe* more than *mama*."

"That's what *Un Kay Kay* means?" I promised myself I wasn't going to cry, but jeez. I was bracing myself for rejection all day, not for getting a new awesome name.

"We've been trying for something closer to *Gabe* all day, but you take what you can get." Keira attempts to sit Shelby on the counter to brush her hair, but Shelby isn't having any of it and starts practicing that no that yeah, she's doing a really good job of.

I pick her up, and she throws her arms around my neck, no doubt trying to strangle me as well as any 16-month-old can. "I missed you, Shel-baby." I feel guilty about being gone the last few months, but I don't have any room to regret it. I can't regret anything I've done. The best I can do is make amends, and I do that by showing up.

"We missed you, too," Keira says, and I can tell she means the whole family. She lowers her voice. "I've apologized to Joss. And I meant it. It wasn't to fix you and me. It was to fix me and her. I . . . Gabe, I had no idea that she lost her baby, and I—"

"Are you talking about Aiden James? Because it doesn't matter whether she lost him or not. She was destroyed by what her husband did. She was destroyed by Wilmington. And you were a b—" I choose to cut myself off, same as I cut her off. I can't let myself get worked up. If Keira's making friends with Joss, I shouldn't get in the way of it. Not as long as Joss wants it.

My silence gives Keira the opportunity to say, "No, you're right. It doesn't matter. It was just what I needed for it to click that she was a victim, too, and I should have been supporting her. I really like her. You need to fix this."

"I am, but baby steps."

Except I'm not a baby stepper. I wear size 14 sneakers. I don't know how to do anything small. So once Shelby and I are settled on the sofa, I fire off a quick text to Joss.

GABE
keira said she talked to you. are you ok w that?

JOSS
Why are you asking?

> **GABE**
> just checking. don't want you uncomfortable if you don't want her around but you don't want to be rude to her

> **JOSS**
> I can tell her off myself if I want to. I'm a big girl.

And prickly, I see. I'm going to ask these questions and offer to fight these battles for her, but she is an adult. She's not afraid to go for what she wants. She's just creative about it.

There's a whole chain of texts here showing her creativity. Like the day she needed boxes brought down from the attic, but then she pulled my pants down when I reached up to the attic pull. Or the time I was tying up some cords in her studio and she bent over a table to get something, only to hike up her skirt and show off her lack of panties.

The biggest struggle is making sure I leave before she kicks me out. She's made it clear this is all she wants from me for now, and that hurts, but I think it would hurt worse if I gave her the opportunity to kick me out every time.

I'm starting to think she's copping extra attitude in her texts to prove something to herself. She knows I'm going to win, but she's refusing to lose gracefully.

> **JOSS**
> I'm out of milk. Are you coming by today at all?

I question how soon I can leave without offending everyone, but I'm not going to tell her that.

Good Guy Gabe

GABE
Sorry, i'm at evan and keira's today. you could come over though if you want

JOSS
I'm not hanging out with you.

GABE
ok

JOSS
can you bring me milk on the way home?

GABE
it's gonna be late. we're having a potluck. i brought tater tot hotdish. huang is pressure-cooking coca cola wings. you should come over.

JOSS
I SAID NO

JOSS
Just bring me milk on your way home

JOSS
And some of those wings

GABE
ok but will you actually drink the milk? we can fuck either way, but i don't want to go to the store if i don't have to.

JOSS
WE'RE NOT FUCKING I JUST NEED MILK OMG

GABE
::wink::

The one nice thing I can say about spending Super Bowl Sunday on the oversized lounger in the theater of the Jugs House is we never expected to make it to the Super Bowl anyway.

Sure, we thought a miracle was happening as the season went on and our record stayed strong, but it would have been a miracle. Just making the play-offs our second year was impressive. The only expansion team in modern history to have done any better was the Panthers, and only by a single game before losing the Division championship. It was almost a decade before they got to the playoffs again, so we have a lot of time to best them.

Some of the guys have picked sides. They're watching the game, arguing plays. The usual. Blaise is next to me, nearly upside-down on his lounger, with a plate of Super Bowl snacks — except it's literally just Vienna sausages for god knows what reason — on his stomach. One leg is kicked up over the back, the other over an armrest. I'm pretty sure his head started on the other armrest, but it's since rolled down to the seat and half off. He's combed his hair out but hasn't gotten it trimmed yet, and gravity is doing wild things with the shaggy afro. One arm is flopped over his head, his limbs so long his knuckles and phone graze the carpet.

He's got an earbud in. He's definitely watching anime.

So I don't feel guilty about the fact that I'm not even pretending to watch the game anymore. I threw a hundred bucks down on the betting pool. I made chili. My phone dinged to let me know Joss was streaming, and it's good for her algorithm if I watch, so I let it play while I watched the game.

But then there was a dull stretch and Joss was making this funny raccoon pattern, so I started reading the captions to hear which story she was telling about Jerry. I kicked out the footrest on my lounger and anchored my feet there so I could set the phone in my lap and bury myself under the big quilt she made me for Christmas. I think it's for my bed, but it's made its home in my chair.

It was fine, but then she said something about making a sandwich — a quilt sandwich, surely — and it hit me that she's said that to me recently. I scrolled through my texts, and there it was, three days ago.

JOSS

Come make me a sandwich

I have a lot of these texts now.

Every stupid text from her is a flash of what we've been doing. I don't need her to text me for me to think about her, but man, it helps.

I scroll through those messages, having stupid happy thoughts of all the times she's touched my dick recently even if I ran off immediately after so she couldn't kick me out. It's better than watching the game, but everyone's been on my case about not hanging out enough. Besides, I'm not the only one dicking around on my phone.

Which is why it's super irritating when I get beaned in the head. If I had doubts about who's throwing shit at me, it's clear enough when the slimy little not-hot dog lands in my lap.

"Bruh," Blaise says, more of an accented breath than an actual word. "Watch the game."

"You're not watching the game."

"New season of *Watashi no Chichi no Fakkusu-ki* just dropped," he says like that has any meaning to me. Nothing against anime, but he watches the weird stuff. I'm lucky he doesn't launch into an explanation of it.

I flick the sausage back his way before yawning and pulling my blanket up to my neck. My eyes glaze over the moment they hit Merrick's full-wall screen. "See, watching the game."

He eyes me up skeptically. "If you go vanish to your room to whack it, I'll tell everyone you got so hot and bothered seeing everyone else's ass in their uniforms that you couldn't keep your dick down."

I slowly pan my head his way. "What the hell sense does that make?"

He shrugs, but he's still mostly upside-down. It's hard to translate the gesture. "I gotta look at your fat ass all the time. You owe me this."

I lean over in my seat to get closer to him, lowering my voice to conspiratorial levels even though the game's so loud we've been talking normal volume and no one's heard us. "Do you struggle with keeping your dick down when you look at my ass?"

I get another Vienna sausage between the eyes. "Bruh, I'm a fucking pro."

"Pro at checking out my fat ass."

Blaise grins at that like he's actually achieved something, which makes it even stranger to me that the next thing he says is, "You need to get laid."

"I got laid yesterday."

"Yeah, but by a real girl."

"She was a real girl."

He rolls over, but he's still thrown all over the chair, so now he's contorted in a pretzel pose. One leg remains propped up on the back of his chair, but it's crooked at the knee, the foot dangling dangerously close to his head.

If he kicks himself in the head, I'm here for that.

"Yeah, but not to you. You're putting too much energy into Joss."

Crap. I did tell Joss I wasn't going to mention this to anyone, and Blaise is a blabbermouth. "No, what? I'm not fucking Joss."

"Yeah, you are. And you're being a simp about it. She's using you for that fat ass."

She does, in fact, like my ass. But that's not why she calls me over every day for sex. She said it herself: she can go get any guy. I'm not a simp. I'm rebuilding.

"You got something you wanna share with the class?" Merrick says from behind me. He puts his hand on my shoulder like he thinks I'm about to stand up and shouldn't. I wasn't going to stand up, but now I'm thinking I should.

"He's not going anywhere," Blaise says, which gets Merrick patting my shoulders casually. "She's streaming right now. Made a whole thing about it like she's saving women from Super Bowl Sunday. And before you get shitty, Gabe, I have the platinum subscription and I used my real name. I'm not stalking her."

That still sounds like stalking. And this is feeling weirdly like an intervention, especially when several others casually make their way toward the snack table, conveniently next to me.

These assholes are blocking me in.

I know a fucking play when I see one.

"Listen, dicks, Joss is having my baby, and I love her. We're going through a bad patch, but we're getting past it." Positive affirmations. I don't know how to fix this. I'm not sure if continuing to do the same thing will get me there, and I'm not sure what else there is. But I haven't given up yet. My NFL career may be over, but I'm not giving up on everything else. "And we're going to get married, so you better not say shitty things about her."

There's a lot of silent communicating happening around me. I've been the one silently communicating enough times to know that Blaise has no idea how to do this. I smirk shamelessly when everyone's eyes end up on Blaise, who's either flagging a plane or relaying signals from the baseball coach to the pitcher.

No one moves, but Blaise ultimately nods and says, "Yes, this halftime show does suck and I do think we should go toss a ball around. Great idea, guys."

The entire party, fourteen Jugs first-stringers, ends up on the front lawn. We tell ourselves this is going to be a gentle football game, hardly anything more than flag football, but come on. We only know one way to play this game.

The Super Bowl Halftime Show must be garbage because several of the neighbors watch from their porches. A couple wander toward us.

We don't have a balanced team. There are no running backs here, just Merrick. We have our punter, Donnie Thompson, who's brave enough to take over that role, and then we don't have any of the defensive back field, just the line, but that makes Merrick happy. "Thank fuck Allore's doing family shit with Morales," he jokes, although he's not laughing. He's not a laugher.

Allore is batshit on the field. He's a great safety for it, but the best thing about being on a team with Allore is he's not on the other team. I'm not sure he wouldn't accidentally wreck Merrick in the heat of the moment.

The game is simple: we see how long it takes to make a touchdown, the touchdown being the neighbor's driveway. We figure that'll be enough shenanigans to get through the halftime show, and it'll burn off steam. Thompson and the defense — heavy for the first play, not that anyone's counting — line up in the neighbor's yard, Kai holds the ball, and Thompson kicks the crap out of it, sending it all the way to our driveway, narrowly missing Bodley's Camaro.

"Shenanigans!" Blaise yells as he slides his ass right across the hood to retrieve the ball and make a run for it.

Chaos. Blaise doesn't run balls, and now I'm seeing that this was a strategic move by a coach of eons past who likely didn't recognize the value of his arm so much as the impossibility of his running. Instead of attempting to gain any yardage whatsoever, he darts in and out between the vehicles, leaving four of the D guys chasing after him as it turns into a game of protect-the-property-value. He gets blocked by Bodley and Thompson — the other Thompson, Rydell — on either side of Vedder's lifted truck, so he drops down and crawls under it, popping up on the other side. He sprints across the lawns, hitting the neighboring driveway and spiking the ball before breaking into the Chicken Dance.

"Can we fine him for that?" Donnie Thompson asks with a chuckle.

"For what? The idiot didn't score," I point out.

"Get your ass back here!" Merrick yells.

C. B. Alice

From across the lawn, Blaise shouts, "We're done! I won!"

"You literally had your entire body and the ball on the ground."

Even at this distance, I can see his grimace. "Right, yeah. I guess Vedder's truck's the line of scrimmage."

"No the fuck it isn't!" Vedder yells, and we settle for the mailbox a couple feet up from the driveway, just to give us a bit of space to work. The second play goes far more cleanly, with Merrick catching the ball and Rydell herding him into the street, out of bounds, about twenty yards down the lawn.

The next play, Blaise passes it off to Donnie, but Vedder accidentally hits him hard enough he fumbles the ball. It hits the grass, and instincts take over. Everyone scrambles for the ball, and Rydell ultimately comes out of the pile with it.

I pivot to chase after him. Again, instinct. We didn't think this game through clearly enough to know what will happen if he gets back to the driveway — or worse, if he doesn't, and then defense is playing offense and we end in some Stranger Things nonsense — but I give chase.

My entire body turns.

Except one foot, snagged on a sprinkler.

Right as Vedder plows into me, a totally friendly hit if my knee wasn't pivoted the wrong way.

I go down screaming.

Chapter Thirty-Two
JOSS

I always get nervous in hardware stores.

It's the way employees go out of their way to be helpful. Not that I don't appreciate it, but I'm always on edge when I'm out in public, and I swear the employees pop up everywhere. It's like they're all watching the aisles from security cameras, prowling for women who look lost to pounce on.

I'm not lost. Not any more lost than usual. The only difference is most times I'm wandering the aisles, I'm looking to jury-rig something. Expanding shelves or repairing tables, the unending fight between filming equipment and necessary quilting space. This time, I don't have anything I need to get done.

I stare at one of the display doors. It's pretty. A nice shade of light green with a big oval window, etched with a floral pattern. Jeff just kicked me out of the apartment so he could get to work taking out that section of wall in my kitchen, so I'm betting there's already a door for that spot, but I wonder if I could trade out the one at the bottom of the stairs with this. Or put this at the top of the stairs. I have no idea how doors are installed, but I bet Gabe could do this.

I just have to text him.

"Can I help you find something, ma'am?"

I nearly jump out of my skin, realizing my mistake of slowing down to consider this. It's not even a good option; the door is almost $2000 and I didn't bring dimensions with me.

I turn to shoo the employee off, but then I have a second thought. I'm expecting a geriatric or a pimply teen, what I'm used to at this particular store, but the man behind me isn't much older than me, with enough gray in his dark hair to be intriguing, an inviting twinkle in his brown eyes, and lines cut in his face from smiling.

What a smile, too. He's darker skinned, and his perfect white teeth glow.

Handsome. Aging well. In great shape, that's clear from his snug gray sweater and slacks. No rings on meaningful fingers, no apron. He doesn't work here, he was just offering to help because he's kind or I looked desperate.

Or he likes how I look.

"I'm . . . just browsing," I tell him, my voice uncertain. I don't mean it to be a test, but I can't deny that it isn't.

He lifts an eyebrow. "I could help you."

He is hitting on me.

I'm single.

I don't need Gabe to come over and . . . do some undefined task. I don't need Gabe at all. I'm just a hormone disaster, and any man can help with that. I'm not good at dating or casual stuff, but I bet if I showed this random guy who's at the hardware store at 11 a.m. on the Monday after Super Bowl even the slightest interest, it would be next to no effort to convince him to take me to lunch and then have sex with me.

He could be a nice guy. He could be my casual stuff guy. I don't need Gabe for that.

"If I'm not imposing," he adds with a far more obvious look at my ring fingers than the glance I stole at his.

This could be so easy. I should do it. Worst case scenario, I'm misreading the situation and I never have to see him again or he's a jerk but I get laid.

He's not super tall or super big. I'm not super tall or super big, either, so that seems well matched. I don't need super tall and super big. And he called me ma'am, so that's a perk.

Except it isn't. It didn't hit right. It didn't hit at all.

I rub my belly casually, like I'm not trying to draw his attention to the bump, and laugh politely, "Oh no, but thank you. I'm just figuring out some nonsense for my boyfriend to do because he's in the dog house right now."

I wink and continue down the aisle at a faster pace this time, making half a lap around the store before I cave and find a shelving unit that looks like a pain in the ass to put together. Visions of Gabe fighting it for a couple hours, working up a sweat and a mad before he burns off his frustration with some absolutely punishing sex that leaves me limping fills my head as I take a photo of the box once it's loaded into my car. While an employee ties my lift gate down and sticks a plastic red flag to the shelf, I send it and a text to Gabe.

JOSS

> You need to come put this together.

C. B. Alice

I don't know where it's going, but he wasn't on Jeff's crew this morning, so I figure I've got time to find a home for it.

GABE
i'll let jeff know.

JOSS
Let him know what?

GABE
that you need it put together. he can do it.

JOSS
So can you it's just a shelf

GABE
i can't come over today.

I flop down in the front seat, debating how willing I am to push it. I don't *need* sex. I'll be fine. I was fine for years. I've got this. I'm not going to be pathetic.

JOSS
Just come over tomorrow then

GABE
can't

GABE
jeff says come get him when you get home and he'll put it together for you.

My sinuses prickle. This is dumb. I'm not going to be a whiny baby about this. But I don't want Jeff to put it together.

> JOSS
> You can do it next time you're over it's not a big deal

> GABE
> idk when i'm going to be over next. just have jeff do it, ok?

My head fills with all these explanations for why Gabe isn't going to come over, from silly incon-sequential stuff, like a training camp or a quick trip, to him leaving Wilmington entirely.

Or staying right where he is but refusing to come to me.

Or like he's over me and moving on.

My stomach churns in a way that's absolutely not morning sickness, and the only thing I can do is tell myself this is good. Great. I don't need him anymore. I'm over him.

Really, I am.

"I wonder if it would be easier if we set this up on the longarm," I posit as casually as I can as Iris, Rose, and I wrangle the quilt back over the thickest cut of batting I sell. I'm about ready to suggest I do this entirely by myself because Iris and Rose are acting like they've never sandwiched a dang quilt before and this is taking about fifty times longer than it should. This is our fourth attempt at lining the backing up with the batting, each time dousing it in basting spray again. I'm starting to get concerned that it's going to gum up a needle. Basting spray isn't supposed to do that, but it's also not supposed to be layered half a dozen times.

"No, no, I want to be able to work on this at home," Rose insists. She smooths the tiniest bit of corner but doesn't hold the fabric as she does it, so she ends up making a wrinkle. "Oopsie."

I keep my feet planted so I don't stomp over to her side in a huff. It's not her fault I've been in a foul mood the last few days since Gabe's started dodging me. I swear everything he's done lately is calculated to mess me up as much as possible. "You have a longarm at home."

She stares blankly at me like she's completely forgotten the seven grand she wrangled out of her husband for the extravagant self-gifting two Christmases ago. Finally, with a blink, she says, "It's broken."

"Since when? Why didn't you tell me? You have a five-year warranty on it!" Now I'm irritated with myself for recommending the machine to her. Two of the longarms in the barn are the same model, and I've never had an issue with them. I sell them to everyone I can because I trust them so much. If they're breaking after two years, I need to know.

"Oh no, no, no," Iris blurts out over top of whatever Rose is about to say. "She dropped it."

"You *dropped* a longarm?" I repeat as Rose gives Iris a bug-eyed look. "I don't—how did—? I don't understand."

"I . . . was . . . cleaning." Rose glowers at Iris. "I tried . . . picking it up, and . . . oopsie?"

That's clearly a lie. Not that Rose isn't an obsessive cleaner to the point where I've had to lecture her about what should and shouldn't be used on sewing machines and how she doesn't need Carl to take them apart for her after every single project so she can remove every speck of lint out of them — I go into the chassis of my longarm once a season at most, and this is literally what I do for a living — but she's a terrible liar.

I just can't for the life of me figure out why she'd lie now. I drop my side of the backing, wanting to be dramatic but still laying it down as gently as possible so it doesn't actually adhere and create more problems. Then I anchor my fists at my waist, thankful it still exists because the baby bloat is not easing up and I'm growing more concerned daily that the obstetrician is lying to me and I'm going to birth an actual monster baby. "Okay, you two. Fess up. I know for a fact you did not pick up your longarm and drop it."

Rose looks relieved at this. Probably because I know these two well enough to know they would have actually dropped it, repeatedly if necessary, just to make the lie work.

"So there's no reason on Earth that we've spent the last—" I glance up to the clock— "hour now sandwiching this and not made any progress on it unless you two were up to something. What is going on—*oh god.*"

"Are you okay?" Rose asks, startled, as Iris rushes to my side.

I shrug her off. "It's Valentine's Day! And you two are thick as thieves with Gabe. Is he plotting some ridic-ulous thing? Because I don't care if it's Valentine's Day—"

I silence myself when the initial sheepish looks they get sink into pity. I bet they think Gabe has forgotten what day it is and I'm imagining a surprise plot. I haven't told them we've broken up.

For a second there, this whole fantasy flashed through my mind that the reason he's now blown me off several days in a row — because apparently I didn't learn my lesson at the hardware store — is he's planning something big for today. It makes so much sense. He's such a manipulative jerk that of course he'd pull some gaslighting nonsense like this.

I hate him so much.

But I want chocolates and flowers and a giant fancy dinner. I want him to beg me to take him back. I need it.

"He's not plotting anything, is he?" I ask, madder that he isn't than when I thought he was. Completely ridiculous.

Iris takes my hand and gives it a squeeze. "Honey, we know."

At my peevish look, Rose clarifies. "That you and Gabe broke up. Rachel told us."

"How does Rachel know?"

"She overheard you talking to that nice cheerleader lady."

Keira. She's stopped by a few times recently, checking in and offering me hand-me-down baby stuff, inviting me out for lunches with Cadence and Wren, but I haven't been brave enough to accept the invitations yet. I'm warming up to Keira, I truly am, but I don't know if it's smart getting close to her when I don't want to reconcile with Gabe.

But every one of her invites is more inviting than the last.

She's been around a lot lately, but it must have been that first time Keira was here that Rachel overheard her. I haven't seen Rachel much this past month, so I doubt her and Keira's paths have crossed since then.

Everyone's known for a month now that I ended things with Gabe. Everyone's also seen how many times I've casually excused myself to get 'something' from my apartment and Gabe's followed after me. Lord, give me strength.

"And between you and us," Iris continues, "you've been a bit crabby this week—"

"I have not!"

Both ladies smirk, identical enough I'd think they were twins if not for the fact that visibly, they couldn't be any more different than Jack Sprat and his wife.

"Okay fine, I've been crabby this week. I'm sure it's second trimester hormones." With a sigh, I take over the sandwiching, getting the backing on in a couple minutes. "You guys don't need to be here if you don't want to be. I'm fine, I promise."

"We do want to be here," Iris assures me.

"It's Valentine's," I laugh. "Go be with your husbands!"

Rose snorts. "They're at the grocery store fighting off all the other husbands for the last Russel Stover's heart. We need to give them at least a couple hours to figure their messes out."

The door chimes to let us know someone's walking in, and I look up, expecting a customer or Barb. "What are you doing here?" I ask, surprised to see Blaise.

And also just how giant his afro is.

"He's even cuter with off-season hair," Iris says like they were fully aware that Blaise untwists his hair when the season ends. It's one of those reminders that Gabe may be an entire chapter of my life, but it's a short one. I have no idea what off-season is like.

I don't even know if Gabe is going to be playing for the Jugs next year if it all. Part of me has quietly hoped that he's getting transferred to another team. He'd be hundreds of miles away, I'd be here. Problem solved.

"It's Gabe!" Blaise blurts out, his voice winded like he's sprinted the three miles here from the Jugs House. "He's been injured."

The words I feared all season. Every single game, every time he lay on the field a second longer than he needed to, every time he was wobbly standing up. But the season is over. It doesn't make sense.

Except I don't know what off-season is like. He talked about having more time and that it was a good thing that my due date is in the summer because he'll have a couple months to bond and care for the baby before things get crazy again. That doesn't mean the off-season isn't rough, though.

"How bad is it?" I ask, fighting the urge to vomit.

Blaise's eyes are watery, his bottom lip quivering. "It's bad. It's really bad. He's asking for you."

"Oh god," I whisper, unable to say anything else. My knees buckle, and poor Rose and Iris have to keep me upright until Blaise makes it to my side to take my weight off their hands. "What hospital is he at?"

Blaise shakes his head. "He's at home . . . if you want to see him. You don't—"

"Of course I do!"

We leave behind Rose and Iris, who are wringing their hands.

Chapter Thirty-Three
GABE

No fucking clue where Blaise ran off to. Literally ran off down the street like a psycho. There's a Jugs social thing this afternoon that Blaise bailed on to hang out with my crippled ass, and then he just ran off. And I'm losing my mind.

With boredom.

I adjust myself in bed, grunting when my knee bends the slightest amount and pain shimmers through me, pushing the outer bounds of my pain killers. Blaise was lying next to me like we were having a damn slumber party, watching one of his weirdo animes with subtitles. Focusing on them is giving me a headache. So I spend at least three minutes feeling around for the remote where Blaise was sitting before realizing that it's on the opposite nightstand.

Joss's nightstand.

C. B. Alice

Valentine's Day sucks when there's an actual person to spend it with but they're across town and there's no way they're going to come over here.

I seriously consider making the trek across the bed, but laziness and malaise win out. I fish around my nightstand to get my glasses and start reading the screen.

It still hurts my brain. Not the reading, but what they're actually saying. There are two characters on screen, except one is some sort of clunky office equipment, I'm thinking a printer, and I'm not sure if it's sentient or if the other character, a supposedly teenaged boy, is psychotic and hallucinating the printer's side of the conversation. And I say *supposedly* because he may look young, but he's definitely a villain who's already murdered a bunch of people and is discussing with the printer who he should murder next.

Or possibly not discussing because, again, it's a printer.

Also, and this might be something that would make more sense if I hadn't been tossed into the middle of this insanity, they appear to be in a fantasy setting. Like, they're in an old castle and the boy has a sword and a cape and a magical amulet.

The stupidity sucks me right in, just trying to figure out what the hell is happening, and it's two episodes later that I hear someone running down the hall. Not unusual in this house, but the guys all left together and I don't hear the usual commotion of everyone walking in at the same time. Not Blaise, either. He'd be going way faster. His perma-zoomies.

It sounds more like Merrick jogging at a pace that could pass for normal human speeds, except the shoes sound all wrong. Light footfalls, but striking the ground sharply like the soles aren't as flexible as his sneakers.

This is what my brain's turned into in the last five days. In-depth analysis of footfalls.

"Gabe?" Joss yells in a panicked voice.

Oh fuck.

I haven't even had the chance to get my legs off the side of the bed before Joss rushes through the doorway, her face red and tear-streaked. "Oh my god, what happened?" she sobs.

I'm so thrown by her clear distress that I get myself even more tangled with the stack of pillows and blankets that have been crafted to prop my leg and back up in the absence of one of those fancy beds that do it automatically. Joss bodily throws herself over my torso with a shriek to stop me.

I gently ease her up with a hand against her collarbone. "Gentle!" I warn, careful not to state my concern over the baby, having learned that lesson the hard way. "It's my MCL. It's fine."

She's still crying, though, and if tearing an MCL is what it takes to get her to throw her arms around my shoulders to hug me as fiercely as her scrawny little arms can hug, I'm happy. "What's an MCL?"

"A knee ligament. There's a bunch of them. ACL, LCL, PCL, you know, just knee stuff."

She's still crying as she lifts her head back up. "Are you ever going to walk again?"

"What?" I snort and then do my best to reign my laughter in. "Ma'am, I can walk now. The team doc wants me to use a crutch for the next couple of days, and I'm kinda stuck here because the guys hauled me up the stairs when we got back instead of setting me up on a sofa, but I'm fine. Ligament tears happen. It's really not a big deal. I mean, it *can* be career ending, but it's usually a couple weeks of recovering. I'm—

hey, hey, hey," I say quickly when her bottom lip starts to tremble again. "I'm fine, I swear!"

She smacks my chest, but I'm pretty sure it's more of an irritated swat than anything meant to harm. "You scared the crap out of me!"

"How?"

She climbs off me but stays on the bed, sitting crisscross next to me with her arms over her chest and the sweetest pout on her lips, her cheeks bright red and her blond hair falling out of the clip it was pulled back in. "Why didn't you tell me?"

"Because it's nothing to worry about. They put me in PT to make sure it heals right, but I'm mostly just going to be in a brace for a few weeks."

She chews on her bottom lip. I can see she's still working on her mad, but she's sitting here next to me, close enough that if I shimmy my good leg over a couple inches, I'll feel the warmth of her knee. "So you've been lying to me all week? Every time I texted you and—"

"No! Fuck. No." That's the last thing I need, her thinking I'm lying about more stuff. "No, I promise. It was dumb and not a big deal, and honestly, I was embarrassed." I give her my most sheepish cringe and admit, "We were dicking around on Super Bowl Sunday, and I tripped over my own foot in the front lawn."

"You—!" Joss's face scrunches up. Her hands ball into fists. Her nostrils flaring like a petite, adorable, raging bull. "You tripped over your own feet and tore your-your-your whatever ligament? Why do you drive me to violence? Never in my life have I ever wanted to hit another human being except you, and now here I am ready to punch you because you're so stupid! Why am I like this with you?"

I take a gamble. It's a big one, but it's the moment for it. Besides, since it's the off-season and I have a good track record of not misbehaving while injured, they gave me opioids for the pain. I'm feeling pretty lucky right now. I take one of those fists and bring it to my mouth, kissing the knuckles knowing that there's an outside chance I'm about to lose a tooth on them. "Because you love me?"

She snatches her hand away only after I say that, and I consider it progress. "It doesn't matter. I can't just forgive you, Gabe!"

"I fell in love with you that first moment I saw you in your studio, and not a single thing you've ever done has made me doubt that. But you're so nice and smart and talented and beautiful that I thought once you met the rest of the team, you'd realize you were too good for me, so I did what I had to—"

I saw her softening up slightly somewhere in the middle, but she smacks me again at that. "Why do you always say stuff like that?"

"Because I mean it. You're incredible."

"Not that!" she huffs. "What do your teammates have to do with anything? What have I ever done to make you think I'm with you because you're a football player?

"Because what else am I?" I sigh at the weight of my own words. "It's the only thing that ever mattered to me. I threw away years working bullshit jobs instead of building a career because I didn't want work to get in the way. But then my dream came true, and I had a couple good years, but now it's over, and what am I?"

"You got cut?"

I shake my head. "Not officially, but no contract. Someone else might pick me up, but then I'd have to leave Wilmington and . . ." I shrug.

Joss thinks on that for a long time. She gets distracted momentarily by a thread on the quilt beneath her. I think having a place for her eyes to go is enough to get her to say, "Well, you're definitely going to be a dad soon. And that's something, right?"

"That's a lot. That's huge. I don't want to lose a second of it that I don't have to."

She swallows. "That's not fair."

I rest back but grab her thigh, taking what I want, tired of this notion of fair. "I'm not going to say I'm sorry, because I'm not. I was sick with stress when I found out about your Aiden James and realized another pregnancy could be traumatic for you, but it isn't, not for you, so I'm not sorry. Maybe that's not right, but I don't care."

"You rewrote my life without my permission!"

I look her dead in the eye, claiming every ounce of her anger. "You keep saying you can't forgive me, but what you're doing, your actions? That's not what they're saying. I mean, you were having a whole meltdown because you thought I was hurt, and I'm pretty sure you're mad I blew off a couple booty calls."

Joss groans and pitches forward, faceplanting on the pillows next to me. "My body is dumb and makes bad decisions."

"Then make a bad decision! You're fucking right, I rewrote your life without your permission, but did I not give you exactly what you wanted, when you wanted it?"

She doesn't answer.

"Your Christmas and Valentine's Day presents are right there in the closet. Why don't you see what else I'm giving you?"

She drags her ass off the bed dramatically and pulls the first package out of the closet. It's wrapped all proper-like with a bow and everything, but the moment she picks up the giant gift, she says, "This is a bolt of fabric."

"Yeah, obviously."

She wants to tell me to piss off and die, I can see it clear as day. "I own every bolt of fabric on the planet," she mutters as she tears through the paper. "Why would you think I need m—*oh my god,*" she gasps as she reveals the pattern of dense, intricately arranged orchids. "I've never seen this before. Where did you come across—?" She looks more closely at it and struggles so hard to stay irritated and not laugh that she nearly spits on it.

"Saw the chicken wings, did you? I commissioned it. Charged me a small fortune, but it was worth it. Now go on, your other present is behind it."

I see the dampness in Joss's eyes, the tremble as her emotions get jumbled. "This isn't—"

"Fair. You keep saying that. Ma'am, the decisions I made for you, I didn't make them because I thought you didn't want them, I made them because I knew you did. Yeah, it was shitty of me to push my issues on you. I'm a coward, okay? I wasn't even brave enough to fucking ask if I've got a spot on the team next year because I didn't think I could handle being told I don't. I promise I'm going to try to do better, but there it is. Open the other present."

Joss swallows a lump in her throat before tearing the paper off the quartet of fabric that matches the first bolt. "Is this for the baby?"

She's smiling, but now I'm grouchy. At myself, but it doesn't matter. "Got charged a much larger fortune for raccoon themed baby prints."

She traces the happy face of the gray and black bandit. "Crud," she grumbles. "How am I supposed to not forgive you after this?"

"I'm pretty sure you're supposed to forgive me after this." I pat the bed next to me casually, but my heart is pounding with the need for her to just be here, right here. Holding me. "Come give me a Valentine's Day kiss, and I'll order us some Valentine's Chinese."

She's not sold, not entirely. But she curls up in bed next to me and says, "Those glasses make you look smarter than you are."

I don't know why I ever worried about another guy stealing her from me.

Chapter Thirty-Four
JOSS

One time early in our relationship, Brian forced me to end my friendship with a college friend. He told me he'd overheard Josh saying inappropriate things about me. Brian was also a lot older than me or any boyfriend I'd had before him and insisted we do things in the bedroom that made me uncomfortable. He said it wasn't because I didn't like them, I was just inexperienced. I needed to grow up.

When I did inventory of the medication in his practice, the numbers were always off, but he had a reason every time.

Brian always blamed the patients when I asked about whether they needed sedation because the insurance companies were forever denying claims. He said teenage girls were babies who couldn't handle a little pain.

I'm cautious with Gabe, but I'm not sure it's a bad thing. I fully trusted Brian and spent many years blaming myself for not recognizing all those little incidents for what they were, but I was young and naive. I am now less young and less naive.

Every time Gabe takes my hand, I feel this peace settle over me like I made the right decision. I think we're going to make it.

Gabe squeezes my hand to get my attention. "What's got your eye there?"

I look from the wall of fabric in front of me and the swatches of the baby fabric. He's been glued to my side all afternoon. At lunch, he even insisted on sitting next to me at a booth that was absolutely not big enough to sit three people on one side. And no, I'm not claiming the baby took up an entire seat; Gabe takes up two. It was sweet, though. If I tried to pull away from him, I have no doubt he'd say that in his walking brace, he needs to lean on me for support.

I have a feeling he's going to be running that line through March.

I slide the swatches over the line of fabrics the designer matched the custom prints to so it'd be easier for me to pair everything up. I keep pushing my hand to the yellows and greens; my hand keeps springing back to the pinks and purples. I know I'm blushing because we've spent the last week committing to gender-neutral colors when I say, "I know what we agreed on, but don't these prints match so much better to the pinks?"

Gabe chuckles and leans down to kiss the top of my head. "You can say it. Now that you know we're having a girl, you want to do girl stuff."

"I'm not this shallow!"

"Well then, I'm that shallow. I found out two hours ago that I'm going to have a girl, and I'm so dang shallow that I demand all the pink. Every pink. Pink everywhere." He reaches behind himself, taps the shoulder of the lady shopping the notions rack, and says, "We're having a girl. Just found out. We were going to do the gender-neutral stuff, but now that I know it's a girl, I want girl colors. Which pink should we go with?"

The poor lady, whom I don't recognize, so she's either a quilt tourist or a new customer who's probably never coming back, looks at the fabrics I'm debating between. "Oh, that print is absolutely precious with those little raccoons! I've never seen it before. Is it sold here, too?"

"I had it custom made," Gabe boasts. "Got sixty yards of it."

The lady recoils at that. A valid response. It's an unholy amount of fabric for most. Not that most quilters I know aren't sitting on that much fabric, but you don't just say something like that.

"Oh, hi, he means he bought me a bolt of each. And . . . I own the shop, so it's not actually crazy."

"That makes sense." The lady nods and points to a blender pink with tiny swirls and hearts on it. "That matches really nicely, I think. Your shop's amazing, by the way. I just moved here from Salem. I wasn't expecting anything like this when I was told the best shop in Wilmington is all the way up in Camden."

I blush and sink into Gabe at the praise. I know people recommend my shop, but I don't hear it that much, and the recent string of vandalism had me worried people were getting run off again. But there hasn't been an incident in a month and a half, since that day Keira came by, so maybe things are getting better.

Am I suspicious that Keira really was behind all the incidents? Yes. But as long as they're not happening anymore, I truly don't care.

"She's got the seventh-biggest online quilt shop in the U.S.," Gabe boasts, having heard that a dozen times by now probably.

"Oh, that's wonderful! Well done." She looks ready to step out of the conversation, but then she eyes us up more scrupulously, her gaze bouncing between us. "You two look familiar."

"She's famous," Gabe tells her.

"So are you," I remind him.

"Yeah, but you're quilt famous. This is Joss Page right here."

"Oh lord, I do know you," the lady laughs. "I've got a couple of your FPP patterns. Do you teach at all?"

"She teaches so much!" Gabe says loudly enough that everyone in the shop looks at us.

From the back hallway, one of the storage rooms we let our regular customers into for stuff like batting remnants and leftover packaging, Rachel pops her head out. "Gabe?" she says, surprised.

"You're one of the Juggernauts," the newcomer says as I hold up mine and Gabe's hands to Rachel. I'm not angry with her about blabbing to the rest of the quilters about how Gabe and I had broken up, not angrier than I have a right to be because I get that it was hot gossip and we are public figures. Still, I want to make it clear right now that Gabe and I are together, working things out, and it's not anyone's business what's happened behind the scenes.

I swear I see Rachel scowl like she's upset about this, but then she lights up and shoots us a big thumbs-up.

Gabe grunts. "I know this is going to be a weird thing to say, but I don't think Rachel's going to be making me cookies anymore."

"Nobody's making you cookies anymore."

"Because I'm not on the team next year?"

I slug his arm. We don't need negativity today. "Because you're mine. So I'm the only one who should be making you cookies, and I don't know if you deserve my cookies."

He spins me to face him in a quick, weightless swirl, his giant hands taking mine and pulling them behind my back so I have nowhere to go except against him. Right where I want to be. "Ahh, and that's just about the kindest thing you could have ever said to me because I have it on good authority that you haven't yet met a cookie dough that you didn't burn to a cinder in the oven."

"That's me!" Barb pipes up from behind the cutting counter. "I warned him!"

Grinning, Gabe tugs down on my hands, forcing me to bend back and tilt my head up for a kiss that's highly inappropriate in front of my customers and employees. And once I'm breathless, he whispers in my ear, "I have a secret for you. I make the best snickerdoodles you've ever had."

"Why don't we test out that ramp, see if we can get you up to my place so I can try some of your snicker-doodles?"

Whether he takes that to mean rummage through my cupboards for the ancient bag of flour to bake cookies or just experiment with sex positions that don't mess with his knees, I'm good.

Chapter Thirty Five
GABE

"That is looking incredible, Shaunessy. I wish Sinclair was as easy a patient as you."

It's because Blaise lacks patience, but I'm not about to have that conversation with Doc Keltner. Instead, I'm going to be really happy with the fact that we're only a week into March and my MCL is already getting an 'incredible.'

"Seriously, I wish this was the injuries we were getting during the season," he continues as he takes hold of both sides of my leg and flexes it. It's stiff, but that's from the brace. The only reason I haven't been taking the stairs at Joss's place is she gives me that look. She's personally taken it upon herself to decide when to clear me for construction, too, so it's been a lazy few weeks. "Out one game? Medical advisement the second, good to go by the third? Can't ask for better. I do want you to go easy on the running, stick to the elliptical for your cardio to help on the impact, but once practice starts up again? You're clear to go."

Clear to go. Doc Keltner doesn't know anything about what's going on upstairs, he just knows that I needed my knee fixed and my badge is getting me into the clinic to get it worked on. When I went down on Super Bowl Sunday, we called Coach Keenan, who made Bodley hand the phone to each of us so we could all get yelled at before he ordered Vedder to throw my ass in the back of his SUV and drive me down to the facility. His professional assessment was that because I was talking on the phone, I didn't need an ambulance, just a ride. Doc Keltner's been treating me ever since.

If this is my last hurrah here, I guess it's a good one.

I'm in the middle of some PT, on that elliptical that I've graduated to from the aquarobics the guys have been razzing me for, when Maurice Bradley, the GM, pops in and heads right to me. "You got a minute to talk, son?" he says, and my soul withers.

This is it. Every time I come here, I feel this dread. I can understand waiting until the end of the season before telling me I'm not coming back so I didn't pull any nonsense on the field, but I figured it would have happened right after the end, not almost two months later.

I want to tell him no, just so I can cling to this stupid elliptical another couple minutes, pretend that I'm still a pro football player and I don't have to figure out what's next yet, just play ball and be a dad and make Joss happy. But Doc Keltner claps my shoulder and says, "He's all yours. That MCL of his healed like a champ."

"That's great," Bradley says without inflection.

Good Guy Gabe

I trudge behind him to the elevator up to the corporate offices in silence. In the elevator, he says, "Heard a rumor about you."

I swallow to make sure my voice doesn't sound all sad and mopey. "What rumor?"

"Heard that gal of yours is expecting."

"She is, yeah. We're having a girl. Due at the end of June."

He raises an eyebrow like he heard the panic in my voice that time, but he must misunderstand it because he laughs and gives my shoulder one of those fatherly squeezes old coaches give you when you slip up and admit you have a personal life you're actually concerned about. "The first is always terrifying, son. But I can tell you're going to love that little girl."

"Yes sir. She and her mom are my world."

"That's great. Glad you're settling in to Wilmington."

Probably because it's easier for former players to move on after they're let loose if they still have some connection.

I'm despondent by the time we reach his office. He gestures to a chair for me to sit in, and it looks flimsy as fuck, but I'm surely not the only linebacker to have sat here. I ease myself down, cringing at the creaking but feeling solid once I'm settled. I'd hate if my final act as a Jug was landing my ass on the floor.

Bradley pulls an old-school manila folder out of a drawer and pitches it across the desk along with the pen. "Alright, now. You've had your fun. Stop dicking around and sign this before Accounting rips me a new asshole."

I don't have anything to say. I'm guessing this must be my severance package, but that's a set number. It's not like Accounting doesn't know exactly what it'll be. I go ahead and open the folder, wondering if there's stuff I don't know about leaving the NFL.

There's a new contract inside.

I look up at Bradley and frown. I should be happy — I will be happy in another couple seconds, I'm sure of it — but for now, I'm holding back the need to freak out over the stress he's put me under.

I'm staying another . . . however long. I didn't actually look. I glance back down, the words blurring together, but I finally locate a 3 (THREE). Three more years. This is it.

Bradley groans. "Please tell me you're not retiring and have just been dodging my messages!"

"Your . . . messages?"

"I've been texting and emailing you about this for five months, since we got this hammered out with your agent!"

"I—what? I haven't received a single message. I thought you were letting me go, Maurice! What the hell?"

We stare at each other. I probably shouldn't have said it that way, but Bradley's used to hotheads. He keeps his cool as he finger-pecks his way through his computer and then turns the monitor to face me. "Look, we've been reaching out to you since November."

I do see a string of messages, both texts and emails, sent weekly. Marked as opened by receiver but no responses. I definitely haven't opened them. I look more closely and see that although this is a tab with my personal information, only my home address is correct. I don't recognize the email address, and the phone number isn't even my area code. "This info is wrong!"

Bradley takes a look at it, then shrugs. "It's what your agent gave us," he says defensively.

Good Guy Gabe

I glower at him as I whip out my phone and dial the number on the screen. Caller ID gives me the name, but I go ahead and hit CALL and turn the ringer on.

"'Sup, broseph," Vedder says on the other end, and Bradley grimaces.

"Hey man, have you been receiving a bunch of texts and emails about me needing to go get my contract straightened out with Bradley?"

"Yeah, bro. You get that done?"

"We don't even have the same agent," I inform Bradley as I hang up on Vedder.

I look back down at the contract. It's a mountain of pages with little flags all over the place, a million things for me to sign my life away on in the National Football League's behalf. There's a page about money, and numbers are thrown all over the place, the magic of that Accounting department working to pay us our market value while circumventing the NFL's salary caps. I scan through it, but math's not my strong suit. I find the box that matters, the bottom line, and my jaw drops.

"You're giving me another nine million over three years?"

Maurice Bradley snatches the document back, fishes out a decaying bottle of liquid paper, and dabs it on a couple numbers. He writes over them and passes it back. "Ten million. Sorry about whatever that was. And Gabe? Please tell me you're not retiring."

"Nope, definitely not."

We both let out huge sighs of relief, and then Bradley says, "Why the hell didn't you ask someone about your contract?"

I cringe and look away sheepishly.

"Fucking millennials. Go see the team therapist and explain it to her."

"Yes, sir."

I groan as Joss straddles me and takes hold of my cock. "Why do I get the feeling that you're trying to keep me here all day?"

Not that I'm complaining, but she's got a list of stuff she insists has to be done today, and instead, it's nearing noon and we haven't even gotten out of bed yet.

"I think we should test the frame while it's under warranty, Mr. Starting Center For Three More Years," she says, as though it's the most reasonable thing ever. As soon as I told her what my next bonus will be, she took me bed shopping so we could finally get her mattress off the floor.

It's a fresh start for us both. Out with my bachelor furniture and the emergency stuff she got when she had to sell everything. Out with Cora's dressing studio — which is getting moved to the barn, where I'm betting the quilting crew will love it anyway, since some of them do dressmaking on the side — and a complete makeover of the nursery. When the new furniture arrived yesterday, the first thing we did was move the urn to a special cabinet we ordered specifically for it. There's a spot for the baby blanket she made beneath the urn, and I'm having a plaque engraved. We're moving on, but there will always be room in our home for his memory.

But this moment is about us and Joss's obvious deception.

And I'm going to take advantage of it.

"Ma'am, you weigh 148 pounds. We're never going to be able to test the bed like this."

She glares at me for giving the exact weight that we got from her appointment two weeks ago, so it's probably not even accurate anymore. "What, you think I can't make this bed shake?"

I grin and grab her by the waist. She might be nearing the 150 mark, but she's still featherlight in my hands as I pluck her off me, set her on her hands and knees on her side of the bed, and smack her ass.

She squeaks and looks back at me. I love the way she looks like this, her ass and pussy on display for me, her face rapidly reddening, a fire in her eyes that never existed before the big disaster, but I love it. I'm not going to say what I did was the right thing or a good thing, but the baby isn't the only right or good thing to come out of this. There's a temper to Joss, a passion I don't think she let herself feel before. There's a bite to her words when she says, "Don't you do it!" that makes the tease so much more worth it.

I slide a finger into her pussy and crook it.

"No!" she screams, but if she really meant it, she could pull away. I'm not holding her in place.

And I'm only teasing. She'd love to force us to waste more time today stripping the bed. Again.

Instead, I bite her ass cheek, give it another smack, and mount her roughly enough I bet she regrets telling me to stop fingering her so soon.

She groans and drops her head into the pillows, and I take hold of the wrought iron headboard and give the bed the test it deserves.

It survives with barely a squeak, which is actually a little sad until I remember that one day, in only a few years, we're going to have at least one kiddo running around who's going to start questioning the sounds coming from mommy and daddy's room.

I drag Joss out of the bed — again, to protect the bedding — and haul her into the shower. It's barely big enough for me, let alone us both, but I make it work while I plot a complete remodel. I have a feeling, or at least a hope, that we're going to outgrow this apartment someday, but I'm going to spoil us both until then.

She tries to distract me in the shower, but I refuse to let her drop to her knees when I'm not even sure she's going to be able to get back up. She's in a playful snit by the time we get out, huffing off to make coffee, shaking her ass the entire way down the hall. She's taunting me, trying to distract me for another half hour, and my dick is definitely interested, but I tell it to shut up. "It's not going to work!" I yell at her. "You want to tell me what you're up to now?"

"Of course not!" she calls back, which isn't even a little bit of a denial that something is going on. And listen, I know I shouldn't be getting irritated that she's hiding something from me. I deserve it. But my nerves are still recovering from my meeting with Bradley. She's going to be the death of me.

What a wonderful death it will be.

"We should make pancakes," she continues, meaning I should make pancakes. "I've got this new—*oh no.*"

I head down the hall to the kitchen in no rush. Her tone isn't saying disaster so much as I'm about to run to the grocery store for maple syrup. I only ask, "What's wrong?" when I see her looking out the window at the barn.

The grass, brown and dormant but clear of snow since the recent warm spell we've had, has been spray-painted. In great big neon pink letters, it says LEAVE WHORE. Surrounding it is a bunch of weird wire frames. I'm not sure I've seen anything like it, but then I look closely at one and see something in it.

"Go back to your bedroom and call the cops," I say softly, not wanting to alarm her too much. "Stay there until I come get you."

"But—"

"Please, let me take care of this."

Chapter Thirty-Six
JOSS

"You should have told us sooner," Officer Vega says, but he's young. I bet he has no idea about my past or the history of this property. "We take vandalism very seriously here in Camden."

Of course they do. We're in the wealthy suburbs. It's a boring area to be a cop, and they'd love to get more calls of any sort.

"I'm sorry," I lie, swiping a tear of frustration away. I'm not scared, I'm *pissed*. I ignored Gabe, of course. Made the call about the vandalism, told them I was worried something serious was happening, and rushed down.

To find Gabe wearing bloodied gloves and carrying a wire kill trap in one hand, a trash bag with a dead animal inside it in the other.

There was only a half second of panic — but I can still feel that half second in my heart as I talk to the cop — before Gabe saw me and blurted out, "It was a possum, not Jerry."

The lawn was covered in kill traps, at least a dozen of them, and although nothing else but that poor possum got caught up in them, Gabe had to assure me repeatedly that he saw Jerry in his little house under the new deck. The only reason he wasn't still there was because Gabe ran him off the property so he didn't have to keep an eye on Jerry while he disabled the traps.

It's painstaking work. These things are brutal enough that he's triggering them with a stick instead of risking his hands disarming them. I keep one eye on him as Vega takes my statement, but he's being careful.

"How long would you say this has been going on?" Vega asks.

"That's . . . a trickier question than it should be." I laugh, but it does little to temper the statement.

"Why don't you start in the beginning?"

"You new to Wilmington in the last six years?" I ask. "This house doesn't have a great past. I don't have a great past. So there was a good three, four years where this was a regular thing, not worth addressing. And then it stopped, and I thought it was over, but then there were some incidents this past fall."

"What changed?"

I nod to Gabe. "We started dating. My picture got in the news. People remembered me. It was bad for a while, a few times a month. But then they stopped again in January. Until this."

"Did anything change this time?"

I shake my head. It's been a weird couple of months. "I got pregnant back in October, everyone knew by December. Gabe and I broke up in December, too. But it still happened a few more times. And then nothing for the last two months . . . until Gabe and I started seeing each other again."

Officer Vega looks over at Gabe, diligently clearing the traps. His eyes narrow. "So this has only happened while Gabe was here?"

"Well, not *here* here. Sometimes he is, sometimes he's— *oh!* Are you thinking Gabe is doing this? No. I mean, I know people are crazy, and trust me, I don't take things lightly or ignore red flags. But he literally built a cubby for the raccoon that lives here. He would *never* put these traps out."

I can tell Vega doesn't agree with this argument, and I get it. He doesn't know Gabe like I do. He didn't spend two months trying to convince himself that Gabe is a bad guy based on one incredibly inappropriate decision he made that reflects something far more important. He's looking at a woman who might be easily duped by a man who could be a run-of-the-mill sociopath who feigned a humanitarian streak to manipulate her into thinking it would be impossible for him to harm an animal.

But it doesn't seem impossible to me that he would lie to me to get me pregnant, and it is impossible to me that he'd try to kill Jerry.

"And you have no security system to prove he didn't leave your apartment while you were sleeping? No cameras out here?"

"I'm sorry. I swear, I was going to get one of those doorbell cameras, but then the vandal stopped and it slipped my mind."

"And you?" Vega yells to Gabe. "Mr. Shaunessy? You didn't see anything?"

The look Gabe gives me isn't the one I'd expect right now. He's gotten on my case numerous times about getting cameras, so this would be the perfect moment for him to look vindicated. But with the pregnancy, the threat on Jerry's life, and everything else, I could really go for supportive right now and maybe save the told-you-so for a later date.

He's looking oddly sheepish, though, as he says, "Well, not me personally, no."

Vega raises an eyebrow. "Do you know someone who did?"

"Jerry did." His phone buzzes in his hand, and he holds up a hand for patience as he answers it, putting it on speakerphone for us. "Jeff, buddy, tell me some good news."

"I do, in fact, have good news. But good god, man, you could have warned me I was loading a snuff film."

Gabe mutes the phone to explain, "He means the possum," before unmuting and telling Jeff, "You got a good look at the vandal's face?"

"Yeah, bitch got a close-up. Was taunting Jerry. I genuinely didn't know a woman could have so much hatred for a raccoon minding its own business. I'm sending you the video, but do me a solid and go give the lens a scrub, would you? Jerry keeps smearing mayonnaise on it."

I watch, stunned silent, as Gabe crouches under the deck in front of Jerry's cubby and scrubs the little circle next to the door. This whole time, I thought it was a silly bit of decoration, a pretend doorbell.

It's a camera.

"Dammit, Gabe, why didn't you tell me?"

"Love you, ma'am!"

I shake my head and make a mental note to start plotting to deliberately do stuff behind his back.

More stuff than what I have planned tonight.

This is just our lives, I guess.

He messes around on his phone as he walks back to us, his gaze stuck on his screen. The way he holds it indicates that he's watching the video Jeff said he was sending him. "If this makes you feel at all better, the feed is going straight to Jeff, and he's promised not to watch them unless we ask for a specific clip. It's for your safety. I figured you'd eventually remember to get a camera installed, and in the meantime, this would be for emergencies."

Officer Vega nods like this isn't a dick move, and I have to remind myself that Gabe's a big bear sort of guy who really is just trying to look out for me. Also, I've been hoping he likes surprise parties, but now I'm kind of hoping he doesn't.

"Whatcha looking at me like that for?" Gabe asks.

I shrug.

He shifts uncomfortably, like he thinks he's sleeping in the raccoon house tonight. "Look here, wanna see how cute Jerry was taking home half a ham sand—*ohhh, shit.*"

Officer Vega and I both flank him to see what he's seeing, and we all watch together as the vandal approaches the house with an apple core, one of Jerry's favorite treats. So although it's devastating, it's not entirely surprising that it's Rachel with the apple core.

I keep watching, hoping that this is just terrible timing and she was bringing Jerry a late-night snack and leaving, barely missing the vandal, but then she says, "You want this trash, you little shit?"

Jeff was right. That's the nicest thing she says to him before he makes a grab for it and she snatches it away and tells him she's going to leave it on a trap for him. I watch in horror as she sprays the lawn and sets up the ring of traps, placing the apple core on the one closest to him.

"I don't understand," I say voicelessly as she disappears from the screen.

"Do you know this lady?" Officer Vega asks.

"Rachel Graves. She's one of my students."

"And vice president of my fan club," Gabe adds grimly.

My eyes are still riveted to the screen, but thankfully, Gabe is protective to a fault, and once the possum ambles into the frame, he presses the phone against his chest.

"They're the single biggest preventers of Lyme Disease," I tell him. "That poor guy didn't deserve—oh hey, are you okay?" I ask when I notice Gabe's cheeks are red, his knuckles white.

He puts his arms around me, pinning me against him, covering me as much as he can. "This is my fault. It never had anything to do with you. That's why she only bothered you when she knew we were together. Dammit!"

Vega hands me a card and starts taking pictures of the spray paint. "I'll need that video sent to me. I need the source though. The dates of the other incidents, if you know them. Any evidence. Did you take photos?"

I guess we should have waited to clear those traps until photos could be taken, but Gabe did the right thing choosing the safety of any animal that might happen through the yard. When I first saw the traps, I thought how lucky it was they chose to do this on a Sunday when Rose and Iris were at a convention so they wouldn't see it. Now it all makes sense.

"I did," Gabe tells him. "The one I was here for. I bet other people did too. We'll reach out to everyone who was around those days, give you anything we can."

"Rachel actually helped me clean her mess up," I grumble. "Twice."

Vega perks up at that. "Has she always come by the next day?"

"Most of the time. It didn't click until now, but yeah."

"You two, sit tight for a minute. I'll be right back."

He jogs around to the front of the house, and we watch as he gets in his patrol car and drives off, only to come back on foot a few minutes later. His instincts are right, and it's only fifteen minutes of the three of us hanging out on the deck, sipping coffee while Gabe signs some Jugs merch for Vega, when Rachel appears below us with a story about dropping off cookies.

Epilogue
GABE

"So he arrested her right in front of you?" Keira asks, as stunned as everyone else has been when Joss has recounted our midday adventure to the partygoers.

As stunned as I was when I discovered the thing she was hiding from me this morning was a surprise party for me. Plenty of us here were extended this year, so I think this is more for all of us, but Joss insists this is *my* party.

She did so with a smug look, no doubt in response to the way I recoiled when a party was thrown at me. Today was rough. Dead possum? Not fun. Traps strong enough to break a twenty-pound critter's neck strewn across the lawn to take out our sort-of pet or any of the neighborhood cats? Very not fun. In general, though, I like surprises. I'm not going to tell Joss that, not when she's basking in her victory over pulling one over me, but I'm always down with surprises.

C. B. Alice

She's spent the last half hour making sure I'm rock hard under the surface in the hot tub with a hand on my thigh that's casually stroked both my cock and my balls repeatedly. Great surprise.

"Right in front of us!" Joss says with a gasp that shows how excited she is about the arrest.

"That must have been terrifying," says Mel. The Cohens usually stick to the Adirondack chairs when they're over, but even Mel's been seduced by Joss's excitement and has rolled up her pants to sit on the edge of the crowded tub. We're at capacity, with Keira and Tilly across from us, Bodley and Wes Foster each taking up most of the other two sides. Squeezed in next to them are Cora and Merrick, who's glaring hard at either Cora or the arm Foster's casually cast across her shoulder. Mel sat right in overflowing water when she plopped down on the corner headrest and then laughed it off. *It's a party,* she said. I'm pretty sure she's drunk.

Most people are. We have another few weeks before the official team activities start back up again. Everyone's mostly rehabilitated, we're just doing our personal trainings, but plenty of the guys are taking advantage of the lax schedule.

Not me. I'm not a big drinker anyway, and my Super Bowl flub put the fear of god into me. Since Joss can't drink, it makes sense that I shouldn't.

"Honestly, it's a huge relief," Joss tells Mel. "It was the norm for so long that it didn't bother me, and even though it kept getting worse and worse, I told myself that no one was physically harmed. It wasn't a big deal. But today's? Someone could have gotten seriously hurt. I feel bad enough about that possum." She gives Keira an apologetic look. "I'm so sorry I accused you of this."

Keira shrugs her off with a drunk hand that Evan, standing behind her, grabs and tucks back under the water before she accidentally smacks Tilly. "'S alright. I deserved it. I'm just glad to know you caught her."

"I still can't believe it was one of Gabe's fans."

I want to agree with her because it is nuts that one of my fans would go all psycho stalker, but Merrick tosses back his whiskey, stares Cora dead in the eye, and says, "We've all had fans that go over the top, haven't we?"

The guys nod. Only so many players on any team can share that spotlight, but most of us were the best our high schools if not our colleges had to offer.

Cora tilts her head like she's not sure why Merrick directed the statement at her, but she finally nods as well. "Some fans just don't understand 'no,' do they?"

The quirk in Merrick's lip tells me that the moment Cora gets out of the hot tub, he's going to chase her down. Cora's scowl looks like she's going to run but not fast enough to escape.

I glance to Joss, curious if she'd want that, but nah. That's not who we are. I lean in close while the other hot tub occupants strike up a pissing contest about crazy fan experiences and whisper, "You wanna go inside for a bit?"

"Gabe, I fully intend on spending at least another two hours in this hot tub."

"Are you sure about that?"

I slide my hand over her thigh, parting her legs enough to get a finger in to the narrow band of bathing suit fabric covering her core.

"Watch yourself," she murmurs right back, unabashedly grabbing hold of my dick.

I bite the inside of my cheek to keep from groaning. The best I can do is give her a kiss that has Tilly splashing water at us.

"Gross. Get a room, you two!"

"See? Tilly thinks we should get a room."

Joss glares right across the hot tub. *"Tilly* is jealous right now."

Poor Tilly shrinks into the water as much as she can, but she's eight months pregnant. Not much shrinking to be done.

Foster says, "You need a man? We can find you a man."

Cora and Keira team up to attempt to drown Foster. To keep Joss from joining the dogpile, I sneak my finger back into her bathing suit and slide it right into her slick pussy. "Don't you think you've caused enough trouble today?"

"Mmm, not quite yet."

"No? What else are you planning?"

She throws her leg over me and hops onto my lap so she can lean down and whisper, "Will you marry me?"

I glare at her. "Are you serious right now?"

She frowns. "What? Do you not want to?"

"Ma'am, I have asked you to marry me twice and you never said yes. Literally the first thing I did was ask you to marry me." In frustration, I tilt my head back and yell up to the sky, "She said yes, we're getting married!" so she can't steal my thunder.

"Mazel tov!" Mel Cohen squeals, falling fully into the hot tub to give us a hug.

BLAISE

I'm so freaking late for the party. I told Joss I had to run a quick errand so she should start things without me, but I promised I'd be there.

I'm in so much trouble.

"I can't renegotiate your contract again," Andy says to me in this helpless voice, like there's absolutely nothing to be done.

So much trouble.

But I knew this already. I know how contracts work.

"I just need more money."

Andy scrubs his forehead on the other end of the video call. He's in his office for some ungodly reason considering the hour, probably because he's in hot water with his wife again. I consider asking him what's going on. Maybe I can help him like I helped Gabe.

C. B. Alice

Gonna suck losing Gabe in the house. It's only a matter of time before he vanishes from my life. First it'll be the move, then it'll be needing to get home after practice. He'll leave parties early, start checking the time more. He'll expect me to hang out with Allore and Morales and their wives and kids. And then we'll be quick nods in the locker room and bland *good game* platitudes.

He loves Joss, and his kid needs a dad. Sucks for me, but worth it.

So I don't offer to help Andy. I need help this time. He gets a crap ton of money off that contract he can't do anything about; the least he can do is figure out another avenue of income.

"Look, usually I'd say more product endorsements—"

"Cool, let's do that."

"—but no one wants to work with you."

"Bullshit. I'm a hot commodity. I'm the ninth ranked overall. Fucking Tuberty got that Gatorade spot, and his ass got dropped. Get me his Gatorade spot."

"Gatorade can't work with you."

"Can't or won't? I didn't get in any trouble this year—"

"You're not allowed to take your shirt off."

I slam my fist — my right fist, the one that's not the moneymaker — into my steering wheel. When I got home, there were so many cars I couldn't get in the driveway. At least out here on curb, no one can hear this conversation.

My horn beeps, and two neighborhood dogs start barking. Someone yells at me from outside, and I look up to see Mrs. Clark from two houses down is walking her Pekingese a couple yards away. Whoops.

"Fuck! Can that be renegotiated?"

Andy's pained look is enough. Part of getting signed on the Jugs was some ridiculously strict rules, including media dress code. One leaked sex tape — okay, four — and suddenly shirts-on for *everything*. I was lucky to get away with the wet crop top bullshit I did last summer, but even that landed me in the hot seat. No visible nipples, nothing below the navel now.

Bunch of prudes.

"I'm trying to help. But literally the only requests that have come in are for—"

"I'll take it. Whatever is. If I gotta be not-so-fresh in a fucking field of daisies, I'll do it."

"Blaise—"

"Actual tampons? I'm down. You know how many times I've had to stick a tampon up my nose? Four times, Andy. Four. Times. And I will do it again."

Andy sighs once I give him the room to talk. I've been told I'm bad at talking over people, but seriously, I will jam yet another tampon up my nose. The last one got stuck. They had to use tweezers and a saline wash to get it out. I'll still do it.

If it'll get me through the next payment, if it'll keep this video from getting leaked, it'll be worth it.

"Blaise, they're all local spots. Car dealerships. Mattress shops. The pizza place down the street. Pennies."

I drop my head back in my seat. It's a nice seat. A custom Ferrari. If I sell it, I could get six figures from it. I can't be driving around in an old beater on my salary – not even for reasons of pride, I just don't have a way to explain where all my money's going – but I bet there's a way I could frame this where management will hire a driver for me on their buck.

"What are you thinking?" Andy asks.

C. B. Alice

I swallow hard. What I'm thinking, what's actually spinning in my brain, isn't what I'm *thinking*.

"I'm thinking my career is over, Andy."

"Are the tapes really that bad?"

I nod. I don't want to talk about what's on the video. I don't want to tell him about how the most intriguing woman I've ever seen in my entire life — from the neck down, thanks to the masks — duped me into saying stuff that out of context makes me look absolutely disgusting and depraved.

I'm not saying I don't have my kinks, but what's on the videos I've been getting sent, the way they've been edited? They sound like I hate the women I fuck. They sound like rape.

I want to vomit thinking about it.

And every time I'm sent a new video, I'm asked for more money. Every time, there's another zero on it. She has to know that I'm tapped out. The payment I just made will leave me on McDonalds until my next bonus comes through. If she demands more next time, I'm sunk.

These videos end me.

"I still have a guy working on this," Andy promises me. I'm sure he does, I'm the Cuba Gooding, Jr. to his Tom Cruise, but his guy hasn't been able to track this girl down yet. I'm running out of hope as rapidly as I'm running out of money.

"I gotta go. Gabe's having a party. I'm late."

"Okay, send Gabe my congratulations. Tell him if he needs a new agent, I've got plenty of room for him. And hey, we'll get through this, okay?"

I hang up on that, unable or unwilling to give him the energy I've been storing up for my appearance at this party.

My appearance. Fuck. Gabe's my best friend. He lives with me. This isn't an appearance, it's a celebration.

Good Guy Gabe

Shots are passed to me the moment I walk into the house. When I ask where Gabe is, Bodley nods down the hall toward the bedrooms. "With his girl. Where you been?"

"Just dealing with shit is all." I tap my empty shot glass on the counter to get Bodley to pour me another one. "It's cool, they'll be out later." After they're done with their lame romantic sex.

I give myself a good shake, screw on my party face, grab the tequila in one hand, margarita mix in the other, and head out the back door. "Mouth margaritas, bitches!"

Most of my teammates are shaking their heads, no, wildly. Thompson's clearly tempted to tackle me when, instead of dumping the booze on everyone else like I usually do — whether their mouths are open or not — I tip my own head back.

It tastes awful.

Fuck, it's all room temperature.

And I'd do it again if Merrick didn't reach out from the hot tub and snatch the tequila from my hand, passing it to the stranger on the opposite side of him.

"Well, I don't want this," she says.

I *know* that voice. I don't recognize the girl, not even a little bit. She's silver-haired with bright green eyes and pudgy cheeks. She's cute. I'd remember her.

"Just take it, Tilly," Merrick says to her. So she's Joss's friend, the one I haven't met yet.

"You can't give tequila to pregnant girls," Allore whines.

The girl stands to lean past him and hand it back to me.

My eyes go to her boobs first because, wow, lots of boobs, but then I look down and notice she's enormously pregnant. Like, I'm kind of worried that standing is going to cause the baby to fall out of her. And alongside that giant, pregnant belly of hers is a tattoo of honeysuckle vines.

I know that tattoo. I've licked that tattoo and said it tasted just like honey.

Joss's friend is the girl I slept with eight months ago at AnimeCon last summer.

She's my blackmailer.

Hiya, reader!

I leave teasers behind. Occasionally cliffhangers, but I warn readers in advance when I do that. *This* is a teaser. I'm not sorry.

I did write a little novelette of Gabe and Joss's babymoon that does further tease at Blaise and Tilly. Still not sorry.

You can find it over on my Ream. It's also the best place to get updates on my upcoming projects, including the rest of the Wilmington Juggernauts series.

https://reamstories.com/cbalice

About C. B.

Idk, man, I'm just here doing my thing. You can find me doing my thing on Instagram and TikTok @CBAliceAuthor and on Threads @chloecomplains.

Printed in Great Britain
by Amazon